ABYSS OF THE FALLEN

DIANA ESTELL

Brimstone
Fiction

ABYSS OF THE FALLEN BY DIANA ESTELL

Published by Brimstone Fiction

1440 W. Taylor St. Ste #449

Chicago, IL 60607

ISBN: 978-1-946758-32-3 © 2020 by Diana Estell

Cover design by Elaina Lee, www.forthemusedesign.com, Interior design by Meaghan Burnett, www.MeaghanBurnett.com

Available in print from your local bookstore, online, or from the publisher at: www.brimstonefiction.com

For more information on this book and the author visit: www.dianaestell.com

Brought to you by the creative team at Brimstone Fiction: Rowena Kuo, Meaghan Burnett, and Jessie Andersen.

Library of Congress Cataloging-in-Publication Data

Estell, Diana.

Abyss of the Fallen / Diana Estell 1st ed. Printed in the United States of America

To my parents
Who believed in me.
To my daughters
My muses.
To my husband Ryan
For everything.
And finally
To the memory of K.C.

ACKNOWLEDGMENTS

How do I thank all the people who have been very influential in my life and with my writing? By pausing and giving thanks to God for bringing life into my soul and redeeming my voice by the written word.

To all the people I've crossed paths with, transected or intersected with, I thank you from the bottom of my heart for enriching my life, both personally and professionally.

How do I thank those no longer on this earth? By pausing and giving thanks to God for my father, Glynn Ray Leeka, whose presence still resides in my soul. Some of his personality are woven in my main character, Dagon. I like to believe he knows about my novel and would be deeply proud. I can almost hear his voice, "What took you so long!"

My character Mary's strength, love, and patience are in part from my mother, Renate Leeka. The love story in my novel is a tribute to the love my mother still carries for my father.

To Scott and Doug Leeka, I love you both very much. These are two great encouraging men, I'm proud to have as brothers.

I thank my husband, Ryan Estell, and my two daughters, Ashton and Darien, for putting up with the creative process. I'm sorry for the times I may not have been present. I hope when you read my story, it will be clear just how present I was. Some of Dagon's personality is from Ryan. My girls will always be my creative muses. Ashton: riding on a white horse, wearing silver armor, and wielding a sword. Darien: my mini me in writing. Your sword is art.

To all my family and church friends, thank you for all your love and support. I thank my friends who believed in me from the beginning, even before I did: Kelly Clark, Diane Lacoppola, Yoko Bradford, Dianne Ortense, Jen Pulins, Jennifer Nelson (a great creative editor), Alice Fong, Cyndi Proffitt, Rachel Okrey, Anne Walchshauser, Dan Aldrin, Barbara Will-Henn, Pastor Marty Schoenleber, Stephanie Schoenleber (who encouraged me to begin writing. "You don't have any more excuses!") Pastor Marty Voltz (A great inspiration for one of my characters), Pastor Frank and Stephanie Taylor (for listening to me about my story), and Dakota Hietikko, whose creative vibe will always be with me.

I thank Colleen Robins for her friendship, guidance, and helping me learn the craft of writing. Your knowledge and wisdom are awe inspiring. Thank you for helping me see there are no age limits with fantasy. Thank you, my Dungeons and Dragons master! I will forever chase dragons.

To WriteOn Joliet, the best writing group on the planet, or on any other planet. Thanks to everyone for helping me learn about myself as a writer and the craft of writing. This group is soul family.

To Joel Pommier, for believing in the "Empire" and helping me with all my computer needs. You're a great key to my success. I thank my beta readers: Joey Fong and Nija Bradford. Your comments helped me be bold in my writing for the young adult market.

I would like to thank my Brimstone Publishing house team. Rowena Kuo, you're the best editor on earth and a wonderful friend. Thank you for all your hard work editing my novel. This book could not have been polished without you. To my literary agent, Cyle Young, thank you for seeing something in my work worth investing your time and energy in. You're the best agent any writer could have. To Meaghan Burnett, thank you for all your hard work on my website. To Elaina Lee, for bringing my characters to life.

Finally, to everyone I didn't mention by name, thank you for crossing paths, transecting and intersecting my life.

PROLOGUE

Bequeathed

"Dreams are a gift to the young, to burn bright and long, bringing hope and light into the deepest darkness."

Thundering gallops split the skies. Magethna, upon her horse of wind, charged through the clouds, her friend and kin, Dorian, astride beside her. Two other Seraphs, Mystil and Raglen, followed in their wake.

The friction from their horses whirled the air around them. Victory's gleaming, pearled hooves and Triumph's sapphire eyes glinted in the setting sunlight as Magethna's hair whipped around her face in brown waves. Exhilarated, she encouraged Victory to go faster. A strand of Dorian's golden highlights flicked across her peripheral vision like a comet.

"Let's race to that farthest cloud."

Dorian said nothing, but his posture said everything as he leaned into the wind.

Neck and neck, the horses sailed through the air. The finish line approached with Victory in the lead. Pawing the air, her horse glided through the cloud, winning the race.

It really wasn't much of a race. As Dorian pulled up short, he became still. She caught the edge of a thought about science and creation but backed out to respect his musings. The air continued to sail past her when the other Seraphs' horses stopped next to her.

"Triumph wishes your attention," said Magethna.

"He most certainly does."

"If you don't mind, could you please read the scroll?"

"Patience is a virtue, you know; a virtue some lack," he said with a wink.

The winded horses panted silvery mist, hovering in place with each other when Dorian rolled out the scroll. As he opened it, she noticed the gauzy paper and how stiff it was in the wind. It remained resolute and statuesque in its purpose. Emboldened words written in ink of light rested upon the document's fibers. As Dorian read the ancient text, she hummed, following the flow of writing on her sword drawn from its golden sheath. Words appeared and disappeared onto the blade, offering hope and a glorious restoration. After the reading, she was refreshed yet pensive, for these words would also seem hostile to humanity.

Triumph lifted his head and shook his mane while Dorian patted his neck. "Yes, my dear one, the words were a river of love, spilling out from the One Voice of time."

Carrying on with her humming, Magethna smiled in response to his words. Her eyes continued to gaze upon the living writings on her sword.

With their mission at hand, Magethna prompted Victory to resume their journey. Fetlocks glistened over powerful haunches pawing the wind even faster around them. The other Seraphs followed her lead, their movements synchronized with Dorian's. From her sword, lethal double-edged flashes of silver arched in choreographed beauty. Words streamed across the swords at a steady pace and never fluctuated. In a fraction of a blink, all swords shot up, arms fully extended as the immortals sang with an ear deafening shout, "To glory!" The horses flew ever faster to their destination: Oak Park, Illinois.

PEARLED hooves alighted softly on the black pavement, casting an ethereal shadow under the moon and streetlights. Shimmering rays bounced off each hoof like points of a crown. Dismounting, the Seraphs viewed their surroundings. This, for a while at least, would be home. Silhouetted houses rested on tranquil, well-manicured, generationally-owned lawns. Budding trees swayed, and passing cars chilled the air as they drove by.

"The black path upon which we stand is called Chicago Avenue," said Dorian, pointing to a street sign above him. "And over there is our chosen destiny, Forest Avenue and the house we have come to protect."

Anything needing protection meant danger was afoot.

"Is it not peaceful here?" said Magethna, taking everything in, not paying attention to the tour guide. She didn't care about details. She wanted to see it all. "So quiet and welcoming. I know the house as well as you do, but just look at where we are." She waited for the lecture on imminent peril.

"Perhaps it is peaceful, quiet, and welcoming."

"No doom and gloom? For a stoic analytical type like you, this is indeed a compliment."

She wasn't sure if he smiled or twitched at her comment. A wet nose poked her back for attention. Time for the horses to leave. Stroking wind-swept manes and patting noses, the Seraphs stepped away and waved their steeds back to the Golden Land. Caught up in a gust of wind, strong legs pushed higher and higher upward. In a twinkled blink, they were gone.

Not even peaceful welcomes last. Fog began to congeal; stealthy fingers spread out on all sides, overtaking the lawns of the houses lining the path. The fog moved toward them with directed purpose.

Both sides of Forest Avenue balked at the presence, and a heated hiss emanated from the concrete. An old, inimical, villainous specter slithered into their midst.

"Servants come willingly into my dominion or are made by my will," hissed the shadows to the Seraphs.

This was no idle threat. Even Seraphs can be swayed to change allegiance.

Undeterred, Magethna led her companions toward the whispers along the battlegrounds toward their appointed assignment.

Swashes of silver arched across their bodies. Lethal blades took aim at a faceless presence, and Magethna stated a fact of intent. "We are not leaving."

Surrender was as foreign as the concrete beneath their feet. The whisperings moved with a murmured hush across her hair, rustling a few strands. Dorian's footsteps matched her own, their swords held with restraint at the attempts that tried to frighten them into retreat, or worse, into submission.

Rolling pavement moved toward them like tidal waves, an attempt to knock them from their course. Could they cave to the powers of this land? Yes. But in weakness, they were made strong, not by their own strength but by the strength of the One Voice who had sent them.

The sidewalk moved against them even harder, trying to knock them over and crush them. Wave after wave pounded them, but Magethna withstood the onslaught until the tides abated. Imperceptible ripples moved over the sidewalk, leaving no effects of erosion behind. Undaunted, the Seraphs faced the old brown house in front of them.

"It is time, for the boy sleeps," said Dorian.

A black, wrought-iron fence wrapped around the house. The Seraphs, who needed no key, passed through the gate.

"I've been waiting for this," said Magethna.

"Our purpose in this land commences," said Dorian.

Just like the fence previously, the Seraphs misted through the front door and glided up the stairs into the bedroom of their young charge, 13-year-old Mark Bennett. Sure enough, Mark was fast asleep in his bed, his legs dangling over the edge. His patchwork quilt half covered one side of his face. Even in slumber, rapid movement pulsed behind blue veined eyelids. Brunette hair stuck out from his quilt like a lopsided porcupine.

"What side do you want?" Dorian asked. "Ladies first, as it is."

"In that case, I'll take the right."

"You know, you always take the right."

"That's because I am always right."

He only shook his head and smiled.

Raglen's lithe frame moved next to Dorian, long blond hair falling across his face as he peered out the window. Mystil laughed at Dorian's comment and stood next to Magethna, like a pale shadow. The Seraphs turned their attention to Mark who was still asleep.

A book lay on the nightstand, words as fresh as when they were first breathed into existence. Fingerprints smudged the black, leather cover. With this discovery, Magethna glanced at her companions, for the reader would witness their homeland in the measure that could be expressed with ink.

Magethna placed a gentle hand on Mark's forehead, paused for a moment, and then waved her other hand through the air, transforming the room to the land in his dreams for the Seraphs to witness.

A CADENCE of musical beauty never ceased. Sometimes the music softened, and other times, it deafened. The voices of the realm sung in unison, a sweet soothing song gliding with crescendos of power. Every spoken word was a

melody. The land filled with never-ending light. Rivers of pure glass flowed with silvery, shimmering water, orchestrated by a mighty One Voice. The streets of glass glistened, delicate and fragile.

Enchanting wildflowers grew in the meadows and tiny white flowers nestled in the thick carpet of grass, intermingled with blades of silver. Mountains glowed with a glittering golden hue, surrounded by lush thick forests.

"This is our homeland. It is good to remember former events to keep them fresh in our thoughts," said Magethna. She and her companions surrounded Mark as he stood among the trees in the forest. Mark picked up a green stone and used it to carve "MB" inside a heart on the trunk of a tree before pocketing it.

"I wonder why he did that. Is this common to write on trees? Does he not use parchment?" Mystil asked.

Dorian drew closer to the trunk of the tree, motioning for them to follow. Peeking out between the branches, they scanned the distance.

"The breeze whispers, listen," said Dorian, easing back one of the black branches. He murmured to Mark, "There is to be a new guardian in the Second Land or 'Earth' as humanity will later call it. A ceremony of investiture will start soon for the last guardian to be knighted by Savila. In this ceremony, the guardian receives a special title. The only other guardian to bear a title is Savila herself."

Four golden-haired Seraphs chorused in the clearing, their voices communicated like an opera with dramatic vibrato. Many more similarly-haired Seraphs interrupted the four, speaking with angry gestures. Their speech sharp and dissonant, they threw their fists in the air. Some of them did not talk at all but fold their arms and nodded in agreement.

Another golden-haired Seraph joined the fray. This one wore a vibrant, white-hooded cloak over a long white garment. The Seraphs grew silent in her presence. She was beautiful, perhaps the most beautiful of all. She carried herself with grace and confidence.

She waved long, dexterous fingers as she drifted among the other Seraphs. Her voice and mannerisms persuading calm. She leaned toward the tallest of the four original Seraphs, who seemed to be the leader.

"That is Savila as she was," Dorian whispered to Mark.

As if hearing him, Savila directed her attention toward Dorian and Magethna, all eyes following in the direction of her gaze.

One blink and Magethna stood before Savila, Dorian beside her. Magethna glanced over her shoulder at Mark, wide-eyed, flanked by Mystil and Raglen.

Savila's kin became silent, all except the tallest. This Seraph stood proud, defiant.

"Why do we follow these two?" said Lunion.

His poisonous, contagious words spread, for soon other voices grew brave and roared in agreement. In unison, hands moved to their swords, which were sheathed in what looked like thick strands of hair.

"We have just as much authority as Magethna and Dorian have," Lunion continued over the voices. "More, if it comes to that, for it was our kind that forged the vials of the eternal flame. It should be we who lead."

Savila laughed before becoming abruptly still. She stroked the hilt of her sword, her fingers within reach of unsheathing it.

"My sister comes," said Savila. She smiled at the approaching Seraph, though not in a pleasant way. "Nuvila, I will never deny you a place by my side."

"It is not yours to offer," said Nuvila. Raven curls to her waist, her gown of deep blue, Nuvila turned and faced the onlooking Seraphs. "I am Head Guardian and can offer power to whom I please."

"What power do you mean, m'lady?" said Dorian.

"Guardian of Wisdom and nothing more," answered Nuvila. She turned to Savila and lowered her voice. "You have always been too ambitious."

Instead of replying, Savila pushed her way between Dorian and Magethna as if opening drapes to look at Mark. "How sweet to see the boy here."

THE DREAM PAUSED as Mark rustled his sheets, breaking Magethna's contact with his forehead. A breeze carrying a fine scent of gardenia blew through the half-opened window. That meant—

"Focus, Magethna," Dorian interrupted. "We came here for the sole purpose of guarding Mark Bennett. Nothing more. Show us what he sees."

She breathed in the scent of gardenia and again placed a hand on Mark's forehead.

∾

THE SCENE SHIFTED.

Inside a spacious sanctuary, a tidal wave of wind rushed over the audience of Seraphs, filling the place with a splendor of warmth. Five thrones stood against a wall of bright flames. Savila stood in front of them, waiting. "I present your new guardian, Lord Dagon!" Her voice resounded throughout the sanctuary. A deep rumble ensued as the One Voice spoke. Mark, who sat next to Magethna in the back of the sanctuary, covered his ears.

The multitude of angelic beings stood, and Magethna drew Mark to stand with her. Serene music played when the new guardian appeared. With outstretched arms, the guardian, wearing a long white cloak, somberly walked down an aisle scattered with flowers. He climbed to the top of the raised platform and turned to face the throng. Bare feet peeked out from his ceremonial attire. Being light-complexioned and fair-haired, the guardian resembled a pillar of light.

Like ring bearers in a wedding ceremony, Dorian and Magethna with Mark between them, carried enormous gems on platters down the same aisle, gifts they bore for the new guardian. The focal point was a ruby, a gift to humanity and its new steward. Magethna spotted Nuvila in the front row. The light around her glowed safe and warm, in contrast to Savila, whose face darkened with shadows. Placing the platters on a columned stand, they proceeded to stand before Dagon. Rays of red light from the ruby spread over the sanctuary. At the same time, blackened crimson shadows surrounded Savila. Her glory smoldered with the investiture of her subordinate.

Savila took the ruby from the stand and held it above Dagon's head. "With duty comes sacrifice. Lord Dagon, will you sacrifice what you hold most dear?"

Dagon turned and stepped up to face her. "Yes, My Lady, I am ready."

"You know not what you promise." Savila turned the ruby toward the thrones, and a soft light illuminated from it, casting the image of a bridge arching across the sanctuary. Upon the bridge, human figures traveled in throngs back and forth. One figure shone bright as the rest faded in the background. A woman. She paused, holding onto the railing and stared off into the distance.

"Beautiful," whispered Dagon.

"Who is that?" Mark whispered to Magethna.

"Hope," Magethna answered.

"Sacrifice," said Savila. "I will hide what you love within history itself. Only then will I know your heart belongs to me." Savila stepped down to Mark and held out the ruby.

Hands trembling, Mark took the sparkling jewel.

"No!" The guardian's pupils became distorted, a ring of scarlet flames encircling his pale blue irises. His head tilted back, and a burning roaring hiss came from his youthful mouth. In a mechanical sort of way, his head shifted into place. "Mark Bennet, bring the Stone to me!"

MARK THRASHED IN HIS BED, held down and fighting an unseen image.

Magethna stepped back, gasping, hands at her temples. "Wait, that's not how it happened. Dagon's eyes? His words? No."

Mark sat up, dripping with sweat. "Dorian! Magethna!" Mark then flopped down on the mattress.

"Lord Dagon fell. The brightest Seraph among us, and he fell." Dorian placed a hand on Mark's shoulder, easing him back to full sleep. "Lady Savila, Queen of the Abyss as her title is now, sent this dream to frighten the boy as she has with all his fathers before him, all previous custodians of the Stone. Make no mistake, Dagon can be just as frightening as Savila depicts him to be. He was created in the light but has since been lost in darkness."

"But something from the light must remain." Touched, Magethna faced the window at the coming dawn. Mark had not called out to his human family, but to them. "In Dagon's humanity, his heart beats without purpose. By protecting the boy, there is still hope for Dagon."

Just as the sun peered over the horizon, Magethna discerned a faint heartbeat. She turned to find the others listening, too.

Dorian stepped closer to the window. "For the sake of the Second Land, pray he finds her."

1

Dagon

Dagon struck out every day from the Abyss in hopes of finding *her*, unsure if he would meet success this day, this year, this century. Who exactly was she? Well, he wasn't quite sure. He didn't even know her name. She was to be an integral part of a plan to doom humanity. A plan Dagon went willingly along with. A plan which did not include him falling in love with her. Finding her was one hurdle, the second hurdle, they had to be united. United in name only or in love. He hoped for the latter. The worst-case scenario? Dagon finds her, she rejects him, and humanity becomes eternally enslaved. He wasn't quite sure what she looked like as he only saw a brief blurred image of her. His heart saw more than his eyes. Enough to never give up.

His most recent activities centered on watching Mark Bennett, whether sitting on a bench, standing by the boy's house, or following him here, there, and everywhere. Jazzing up his routine, Dagon pretended to be a CIA agent, inventing all kinds of corny scenarios and whacky gadgets that seldom worked. He did, however, become quite good at picking locks. All this to not go stir crazy while keeping surveillance on Mark, the current custodian of Dagon's ruby, half-forgotten within the boy's writing desk. The ruby, coming to the Bennett family's possession by immortal intervention, had been passed down from generation to generation. If prophecy worked the way it was supposed to, why go through all of this? Because Savila liked to torture him, that's why.

But now the boy's house had become infested with boring Seraphs, leaving Dagon on a park bench—*his* park bench—to contemplate sleeping for another century. Not knowing when he would find the woman he had searched eons for, he had reworked his strategy of style and flair to impress and woo her, shoving aside the nagging suspicion that this could all be another of Savila's cunning lies. The 1950s came and went, and then the 1960's flower power generation swirled by, as did the 1970s. The '80s rocked on with its big hair, one-hit-wonder bands, preppy fashion trends, and great rock-n-roll music.

Dagon got up and shuffled along the streets of Mark's familiar neighborhood. Buds had started to open on the trees and flowers. The heels of his black loafers scraped along Kenilworth Avenue, the street behind Mark's house. His silvery trousers fluttered with the spring breeze. Instead of reaching for his usual cigarette, he looked to the crisp afternoon spring air for reassurance. Inhaling refreshed his body but did little to assuage the despair in his soul. With nicotine jitters, he rummaged through his black trench coat, finding a lemon drop. He shuddered as he crunched it, pulverizing it in seconds. He wanted his mind blocked from Savila or any other nosy Seraph. He had laced the lemon drops with his own concoction to aid in covering his thoughts.

Not paying attention and needing a smoke, he found himself at a familiar house when he dropped to his knees, hitting the pavement hard.

There she was, right in front of him.

A rash of goosebumps raced across the skin of his arms. He would recognize her by her eyes, deep blue with flecks of gray along the rims of the irises. The instant feeling that had gripped him when he first saw her on the bridge all those eons ago, flooded his heart and rendered him useless. Scenario after scenario raced through his mind of what he had planned on doing when he found her. None of them showcased cowardly, nervous fear. Bravery planned in darkness is not the same as true bravery in the light. She came out of the house that held many memories for him. It was his heart that recognized her.

Maybe she's visiting someone here? Odd, I don't hear anyone else in the house.

Dagon was not going to use his vision to see inside where she lived. He would have to learn about her the way everyone else learned about someone, by talking. For him, this wasn't the most pleasant prospect. He wasn't even sure what the rules of engagement were regarding communication. How frightening. Who starts it? Who ends it? Is there a natural break, a closer? How long can one talk before mouth paralysis kicks in? *Well, if I survived this long, then surely I can survive some point-blank question and answer sessions. Yeah, it will work out just fine.*

Dizzy, he stared at her. He would walk over any minefield to let her capture and interrogate him, being her prisoner of war any day. Had he known how truly stunning she was, he would have gone completely insane.

Petite, she had flaxen hair, cascading in a shimmering waterfall down the middle of her back in loose wavy curls. Her hair drew his eyes over the curves of her body, which modeled a teal dress. Topping off the look, black stilettos tensed her calves and lengthened her legs.

Compulsively, Dagon looked around for the line of suitors. He was shocked not to see any but glad, nonetheless.

Locking her house door, she shook and turned the door knob several times. With keys jingling in her hands, she moved along the porch.

"Steps!" Her voice shook. Her feet wobbled as she stepped down with black stilettos she clearly lacked practice wearing.

Like a true knight, he recovered from his love-saturated, cowardly, nervous, fearful stupor and walked closer when she stopped. She turned her head toward him, practically stopping his heart. She looked at him and smiled. There was no way she could have seen him, as he had rendered himself invisible, but still her smile seemed directed at him.

On what might as well have been a skating rink, her stilettos navigated the treacherous concrete stairs. He placed an arm around her waist. Giving her support, he guided her down the steps. To his relief, she straightened up and found her balance.

At the bottom of the steps, she walked on a concrete path, which wrapped around to the back of the house. Her house. His arms quivered, and for once it wasn't because of nicotine jitters. He followed her behind the house and over to a two-toned blue car. Like a gentleman, he helped her open the door. She smoothed her dress. He diverted his attention from her hemline, which was too short and too distracting, and he was way too close to her.

The keys accidentally dropped on the ground, and Dagon picked them up along with her and placed his hands over hers. With the keys in her hands she stopped, and just as before, she appeared to be looking at him. Face to face when a breeze kicked up, the waves of her hair blew in his face. The scent which lay on her skin, to his amazement, was gardenia, which happened to be one of the fragrances in his personal blend of nicotine. When he had designed his cigarettes, he wanted something feminine in honor of her, and here she was wearing the exact scent he had chosen to represent her. Incredible.

It appeared she stared at him for hours, but mere seconds later, she closed the door and started the car.

"So, you found her?" said a Cherb, as three others materialized out of the ground.

"Yes, I found her." Dagon sighed. "Mr. Cool, don't you fellas have anything better to do?"

"Heck no, we have to keep up with the times. Always changing and rearranging." Blond spikes stood up from the top of Mr. Cool's short-cropped hair. "Do you like my snazzy tailored silk suit? Razz found a BOGO."

"Check out the bling." Razz looked like Elvis Presley as a rapper. "The brighter the better. Sledge tore up my last suit."

"I still enjoy crashing, breaking, removing, and fixing stuff." With the word "Sledgehammer" stitched onto the name patch of his zippered, one-piece suit, his jet-black ponytail convinced Dagon that Sledge was the lovechild between Thor and the janitor. "I needed the last suit to fix Friar."

"Got too close to one of Savila's fire pits and singed all the hair off my body." Friar's doleful eyes inspected the flame designs on his leather biker outfit.

"The bald head suits you, but the missing eyebrows will take some getting used to," said Dagon. "Why are all of you ... um ... back?"

"You must need us back," said Mr. Cool.

"You mean, you need money."

"Yes, that, too," said Razz.

"Through all the centuries, have none of you ever asked why your existence has been unharmed by Savila? Why can all of you come as you please in and out of the Abyss?"

"Maybe you should ask the same question," said Sledgehammer.

"I know the answer. It's in my job description."

"And exactly what is your job description?" asked Razz.

"You were at my investiture." Out from his coat, Dagon unsheathed his sword. "Guardian of the Earth. Pay attention."

"You need us," said Friar.

"So why you lot? Is it because I'm the only one who'll talk to you?" Dagon sheathed his sword, tucking it back inside his coat.

"We're special," said Razz.

"Yeah, you're all special." Dagon rolled his eyes. "And now, I'm your boss again."

The greedy, conniving, rambunctious fallen Cherbs said nothing. Their scowls turned into crazy fake smiles.

"Fine. These are your duties. You are to guard that woman's house. This house. Watch for malicious attacks on her thoughts of night. As she sleeps, she has no control or knowledge of what she ponders and, thus, is vulnerable. Stay alert to any human prowlers, be it day or night." Like a commander, he paced in front of them with his hands behind his back.

"Thoughts of what?" Mr. Cool said, ignoring the rest of what Dagon said.

"Thoughts of night," chimed Razz.

"Dreams? Does the boss want us to guard her dreams?" Friar said.

"Dreams? That's boring," said Sledge.

"This job is anything but boring. Didn't you hear anything I said? This job is highly classified, practically undetectable, and highly valuable."

Mr. Cool shook his head. "Nah, it's boring. We get the highly classified and highly valuable stuff. Even the lovey-dovey sentiment is fine, but what's this *practically* undetectable business? It's going to be our you-know-whats hanging out on the line. It's either detectable or undetectable, which is it?"

"It's only highly classified if it's undetectable, while it will always remain highly valuable. If you four slackers take the certain safety measures I invented to block your minds, then it will most definitely be undetectable."

"The ancient junk in those lemon drops is nasty!" Razz insisted. "Maybe they're rancid by now. Hey, what do you mean you invented it? It was a fluke how you came across that mind-blocking stuff."

"Horrible taste aside, they're not rancid, and they work. Fluke indeed, didn't I have to invent how and what to place the ash in?" said Dagon.

"Sounds kind of dodgy." Friar smoothed a non-existing eyebrow. "Before we proceed, we need to know if you have the right to protect her. Because again, it's going to be our you-know-whats hanging out there."

"She is my bonded mate, my earthly wife, hopefully. One day. And I was never commanded not to, so I will protect her."

"What accompanies a job, boys?" Sledge crossed his arms over his nametag.

"Money," said the others.

"This better be a paying job," said Mr. Cool. "Don't try and weasel your way out of this. We don't like freeloaders, or is it front loaders?"

"Yes, this is a paying job, you cheapskates, and I will be using a front loader later for your information. I might just stuff you inside one, if you keep at it."

"We're not cheap, just practical." Razz pinched an imaginary piece of lint off one blinding lapel. "I think if a qualifier like 'high' precedes a word, then the pay should reflect that, and be high."

"All of you will be generously compensated as always. You will also have a new job, for now I will be busy trying to figure out how my beloved and I will stay alive. I want your swords spit-shined to gleaming perfection, the way I would do myself. Dirt, as you know, is disastrous. I will personally clean my dagger. Is this clear?"

"Yes, as clear as the greenbacks that will accompany this new job." Mr. Cool smirked. "Do we have to clean as methodically and neurotically as you do?"

"I may clean my weapons methodically, but I don't clean them neurotically."

"You most certainly do. Why, you're always looking at the metal and rubbing it, like you're trying to get a genie to pop out and grant you a wish." Mr. Cool momentarily went silent. "What kind of ugly car is your beloved sitting in?"

Dagon had not noticed the car. Now he saw it, and yes, it was ugly. A wide white stripe ran along the side of the car, seemingly splitting it in half. Was this meant to be a distraction from the two-toned blue color? To make matters worse, the body was bulbous and wide. The car had a hatchback with a wide fat window that tilted in. Dagon cringed at this obnoxious metal thing. "She's too gorgeous to be riding in something as hideous as that."

"Maybe it was a reject from the car manufacturer," Sledge offered. "Humans can make better cars than this. We've seen them."

Tentatively, she backed her car down the driveway. Checking both ways numerous times, she took off down the street.

"Your guarding duties begin now. All of you will stay and guard my love, who is priceless." Dagon took a step and stopped. "I know you have to make the connection, but you don't need to stand around her bed afterward. Make the connection and get out."

"Can you bring us back some chocolates? Milk or dark, it doesn't matter, just bring it!" they said collectively.

He said nothing but nodded as he showed each where he wanted them to be positioned. Dagon relaxed his posture, his hands now by his side. The four unsheathed their swords in unison and turned the blades over in the light. Pleased with the inspection, Dagon began following his bonded mate in her less-than-beautiful car. He could see for miles easily, watching her car turning down street after street.

"This car needs to be put out of its misery," said Dagon, as the fallen Cherbs shook their heads in agreement.

"Save her, boss, save her from that disgraceful hunk of metal!"

"I plan on it, boys."

The car was parked at a local dance club, which didn't thrill Dagon in the least, for only one type of man patronized it. Bewilderingly, she locked the car. Why would she bother? Who would want it? He was half tempted to melt through the car and unlock the door. Maybe, somehow, it would get stolen. The car contradicted the way she dressed.

Again, he placed his arm around her. They went inside the dance club, which was dimly lit. After running into a couple of tables and chairs, he let go and followed her to one of them where several ladies greeted her with warm smiles. He could discern some of their thoughts, while others he could not. This intermittent mental frequency puzzled him.

"Mary, I saved you a seat."

"Thanks, Linda," said Mary.

He received three gifts today: meeting his beloved, finding out her name, and discovering he apparently could not discern the thoughts of Mary's friends. Uncertain if her family or foes fell into this category, he figured he would find out at some point.

Dagon and Mary ... sounds good. Has a nice ring to it.

He found out through listening that Linda was getting married, and this was her bachelorette party. He then conducted a mental sweep of the room. All seemed well ... so far.

Great, I've heard about these parties. If I see a man come out and start dancing and even begin to take off his ... He won't ever dance again nor do anything else again. Well, I never knew when I would find her or what condition I would find her in, but a bachelorette party?

He found a quiet empty table, tucked away in a darkened corner. Reluctantly, he gave her privacy while loneliness gripped his heart. Pulling out a chair, he sat, never losing sight of her.

In the dark, he sat hidden while his light was nearer than ever. The wait was over, and he was the happiest half-man who had ever lived. In that moment, the length of time it had taken to find her meant nothing, nothing at all. In addition to her beauty, she also carried herself with elegance and gentleness. Her voice was soft compared to all the other women seated at the table. Some of the ladies at the table seemed brash and somewhat rude, but Mary took it all in her patient stride. He gave her credit, for had they been men, they would have known the wrath of Lord Dagon. Mary was beautiful, inside and out.

It was early evening, and the women went out onto the dance floor except for Mary, who sat all alone, like him. He saw her watching her friends as they danced. Some were dancing alone, some with men. She looked sad to him. She watched her friends enjoying themselves. He didn't want her dancing with men if he could help it, but he didn't want her sitting alone, either. What he wanted was to dance with her and her alone.

Some of the ladies made their way back to the table for drinks while a few stayed on the crowded dance floor. Mary stood, and he watched her intently, but she just seemed to be stretching. She was safe, so he kept his mind at simmer but remained ready for anything. Rapidly, it went from simmer to a rolling boil when a man started his approach, but Dagon placed himself between them, gripping his sword.

Here come the suitors. This man was dressed not too badly but not too great either. A stylish t-shirt sagged and bagged over his rail thin frame. His scoffed gym shoes proved he didn't have much style, let alone class. He tossed his head toward Mary in a macho way that made Dagon want to hit that guy in the face. Obviously, he thought he was a gift to all women. Dagon flicked the hilt of his sword concealed in his trench coat. The man began to ask her to dance, but then he shut up good. To his good sense, he walked away.

Yes, that's right, back away while you still have a back.

The second man was not as confident but confident enough. He gawked at Mary from across the room. When he caught her looking back, he adjusted his Goodwill rejects and took a step forward. But halfway across the room as he passed several men bigger and stronger than him, and he cast his gaze to the floor. He shook his body, pumped his arms, took a deep breath and moved toward Mary again. Dagon watched this back and forth as the man struggled with his inner demons of self-doubt. Dagon understood this all too well. The man had good sense. He turned around and walked away.

Her body stiffened, fighting back tears.

If a third man comes around, I will stand aside for just one dance.

No time seemed to pass when his mind found a third man who had his sights on Mary. He seemed neither confident nor shy. He stepped aside before the man reached Mary. He sat back at his corner table, watching this man make his move on Dagon's bonded mate. Unfortunately, she said yes. They danced to a techno upbeat tune, fast and catchy. Dagon tapped his feet under the table, keeping time to the music, marking time for the song to end. As he watched them, he detected a hint of a dancer in Mary. Her moves were reserved but fluid. Her skills seemed held in check. He wasn't sure, but he hoped he had found his own dancing partner.

The song ended, and she thanked the man for the dance before making her way back to her seat. She was almost to her chair, when the same man approached her.

"Dance with me again!"

She politely refused, but this character kept at it.

Dagon didn't have to be a mind reader. The man's persistence made his blood boil. The man would not take "no" for an answer.

Dagon was already making his way over to her as the man continued talking.

"Oh, come on, just one more dance? Come on, dance with me," said the guy, gripping Mary's arm.

"No, I am done dancing, okay? Let go. Please, just let go."

Dagon placed himself between them, his back to Mary. He controlled with his mind who would see him and who would not by using veils. One veil made him invisible to humans. A second veil made him invisible to immortals as well. By reversing either veil, he could alter what people saw. Reversing one of his veils, it was Mary and the guy who could see him. Everyone else in the room, if they were looking at this scene, only saw a lady and an obnoxious guy.

She jumped back as the man's grip on her arm released. The man visibly shook when Dagon appeared right there in his face, seemingly out of nowhere.

No sooner was he between Mary and her antagonist when a hiss came from outside the back door of the dance club. Savila. And she hunted for blood.

He wasted no time. He didn't know if Savila would harm Mary by sampling her blood, but he wasn't going to take the chance. He ran his finger down the length of his coat. He opened it wide, exposing his sword. "The lady said she's done dancing with you."

The guy's eyes widened. "Who walks around with a sword? This isn't England or wherever it is that accent is from. What could you do anyway? There are witnesses everywhere."

"You ask the wrong questions. The question you should have asked is, 'Why am I here?' As to witnesses: No one can see me except you and the lady. I am here to protect her, and this I will do," he said calmly as if he were merely giving directions to someplace or another.

Time stood still. Mary's fingers gently stroked the palm of Dagon's hand. With her fingers, she outlined his ring of investiture and his thumb ring, making his hand reflexively draw in, and for a moment, they were holding hands.

Does she like me or is she just glad I rescued her? He was hoping for the first.

"You will apologize to the lady. Now."

"I'm sorry."

"It's okay," Mary murmured, but Dagon felt her quivering.

"Not good enough," he said to the guy.

"I'm really sorry." The man flinched as Dagon applied pressure on his mind. "I should never have done that ... I'm sorry."

"Thank you," was all she said as she squeezed his hand, and it seemed like she was thanking him and not the guy. It took every ounce of strength not to chuck it all, turn around, and hold her.

A familiar caress of ice flowed down his neck and back.

"I can see he has offended you, Dagon." Savila's voice dripped indulgent affection into his head as if she addressed a favored dog. "Thus he will please me, so send him out. I could use a drink."

"You will leave out the back door," Dagon said to the man.

The guy said nothing, only turned around and left out the back door. Mary's face relaxed. Fighting centuries of loneliness, Dagon didn't know what to do next. All he ever wanted to do was be with her, but his emotions kept him momentarily paralyzed. In a split-second reaction, he replaced his veil, making him invisible again to everyone, including Mary. The music drowned out the blood-piercing screams. Even before he placed himself in front of Mary and before Savila arrived, he intended on making the guy leave out the back door. He had not intended to deliver him to Savila, but he wasn't sorry either.

Mary jumped and turned, searching the dance hall. "Where did the blond guy go?" she asked the few friends who were seated at the table.

"I'm right here, luv," whispered Dagon.

"Blond? We only saw the loser with the brown hair," said one of the women. The other women laughed. Even Mary and Dagon chuckled.

She craned her head to search the room for him. He was right there, looking directly at her, unabashed, smitten, and bitten.

He reached up to brush a stray hair from her forehead at the same time a dancer whisked past, creating a gust of wind. He quivered, for earlier he held her waist, and then her hand in his and now her hair. The tactile sensation was sensory overload for a man who had never been in contact with anyone or been shown anything but loathing. He was basically a homeless, starving man, only just now coming to life.

Mary found her chair and sat. He made a quick decision not to go back to his darkened corner but to join her yet remain invisible. Mary mumbled under her breath,

"I know that I saw him. He's real."

"Yes, luv, we have found each other." He hoped she could hear this in her mind.

Several men came off the dance floor and sat by some of the women. Thankfully, they were all just friends. He relaxed, as three large pizzas were placed on the table: cheese, pepperoni, and sausage. This bachelorette party turned out to be nothing like what he feared it would be. Rather, it was laid back and casual.

Seeing Mary, being with Mary, the pizza and the light banter made this the best day he had ever had, and he didn't want it to end. He just wished for the day to come when he didn't have to remain invisible. He wondered why he really needed to do this. The fact was, he didn't, but he was anxiously apprehensive.

Remaining invisible, he grabbed the last slice of pizza. After all, he was a part of the party now.

"Hey, who took the last slice of cheese pizza?" questioned one guy.

"Yeah, and the pepperoni and sausage are all gone, too!" shouted the other.

The two men accused some of the other men of having trash can stomachs.

"We didn't take it!"

"No, I did," said Dagon as he sat back, munching away, the warm sauce oozing out beneath the mouthwatering cheese. He chased it down with some Coke he had poured into an empty glass from a pitcher on the table.

The pizza was now long forgotten, and the light banter continued. Shaky and edgy, his lungs begged for comfort. It amazed him how he had gone this long without a smoke. He took out one silver cigarette and placed it in his mouth. Seconds before he lit it, Mary also had a cigarette in her mouth. In slow motion, he tapped the end of his cigarette, sparking it to life, just as she took a pink lighter and lit the end of her cigarette. At the same time, they inhaled and exhaled.

"Baby, you shouldn't be smoking, it's bad for you." He puffed out a plume. "I should talk."

Mary didn't respond, of course.

The party was ending. She placed the butt of her cigarette in an ashtray on the table while he flicked the end of his, causing the gold to rapidly recede and sizzle. He helped her push her chair back as she stood to leave. She thanked Linda, told everyone else good night, and walked away.

"We had a fun time. Good night, everybody, and thank you for a wonderful evening," said Dagon.

He followed her back to her house. A security light glowed above the driveway, where she sat in the car for a while. She took off her stilettos and took a deep breath before opening the door then made a mad dash to the front porch.

Once inside, she shut the door with a quick hard push. Making quite a ruckus, she rattled down what sounded like a column of locks on the door. The entrance now secure, they watched her shadow check every window in her Fort Knox house.

"She's obsessive, compulsive, and clearly has a disorder," said Sledgehammer as sensitive as a rusty tack.

"She's scared," said Dagon, perplexed. "Did you see anyone come near the house?"

"No. We wish," Friar said.

Dagon shot him a dangerous look.

"I meant we want to see some action," Friar amended. "But alas, no one came near this house."

"Good, but why is she scared? She must live alone."

"Then go to her, boss," said Mr. Cool. "She's a damsel in distress, so save her."

"I want to, but I can't yet. You four are here for now."

"Did you get some?" Razz said.

"How wicked, I'll give you some, I ought to have you flogged!"

"Did you get some chocolates. For shame!"

"Here are your chocolates."

Saluting him, they savored the chocolate and told him to pay up.

Dagon reached inside of his coat and pulled out a metal briefcase. He took out four rolls of cash and threw one to each of them, whose money-grabbing hands caught them with athletic ease. The individual bills flicked fast. Each counted his payment for services rendered. With a skeptical eye, they inspected the money by sniffing it and then holding it up under the moonlight.

"Is this counterfeit?" Razz said.

"That is legal tender," said Dagon.

"Hold it up to the moonlight again. Does it look real?" Razz asked the others while Dagon tapped his foot, trying to control his temper.

"This doesn't look real! Remember back in Rome? He tried to pass us fake coin slugs. Even with no face of Nero on it, which was a vast improvement, it was fake, nonetheless. Any worse luck and we would have been thrown into the gladiator pits."

"The money is not counterfeit, illegal, or otherwise, but if my money is not good enough for you, then ..."

"It's real," said Mr. Cool. "We knew it all along."

With a sneer at the Cherbs, Dagon put the case back in his coat.

"You need one of those human money stuffers, for as much as you will be paying us, it will be quite a workout constantly opening up that hefty case, not to mention the balancing act you performed. Although highly entertaining, it could be hard on your arms. We're only looking out for your best interest, boss." Sledge held his hands out.

"Yes, and yours."

"Yes, that, too."

"You know, you may be right about a money stuffer."

"We're always right."

Dagon laughed with them then stopped. "Don't you dare try and look at her, Razz. You will wish for Nero after I flog you. I am the only one who will look after it's nice and legal, very legal."

"You know you want to, boss."

"Of course, I want to, and I will, but only after it is proper and legal."

"Can we have a cigarette?" said Friar. "You had one, but we didn't."

Dagon didn't answer right away but walked over to Mary's white porch swing and sat. "You're on duty, and I'm not."

"It was easier living under the thumbs of the pharaohs and the good-for-nothing emperors than living under your tyrannical reign," said Mr. Cool.

Dagon smoked away with his legs stretched out and feet propped up on the porch railing. The smoke tendrils moved with the wind over the night grass.

"Slave driver! Tyrant!"

They hurtled insult after insult at him, carrying on for what seemed like hours. Dagon reached his limit and walked to the all night "Suds your Duds" laundromat to wash his clothes. The guys lost interest in bashing him and instead reminded him to use a front loader and dryer sheets, for clingy clothes would be a fashion disaster. Dagon smirked at their subtly altruistic comments.

2

The First Week

Dagon gave his clothes one last sniff, pleased with the springtime fragrance of the dryer sheets and no static cling. Refreshed, he dissolved through the glass door of the laundromat.

With new-found hope, he made his way back to Forest Avenue and walked through the field, noticing the details of the world around him. Each blade of grass bowed under the weight of his loafers, only to rise slowly after his foot had moved on. In the middle of the field, he stopped at a huge tree. From here, he could see the nondescript bench he sat on for hours while monitoring Mark Bennett. Other benches lined the perimeter of the field, but it was this bench he favored.

Black obsidian steps opened in the ground in front of him, leading into the darkened halls of the Abyss. He descended, and the ground closed behind him. Coming to the end of the hall, he faced a black concrete wall with no door. He touched his ring to the wall, and a silver door appeared. He ran his finger down the middle of the door and it opened. The door sealed itself shut behind him, becoming a black wall.

Out of habit he looked around his private quarters to see if anything had been stolen or tampered with. With everything in place, he relaxed and began putting his clothes away. Each perfectly folded item fit in his drawers. Row after row of equally spaced color-coordinated stacks of clothing lined his cedar shelves.

Taking a quick bath, he got into bed, covering himself with two white furs.

Hours later, Dagon, who didn't really need to sleep, woke up. Sleeping had no effect on him, but it made him feel normal. At least it was relaxing.

He dressed to head back to Mary. He never used his mind to dress himself, even though he could. His jeans, black silk shirt, and black-laced shoes flew on before he put on a trench coat and straightened the furs on his bed. Looking his room over, he noted where he had placed everything and walked up into the brisk yet sunny spring morning.

He followed Mary to work. She wore a pale blue uniform and thick, black, homely shoes, and she looked nothing like she did last night. She could have worn a potato sack and would still have been breathtaking.

He watched her all that day. She would take orders, serve, take money, and bring back change for some nice and some nasty customers. The most demanding patrons gave her small tips despite her kindness. He wanted to punch these cheap customers or at least hold them upside down to shake out the coins he heard clanking around in their pockets.

Customers raved about her coffee. Now, how can a person louse up coffee? You would be surprised, for the other waitresses would leave coffee grounds floating around in a bitter tasting beverage. Faithful patrons had noticed the difference and would ask for "Mary's Coffee" as if it were a menu item. Dagon didn't try a cup, though he really wanted to. He would wait to see if Mary would make him a cup in person.

He watched her at work for the rest of the week. On Friday after coming home from work, she left the house wearing jeans and a baseball shirt along with black flats. She looked cute. Falling out from a loosely pinned up bun, soft curls caressed her face.

He paced back and forth in front of a bakery, trying to pluck up the nerve to introduce himself on her way out of the building.

Her beauty gave him confidence, but with a larger dose of self-doubt thrown in for rotten measure. He waited under a streetlight, hoping she would notice him.

She looked down as she walked, but when she looked up, she stopped. Her cheeks blushed, but, having chosen not to read her mind, he was not sure why. She continued walking toward him. Face to face, she had to crane her neck up to look at him. The love bug bit him all over again. He had so many things he wanted to say to her, but the words caught in his throat.

"Thank you for helping me that night." Mary broke the ice.

"You are welcome."

"I knew you were there. No one else saw you, but I knew that I had." She mumbled the last part under her breath.

"Yes, I was there, luv."

"Why are you calling me, love? You don't even know me." Mary backed away a step.

"British influence. They say that to everyone." Dagon spread his arms.

"Ok ... I guess I've heard that." Mary took a tentative step forward.

"As to why no one saw me but you, I was only meant to help you. Your eyes have not deceived you."

The way her eyebrows drew in played on his heart strings like a harp. "So, no one else saw you, only me?"

"Well, the deplorable man saw me also."

Her eyebrows drew in again. Maybe she was confused. "I like your trench coat. It's unusual, but nice."

Momentarily stunned, he didn't know how to respond. He hoped his coat had style, since he couldn't get rid of it. *She doesn't seem repulsed. But once she finds out what this coat is made of, she probably will be.*

"Thank you."

With a short and polite response, she smiled as she hooked the bags of bread over her arm and opened her purse. Out came a cigarette and the pink lighter.

"I'm sorry. Do you mind if I ..." she said in a mumbled voice, as the cigarette danced up and down to the inflection of her words.

"No, I don't mind. I smoke, too."

"I should never have started." She cupped the cigarette while her other hand flicked the lighter to life, careful the wind wouldn't take the flame away.

"Me either. I plan to quit. One day."

"I do, too. One day."

"I started only after losing a bet."

She snickered, flicking ashes and blowing smoke to the side. "What was the bet?"

"I have to go," he said in a flat, defeated voice as a sheath of ice flowed down his spine. She didn't need to know. Not yet.

"Already? Where do you live? What's your name? Where can I find you?"

Is she interested in me or are these just basic questions? Whichever the case, how could he answer her questions without freaking her out? All the answers led to his home in the "Abyss." What a horrible, unbelievable place for her to find out about.

"I'm sorry I have to leave." He brought her left hand to his mouth and kissed it. "We will see each other again." His heart hammered.

"Uh huh," she muttered while she nodded and stared up at him, her mouth slightly open. Her cigarette held suspended in her right hand with thin tendrils of smoke lazily rising.

Hesitant to leave, he shuffled his feet as he dropped her hand and walked away. The streetlight blazed, illuminating the street ahead. Without needing to look, he watched her walk toward her house. Going dark, he alerted his Cherbs that Mary approached.

Savila, the perpetual happy-zapper, had ordered him back to the Abyss. He had a few minutes before she expected him to arrive, so after Mary made it home without incident, he beelined for a store that had caught his eye earlier. He dissolved through the glass. He slung a pair of leather pants and a black belt with a wide silver belt buckle over his left arm. Next, he picked up two more items: a pair of black boots and an expensive black leather money-stuffer, or in human lingo, a wallet. He dropped cash on the counter, including tax, and dissolved through the door. He placed the items in his coat. His coat could hold an indefinite amount of stuff.

Pleased with these stylish purchases, he plopped a lemon drop in his mouth. He crunched and shook until the pieces broke enough to swallow, keeping his thoughts private.

MARY LOCKED THE FRONT DOOR, placed the bread on the kitchen counter, and put her cigarette out in an ashtray. In a daze, she leaned against the counter, recounting over and over what just happened, if it happened at all. Did she meet the man who rescued her? Was that really him? It had to be. He told her as much. The dance floor had been chaotic, and no one noticed him except her and the creep. Even after seeing him, she was unsure if he was real. Her heart pushed the emotional answer deeper into her soul, allowing other buried emotions to surface. Heat rushing to her cheeks, she closed her eyes, picturing his gorgeous face. He had rings on his fingers, but no wedding band. Her head tingled. Every part of her body became alive, responsive in ways that seemed impossible in any other previous relationship.

Leaving the kitchen, she went upstairs to her bedroom. Once inside, she opened the door to her walk-in closet and stood there for a moment.

Hangers poked out in strange angles with old and new clothes stuffed, shoved, and mixed together in uncoordinated strips of color. Rarely did anything get thrown out; she was a pack rat. Without intending to, she began purging her old life in preparation for the new life she anticipated. Soon, a mountain of clothes appeared on the floor of the closet to donate to a local re-sale shop.

She put the massive bundles of clothes in several bulging bags then dragged one bag at a time down the stairs. Eventually, she packed all the bags into the hatchback of her car. She had worked up quite a sweat, relieved by her accomplishment.

She checked the house door lock one more time and then took a bath instead of her usual shower. Finally cozy in her flannel pajamas, she settled in to watch some television.

With the television show as background noise, her mind rested on the intriguing blond-haired man. She couldn't help but laugh at his eager yet reserved manner, those old-soul eyes in that porcelain-smooth face. Blinking, a few tear drops soaked her eyelashes. Unbidden, more drops welled up. What was his name? Where did he live? *And what the blazes is wrong with me, crying over a man I just met?* All she had to go on was his promise that they would see each other again. She mulled over the confusing points and those she was sure of.

Yes, luv, I was there. I was only meant to help you. Your eyes have not deceived you.

The way he had called her "luv" in that British accent sent chills up her back. Anger and resentment had long ago sealed her heart shut. The excitement of her new life broke the seal.

STANDING in the middle of a darkened corridor, Savila waited in a blood-red dress. Her hemline started above her knees and flowed into a cascading train of rippled waves behind her. Web-like embroidery covered the bodice in a death-defying plunge down her neckline. Dark crimson velvet lined the hood on her head. She wore links of silver chain mail around her waist like a belt. Her sword, sheathed in a carved white-gold dragon skull, sported rubies for eyes. Dagon, as always, tried not to stare.

Her plump lips, still satiated from the blood of the dancer her sword drank from, drifted into a smug smile. In a misty vapor, three shadow kings appeared through a black concrete wall. The kings bowed, greeting Savila and Dagon.

After lighting his cigarette, Dagon cradled it between his fingers and bowed to Savila. His jeans added a touch of informality.

Savila snapped around, followed by the Shadow Kings. She wore black stilettos like Mary's. All five of them walked along the black glass of the hallway. Not even their shoes dared to make a sound.

They walked past cell blocks where imprisoned souls awaited justice, sentenced to eternal incarceration for treason against Savila's dominion. Souls which were honorably transformed into shadow soldiers also languished in torment. Their crime? The memories of humanity still clung to their spirit.

Savila waved her hand in the air, opening all the cell doors. Willingly or forced, the prisoners bowed in front of Savila. Waving her hand again, the cell doors shut behind them without making a sound.

Savila moved down the ranks, her train slithering behind her. She did not inspect her troops but continued walking, followed by Dagon and the Shadow Kings. The prisoners filed out one at a time behind the Shadow Kings. Passing by an empty cell, she sneered, but kept walking. Coming to a dead end, all of them dissolved through the wall and into the Execution Room. Dozens of charred, wooden beams lay in built-up soot of torture and death. Death chains hung on the walls eager to fetter victims with their thin but eternal shackles.

More shadows continued flowing into the room. The last shadows to enter were her Seraph-kin. These shadows always entered last because they submitted to her authority last. Not prisoners, shadow soldiers, or kings, they were reminders of what the price of weak submission would be like. With disdainful respect, everyone else bowed to the shadows of Savila's past.

Dagon blew out a few residual strands of smoke from his burnt-out cigarette while Savila stood in front of the wooden beams, watching in delight as her subjects gathered around her.

"All will see my power on the stones of my dominion. The Seraphs have come from a dream of my power to protect the Boy, who is mine. They have come from the Golden Land to oppose us, but they will bow unto my reign, for nothing can deny me this right. Blood will seal the bond forever. An eternal new order will be established under my authority. This was destined even before the Second Land's creation. Now the old bonds will be broken and under the new, we will reign!" shouted Savila, unsheathing her sword.

Black misty swords unsheathed in honor of Savila and in honor of the commencing of the Golden Land's destruction. Dagon unsheathed his sword. Silver rays from the blade of his double-edged sword ricocheted across the room. A black onyx, which sat commandingly on top of the hilt gleamed, illuminating the darkness.

THE DRAGON within Savila slit its serpentine eyes in longing and scorn over Dagon as he came forth bearing this sword. Only his sword bore engraved branches of the White Tree from the Golden Land. She could still taste the blood of her recent kill, which fueled the burn of desire to see the White Tree fall to ashes. Now she would tighten the love strings around Dagon's neck, fashioning it into his noose.

"TWO GRAINS of sand will fall before the Abyss is opened," declared Savila.

Dagon analyzed this despicable punishment. He had enjoyed one week with Mary, though he was invisible for most of it. The Abyss would be closed for two weeks or two grains of sand to demonstrate Savila's power over her subjects. Suspiciously, her edict coincided with him finding Mary. Savila rarely alluded to human time as it meant nothing to her, but at this moment, she knew it meant something to him.

Savila wasted no words on recounting the trifling dream she had given Mark Bennett. Certain that she created it only for the response of fear it produced, Dagon wasn't sure what his role would be, but he didn't have hope it would be anything less than the star performance he had in Mark's dream. The performance left him with the possibility of being incriminated. Thankfully, his subordinates were up there guarding Mary.

The swords reversed, sheathed in pageantry. In silence, Savila left the Execution Room, and everyone followed her and departed to their own private quarters.

Alone in his room, Dagon moved around ritualistically, preparing for something. Of what, he did not know, but nonetheless, he would be ready. He placed a duffel bag inside the bathroom. Within his walk-in closet, he took off his trench coat, unbuttoned his silk shirt, and hung it up. He paused to inspect two thin white scars that stood out on each of his arms, from the first two times he had cut himself—when he had tried to cut his coat. The coat was never damaged. Lashing out at himself released an overflow of anger, sadness, loneliness, and shame—emotions he had no idea how to control otherwise. It seemed weak to contemplate succumbing to this again yet brave, too. To keep Mary safe, he would rely on every form of control, even this.

Ceremonially, he put his trench coat back on over his bare chest and sat down on an ebony chair with a thud, rocking the chair back and forth. Here Dagon sat, alone once again, even after he had found her. He sprawled out in his chair, looking at his shoes, whose charm seemed pointless. He leaned toward his headboard, picked up a blue bottle, and placed it on the floor.

It may be two human weeks, but right now, it was painfully long. He had found her, placed his arms around her waist, rescued her, placed his mouth to her hand, and kissed it. Savoring the scent of gardenia she had worn on her soft, sweet skin ... two weeks apart might as well have been an eternity.

The preparations now complete, he was the lamb to the slaughter. With an icy will, he withdrew a dagger from his right pant leg. It was a miniature of his sword but just as sharp. Inflicting punishment on himself, he slashed at his left forearm, cutting himself through the sleeve of his coat.

Blood bubbled up out of the fresh burning gash and flowed down his arm. The coat became a kind of bandage, slowing some of the flow.

The wounds he deserved caused him intense pain as he took off his coat. He cringed at the signals his nerves were sending to his brain, reminding him he was part human. The blood loss from cutting always gave him an adrenaline rush, so with determination, he picked up the bottle and flipped the lid open. Silver Living Waters poured all over his blade. The liquid came from underneath glass lakes from the Golden Land. The watery substance clung to his blade like glue, soaking up the blood like a sponge. For precautionary measures, he concealed the liquid in a benign human shampoo bottle.

During the two-week confinement, Dagon inflicted two left forearm cuts and three on his right forearm, always cleaning his blade methodically after each cut.

His muscles ached, and his new wounds needed a soak. There wasn't much to brag about living under the ground, but it did have its perks, for his bath water was steamy hot, compliments of under-ground geothermal heating. He placed his clothes in the duffel bag, then walked over to a crystal vase, which stood along the wall next to an archway. The vase contained small rocks level with the lip of the vase. Silver cigarettes stuck out of the rocks like incense sticks. He reached down and took one, placing it to the side of his mouth, lighting the end with a tap. He left the cigarette in his mouth, puffing away when he picked up a fluffy towel next to the vase, placing it at the side of the tub.

He eased his aching body into the deep hot waters. Fully submerged, the cuts on his arms began to sting, a reaction from the heat and mineral composition of the hot spring waters. The springs were continually being refreshed by a series of aqueducts he had installed, all compliments of Roman ingenuity. He fell in love with this form of relaxation after his first undetected visit to Bath, England. The Roman baths were built during the reign of Emperor Claudius, who was an ambitious builder across the empire. He was an okay emperor as far as emperors went. Nothing like his nephew Caligula or his great-nephew Nero. Those were two devious bird-brained idiots, but Savila was quite fond of them. The baths were one good thing that came from that flea-ridden den of iniquity. Medicinal or not, this felt fantastic. Cigarette still in his mouth, smoke pouring out the sides, he began to clean his wounds. Tilting his head back, he puffed away, pouring water over his head to wash his hair. He flicked out his cigarette as he dried off.

Two weeks without Mary, his heart continued to beat despite Savila's cruel attempt to stop it.

3

In the Light of Dusk

His wounds had healed by the time Savila opened the Abyss. He wasted no time in starting his life with Mary. Taking his purchases from his coat, he removed the tags with his dagger. Opening a suitcase, he pulled out wads and wads of cash placing some in his coat pockets and some in his wallet.

After a bath and dressed in leather, he scanned the room. Throwing a lemon drop in his mouth, he bit into it then shook from the horrible aftertaste.

The sun began to set outside the Abyss. Walking across the field, he stopped at the sight of Mary sitting on a bench with another female from the bachelorette party. The other woman must have been a close friend, for he could not see into her mind. She didn't seem to be paying much attention to anything Mary said, and she looked antsy. He listened in as she asked Mary to a party at her house, but Mary declined. The friend excused herself and left. Mary remained on the bench alone. His bench. A good sign.

A smile played on her face as she tilted her head back and closed her eyes. Soft rays of the setting sun bathed her face with a peaceful glow.

As ready as he would ever be, he walked toward her with jittery limbs. His boots felt heavy as concrete. *Great, I look like Frankenstein.* Not wanting to scare her by popping out of thin air, he went behind her.

He shook his arms to release nervous energy. *It's not like we haven't met each other. Everything will be fine.*

"Mary." His voice came out a squeak.

Fine hairs on her neck stood up. Not a muscle on her petite frame moved an inch.

Can't I do anything right? I scared her.

The wooden slats creaked as her body shifted around. With her left arm resting on the back of the bench, she raised her head up until their eyes met. Her mouth hung open, frozen.

"Mary, I told you we would see each other again."

Still Mary said nothing.

"Are you all right, Mary?"

Mary pulled back from him. "Yes, but how do you know my name?"

Dagon tilted his head, his eyes focused on her remarkable azure eyes, darker than his own. Nervously, he figured out how to explain himself without saying too much, too soon.

"Did I not hear someone calling you this name?"

"Yes, that's right. My friend was just here talking to me a moment ago, and she did say my name."

"Yes, I thought I heard—"

"What is your name?"

"What is my ... um ... what?"

"I didn't mean to catch you off guard. I just ... well, I've been wondering."

"I haven't had anyone ask me this before."

"You mean your name?"

"Yes ... well, no ... I mean ...well ... how you've been wondering," said Dagon, hoping his flimsy response would be adequate.

A crash course into Mary's world began. Startled by her question, he made a huge oversight. Had she been wondering about him or was this a normal question?

"Oh, that makes sense ... I guess. I've been wondering about you ... and um ... your name since we met."

"Forgive me, my name is Dagon."

"I have never heard that name before. It's unusual."

"'Tis an old name."

Her eyelashes fluttered, and her head pulled back.

"Mary, are you sure that you are all right?"

"I'm sorry, it's just ... you are ... I mean, your coat, you look so good in it." Mary held up her hands. Her teeth nipped at her bottom lip.

Dagon did a double-take in his mind. *Did she really say I look good in this coat?* He liked where this was heading. "Thank you."

WHAT DID I JUST SAY? He's going to think I'm too forward. I've never ever said anything so forward to anyone.

"I know this is last minute, but my friend who was just here invited me to a dance party at her house, and I was ..."

"Go on," prompted Dagon.

"I was wondering. Would you like to come with me?" Mary surprised herself with her newly found boldness.

"I would be delighted to come with you."

She held onto the bench to keep her balance. "I can't believe I said that," Mary whispered.

"For the record. I'm glad you did." Dagon smiled.

Heat rushed to Mary's cheeks.

Dagon offered his hand to her, and as he did, she saw his unusual coat pull up from his wrist, revealing some faint scars.

His hand was warm and dry. A black onyx ring sat on his ring finger. Unusually, he had rock and roll themed rings on his thumbs. His coat and clothes were the wrapping on the package. *GQ, eat your heart out.* His chin-length hair moved in the wind over his mesmerizing face.

She stood up, tiny as a fairy compared to his height. "How tall are you?

"I don't know really. I would say, somewhere between dwarf tall and giant small."

Good looking or not, I just met this guy. I should be running from him, instead of... anything than what I'm doing now. It can't be. The more she looked at him, the more she believed her gut instincts, a supernatural connection perhaps. Here in front of her, was the man she had been dreaming about since she was a child. She was always the last girl to get a date, and that seemed fine with her. She shied away from men in general, but not this time. He stood tall like a living sculpture, and together they began walking into the sunset. The word "trophy" came to her mind, but that shallow term could not describe her dream man.

Mary's grasp tightened every time they passed women whose heads turned in Dagon's direction like vultures eyeing a kill.

How dare these women intrude on my dream. The gawking confirmed he was here.

At the house party, Mary sensed a spotlight on them. A hip techno beat pumped throughout the whole house when the hostess came to greet them.

Dagon couldn't believe his beautiful bonded mate asked him out for a night of dancing. *Wake up, Dagon, you're dreaming. On second thought, if this is a dream, I don't want to wake up.* Two weeks of torture seemed to be a healed memory, like his scars.

Instantly, Dagon read the mind of almost everyone in the room. The ones he could read at least. Through verbal conversation, he discovered the hostess's name was Caroline. Caroline flirted with him, making him uncomfortable, so he held on to Mary's hand with both of his.

"So, Mary, tell me everything about your new guy here."

Mary hesitated and clutched his hands tighter.

Dagon saw her looking around the room with apprehension, and he jumped in with the introductions, seizing the opportunity to set the record straight.

"My name is Dagon. I'm her boyfriend." Dagon looked at Mary, waiting for a response. He received it. She smiled.

Caroline's eyes popped, and her forehead wrinkled. "Can I speak to Mary alone?"

"Yes, of course." Dagon gave Mary a quick squeeze and a wink. "See you soon, baby."

Caroline practically dragged her into a bedroom.

Dagon was alone again, and for the sake of privacy, he did not try to see or read their minds.

"SPILL IT! Since when do you have a boyfriend? He's so ..."

"Gorgeous, and he's mine."

"Mary, don't be so antsy. Come on, tell me everything." Caroline rubbed her hands and grinned from ear to ear.

"Would you leave a guy like that out there by himself?"

"Okay, okay, but 'boyfriend'? Since when?"

"I guess since now. I met him ..." Mary trailed off. "I met him two weeks ago, and after you left today, he showed up again."

"And now he's your boyfriend already? Just like that? Isn't that a bit fast?"

"Yes, but it's like I've known him for years."

"It just doesn't sound like something you would do. You rarely date and never someone that you barely know."

"I can't explain this. You wouldn't understand anyway." Mary looked at the floor.

"Try me."

Mary's head shot up. Her eyes slit. "I don't have to." She then shot out of the door.

MARY CAME BACK WITHOUT CAROLINE. To his relief, she didn't change her mind and walk out the front door. A new song started. Dagon stretched his arms across the back of a black leather couch, almost the same shade as his onyx ring. With a thud, she sat down next to him. Her face flushed.

"What's wrong?"

"Caroline is wrong. All wrong." Even whispering, Mary fumed.

"Wrong about what?" Dagon brought his arms to his lap.

"I don't have to explain anything to her." Mary folded her arms across her chest.

Dagon said nothing, just tilted his head.

"But ... she does have a point."

"About what?" Dagon wrung his hands.

"You're my boyfriend, just like that." Mary snapped her fingers. "And you tell someone else before you tell me, privately?"

"I'm sorry, I should have told you alone, first."

"You should have asked me first, privately." Mary held up her hand. "I don't know you, but, yet I do. It's in my dream, when I feel like my life has meaning, and now you're here. That probably sounded nuts." Mary put her hands over her face.

Dagon gently brought her hands down and held them. "It's not nuts. But what about your dreams gives you meaning?"

"It's only when I'm dreaming that I would let someone else hold my hand, like you're doing now."

"I still don't understand why dreams are more meaningful than living."

"Life is cruel ... I've guarded myself ... I ..." Mary looked at Dagon, her eyes melting his. "I swore I would never be with any man. Too much pain." Mary cast her eyes down. "Let's just say, the few guys I did date, didn't turn out so well, but in my dream world, it's different. I feel like I'm not alone. Somehow, my dreams are linking me to this life. This probably isn't making any sense. It barely does to me."

"I would never want you in pain or alone." Dagon squeezed her hand. "You said something about me being here, what does that mean?"

Perhaps what he said perked her up to explain the way she was looking at Dagon. Her eyes didn't leave his.

"You have been in my dreams since I was seven. I feel safe."

"You've dreamt of me?" In slow motion, Dagon pointed to himself. Mary nodded.

If anything, at least she feels safe. Not sure, how long that will last. He detected an uneasiness in Mary around other women. He wanted to reassure her she need not worry over other women. He was a one-Mary-man. His lungs screamed for a cigarette, but he put her needs above his own.

"Would you like to dance with me, luv?"

"Yes."

Dagon led her to the small makeshift dance floor. Together, they savored their first slow dance together.

"I've always wanted to dance to this song."

I did something right; this dance will be ours. I'm glad I made a move before she became scared, repulsed, or any number of other rotten things.

Their bodies naturally moved to the slow romantic lyrics of the song. Dagon listened to the words and let the meaning fill in the cracks of his heart. Content, it didn't seem like the last two weeks mattered. *Maybe she does like me, somewhat.* His pessimistic thoughts softened.

"Are you all right?" said Mary.

"I need a cigarette," Dagon whispered sheepishly.

"I do too; it's okay," she whispered back.

Mary led him back to the couch where her purse was, but Dagon stopped her. He saw Caroline watching them, but more specifically, him. This unsettled him, and he reversed one of the veils to give them privacy. To everyone else in the room, they looked like they sat on the couch.

He reached inside his coat pocket and pulled out two cigarettes.

She took the thin cigarette from him and studied it. "This is strange. Like metal or something." She drew it to her lips.

"I make my own cigarettes. These are—"

"You make your own cigarettes?"

"Yes, and they are 18 karat white gold."

Mary's eyes bugged out.

"Don't worry, even the tobacco is my creation. It has pine, musk, and a hint of gardenia in it." He winked.

The once-bobbing cigarette now fell, which Dagon caught.

"How? How did you?"

"Mary, we will have lots of time for these questions," said Dagon, hoping they would. "Suffice it to say, it's chemically complicated."

"How many are in that case? Where do you get more when they are gone?" asked Mary, disregarding what he said.

"They instantly refill."

"They what?"

"Mary, I could use a smoke right now, how about you?"

"Yes, so could I."

He gave her back the cigarette and placed another in his mouth. *Great, my method of lighting the cigarette would be even more startling.* Throwing caution and who knows what else to the wind, he tapped both of their cigarettes.

Speechless at first, she cautiously inhaled and exhaled. "This is the best cigarette I've ever had. It smells amazing, too."

"As it should be."

Spontaneously, he took her hand. She looked up at him and smiled.

Their cigarettes were almost burned out when he tapped his cigarette and then hers. The cigarettes melted into themselves and disappeared. This was apparently too much for her to handle.

"Okay, that's it! Gold cigarettes which you made? Your own tobacco? They instantly refill? Tap and they light? Then tap and they disappear?" Mary covered her face.

Dagon considered telling her they were under a veil, but this wouldn't be the right time to spring that one on her. "You feel safe, remember."

Mary turned her face, her hands covering most of it. "Yes, in my dreams. This can't be real! You? These cigarettes? I think everyone just heard me shouting."

"There is no need to apologize, luv. I can assure you I am real and so are these silver smoking sticks, and no one seems to have heard you. No worries, baby. I think it's getting late. Let me walk you home."

He reversed the veil of privacy then helped her up. Still holding his hand, she followed him along. They exchanged a pleasant goodbye with their hostess, who followed Dagon with a lingering look he felt burning his backside.

As they walked, she commented on the silver and black flecks in his coat.

"They seem to weave in and out." Her hand hovered above the sleeve.

"Yes, they do. Isn't it nice outside this evening?" he said, changing the subject.

"Yes, it is."

He winked at her, and she smiled.

Too soon they stood at her door. The streetlights cast a soft glow around them.

The Cherbs saluted him and made kissing sounds. It took every ounce of control for him not to scream at them in front of her. He had shown her enough of the inexplicable for one evening. Being immortal had its perks, so he smiled on the outside and blasted the Cherbs on the inside, which made them laugh.

"Where do you live?" Without waiting for a response, she continued. "Do you live around here in Oak Park?"

"Something like that, luv."

A sudden chill brushed the nape of his neck. Savila called him back to the Abyss. He just hoped he wouldn't be locked in for two more weeks, but he didn't place much hope in that.

Mary was still talking to him, inviting him to come inside. He was shocked, for Savila had unwittingly helped him to honor Mary by not going into her house at that time. He wanted everything to be done right. He fought to have control despite his racing desires. *How egotistical can I get? I don't even know if she feels for me in that kind of way.*

"No, not tonight. Perhaps another time."

"Will I see you again?"

"Yes, we will be together again. Thank you for a wonderful evening. It was one of the best evenings I have ever had."

"It was the best time I have had, too. Thank you."

"You're welcome."

He stroked her cheek with a shaky hand, which was not from needing nicotine this time. She reached up and steadied his hand with hers, and she pressed his hand to her cheek.

Painfully, Dagon had to let go.

"Guard her, boys!" he said to his Cherbs.

"We will, boss! You should have planted one on her. We would have."

Leaving her cut into him worse than any dagger blade ever had. In the light of dusk, she resembled a sword with the silver of her clothes molding into steel under the glow of the streetlights, blending with the sharp edges of the moon which was barely starting to peek out. From another angle, she appeared like an angel, standing in absolute strength.

Once he was out of sight, he replaced his two veils, making himself again invisible. He took out a lemon drop, popped it into his mouth, and cringed. He was grateful these candies also instantly refilled. The defilement of evil was a renewable resource.

Mary was at home, and Dagon was back in his private quarters. He was sitting on his ebony chair. He hung his head, for he was imprisoned.

This two-week confinement was worse than ever, for Savila had told him he would be the first one the Seraphs would see when Mark would be taken. Savila would manipulate the moment yet again to make the Boy fear him even more.

He again spent most of the time in the ebony chair with his shirt off and his coat and pants on, just staring into space. His dagger cut into his forearms five more times, and again they healed. Mary's scent lingered right where he needed it to. The slow song that he and Mary had danced to echoed in his mind.

4

The Passageway

Savila opened the Abyss, and Dagon half-heartedly went above ground into darkness. His feet sluggishly drifted through a black, formless alien place. Faint moonlight crested above Mary's house. On one of her windowsills, a candle flickered. Its faint glow parted the dense fog in its vicinity. The small light illuminated his blackest night, raising his spirits ... a little. Though no shackles bound his hands or feet and no metronome metallically marked the hour of doom, he remained a prisoner, chained to Savila's will.

No recourse, no arguing, or opinion could release him from confronting Dorian and Magethna with Savila this night. His life with Mary, postponed.

Pragmatically, Dagon walked toward the antagonistic Seraphs, his metaphoric chains lightened at the source of what would release him and Mary: Mark. With Mary's approval, even his good-for-nothing coat gave him confidence. Shielding his thoughts, he nonchalantly chewed on a lemon drop, causing his lips to pucker.

The soft staccato clack of his boots clipped along the sidewalk as he made his way to Mark's house. Face to face, he arrogantly smirked at the goodie-two-shoed babysitters. They would have to acknowledge Savila, which he looked forward to.

A few inches away from the gate, a deafening scrape of blades unsheathed, sounding like metal sharpened on a wet stone. An entourage of four Seraphs guarded Mark's house. They were not honoring him or giving him a welcoming salute.

His group of fallen Cherbs were vastly different than Mystil and Raglen. *What would it be like to have these unfallen Seraphs instead of mine? Quiet, that's what it would be like. Honest to goodness quiet. Golden silence.*

"Hey, that door swings both ways you know," said Mr. Cool, appearing next to him.

For better or worse, he would much rather have noise, for noise meant life.

"Yeah, we'll keep you, too, as long as the green keeps flowing our way." Sledge popped in on his other side. "No worries, boss. Razz and Friar will watch your lady. Looks like you need us more."

With sharp blades pointed at him, Dagon stood against the gate and waited. Digging in his coat, he pulled out a cigarette and tapped it to life. Orange embers crackled away from the burning tobacco. Glinting ashes floated to the ground. The gold melted back even further after each deep drag. Playfully, he created smoke rings with each exhale.

"You know, smoking is not good for you," Dorian chided.

"And it's smelly," added Magethna, her free hand waving the smoke away.

Dagon was surprised that Dorian knew so much about smoking.

"Well, it's good for me." Rapidly, he shook the cigarette. "Calms the nerves, and, trust me, you want me calm."

Savoring the dramatic moment, he inhaled deeply, releasing the smoke in their faces.

Dorian said nothing, waving his hand around, trying to remove the smoke from their presence.

Only Mary's opinion mattered, and she liked it.

A few more ashen silver flakes fell to the ground before his cigarette burned out. One lone ember fell to the pavement as the Seraphs' swords shot up higher, silver steel piercing the fog like a flare, a call for help, perhaps. Bright silver flashes surged from the tips of their swords. Words continually wrote and faded away on their blades. The letters fading away only meant one thing to him: "Defeat."

The battle lines were drawn. The pavement shook, causing all of those present to turn their heads toward the epicenter, the intersection of Chicago and Forest Avenues. The Seraphs sang when the pavement shook more violently. Why would they be singing, unless they wanted to end their existence on a high note? Just then, a film of light flowed around Dorian, Magethna, Mystil, and Raglen, giving their bodies the appearance of armor. Nothing, though, could protect them from the wrath of Savila.

A rumble penetrated and pulsed stronger under the concrete. Pressure pushed the sidewalk up into strange angles. Now the same film covering the Seraphs flowed over the Bennett's house as crack after crack tore at the earth's crust, causing dirt and rock to fall into fine fissures.

The people in the surrounding houses slept unaware of the earthquake taking place. Trees, cars, and houses sat as they always had ... quietly. Even the odd driver coming down the nearby street, radio blasting with the window rolled down, would not notice the raging battle.

No armor of light surrounded Mary's house. Probably for being associated with him. Angry, Dagon grew callous and staunch, for he would defend her regardless of anyone else's action.

Momentarily, the shaking stopped; they were in the eye of the storm. In the calm, Mary's voice wafted up to his ears. She was singing in her sleep.

"I love him, his name is ..."

Dead silence. He waited to hear his name anywhere in her sweet song of night, but only her steady heartbeat as she slept.

Just a dream.

The Seraphs stopped singing. Dagon stiffened his shoulders and stared back at Dorian. Then Dagon softened, for Magethna smiled tenderly, causing him to falter and put a smile on his face.

The eye of the storm passed, and the ground shook with such force the air became charged with static. Wave after violent wave trembled beneath them as thunderous booms rolled from deep within the earth. Splitting the ground in two, pent up energy released to the surface. A deep jagged crack split with lightning speed down the length of Forest Avenue, with no end in sight. The ground thrashed as cement split and fell into the crack. Rocks and dirt fell fast into the widening crevice. The ground swayed severely. The crack kept racing ahead, widening into a gorge.

A tiny fleck from the concrete caught his attention. Why he focused on something so insignificant, he couldn't say, but this small light still shone brightly though it was caught in the crevice.

One fleck of light could not remove centuries of crusted bitterness in his heart. Adding acid into the emotional mixture, Henry Bennett and his wife, Frances, stood looking out of a large ornate window of their home. The Seraphs smiled at them.

What do they think they're watching, the moon? Yeah, their doom.

Any moment, Savila would make her grand appearance, and the smiling couple's faces would be wiped clean.

Henry Bennett closed the curtain and picked up an heirloom gold pocket watch. His fingers warmed the gold within his hand as he paced back and forth. "About to storm."

"Henry, he will call. He's probably in class. Besides, with the six-hour time difference in England, he wouldn't want to wake us," said Frances.

"In a time like this, he would call. Frances, the watch is—"

The phone rang, and his wife smiled. Henry reached for the

earpiece of his outdated phone. Taking a deep breath, he composed himself.

"Dad, are you there?"

"William, according to your mother, I have very few gray hairs on my head, but I do believe more are cropping up for the worry you gave me. Your mother and I know you are well, but to hear your voice … well … it lightens our hearts."

"Yeah, I'm fine. I wouldn't want to be the child responsible for your gray hairs. I'll let Mark do that." William paused. "I felt the shaking all the way over here, but of course I'm the only one who feels it. You know, it's not a clever way to meet a girl when you ask if the ground is shaking underneath her feet, and she doesn't feel it, but you do, and then she leaves, thinking you're either egotistical or crazy! I would have buzzed sooner, but I was in class."

"Yes, your mother said you probably were. The second hand on my watch is ticking … counterclockwise."

"Yeah, mine has begun moving backwards, too. This is wicked, Dad, wicked!"

In slow motion, Henry pulled the earpiece away from his ear.

"What's wrong?" Frances whispered.

Henry only shook his head.

"Remember from where our hope comes, son, and rejoice in its certainty. We love you and miss you."

"Backatcha, Dad, and I hear that. Buzz you soon. Love ya!"

Henry had never heard speech like that before. He muffled the phone and looked at Frances. "Is our money funding a new language in Oxford?"

Frances took the phone and briefly spoke to William, and her face looked as puzzled as his must have looked. She hung up the phone, and they both readied to return to bed.

"He is becoming independent as all children do, and I attribute his adventurous streak to my side of the family," said Henry. "I only need to look at myself for the similarity. What my mind ponders is how his independence, his adventurous nature, will be used given the storm waging around us. It is not William my mind dwells upon, but

Mark, for I believe his nature will be challenged, refined. His thoughts are slipping from me. We cling and press forward to the one great hope and there, my love, will we rest."

"I worry for Mark. He's been through so much." Tears streamed down Frances' face. "To lose his mother so young he never knew her, and when your brother ..."

"I would give anything to bring Arthur back for Mark, for you, for us. But Mark has us now."

"He doesn't possess the angelic nature your family has been gifted with." She smiled through the tears. "He's quite a challenge."

"Right now, he's meant to be in our care." Henry kissed her on the cheek and glanced toward the window. "I'll be right back."

As he walked down the passageway, he passed his father's and grandfather's portraits before stopping in front of the portrait of his older brother, Arthur William Bennett. He was a man whose presence in life would have never fit into a frame, for he was a formidable force in how he dealt with others: how he conducted his life in their jewelry business, with his family, and within his social circles. He had been a living example of duty, honor, and steadfast purpose. A bond of strength born by his inherited status. He was as gentle as he was strong, generous as he was duty bound. Arthur had exhibited all these qualities as a hallmark of his inheritance, unified by one voice, preparing the way for freedom.

A line of light shone from under Mark's door. Henry's soft knock brought a reply to come in.

"Hey, champ," Henry said as he entered the room. "Having trouble sleeping?"

Mark sat at his desk, an opened book upon it. "You can say that. Uncle Henry ... I've been having strange dreams."

"What kind of dreams?"

Mark shook his head and would not say more despite Henry's patient queries. "I'm going to read a little more before going to bed. Good night, Uncle Henry."

Henry continued down the hallway toward his study, following a line of portraits. The gravity of Henry's inheritance gave him pause, an inheritance that had been shouldered by others, those whose portraits arrayed the passageway. Portraits that followed Henry's entire line back to the beginning, to paintings that would be considered religious. The final painting, which looked as fresh as if it were just painted, depicted Dorian and Magethna in full angelic garb, escorting the Fallen from the Golden Land, his own ancient ancestor among them.

5

Fire and Ash

In preparation for Savila's entry, Dagon unsheathed the sword from within his coat, held it up, then twirled it twice. He lowered the point to the ground. Black scales wove in and out on the grip of his sword, which he rested on as he bowed and dropped to one knee.

Thunder split the ground when a beastly dragon with silver scales emerged from the gorge at the intersection of Chicago and Forest Avenue. Fire and ash spewed as the dragon soared upwards. Its wings unfolded to resemble that of a bat. Claw-like fingers retracted in and out around each wing. Two prominent horns stuck out at each of its temples, curving as they pinched in and out like weapons as strong as a vise. The movement of the horns pulled the muscles of its face tight, exposing the cheek bones. Its arms and legs had talons as long as swords. Its tail swept sideways, destroying anything in its path. Soulless eyes tore like fire at its target: the house where the Seraphs were standing guard. The dragon landed at the intersection, mocking the Seraphs as it evaluated the battle ground before it. This dragon was not of this world, transformed into a killing machine by an immortal *coup d'état*.

Dagon did not move, did not even look up. The wind picked up and swirled like a tornado toward the dragon. The beast opened its mouth, revealing alternating rows of razor-sharp steel teeth, the most vicious dinosaur paling in comparison. Its vast wings beat faster, spreading its arms out wide on both sides, expanding its lungs. The wings savagely thrust up and down, focusing the air around the wings into a tornado, plummeting the air pressure.

The Seraphs faced their adversary, the dragon. They planted their feet firmly for combat.

No sooner were their swords set when the dragon reared its head back and snapped it forward. The jaws opened wide, expelling a putrid stench of sulfur, fire, and ash. A blood curdling roar of grating metal reverberated across Forest Avenue, the gaping hole in the street revealed the entrance to the dragon's lair. Its head gyrated back and forth from the pressure of the vulgar steam which spewed from its mouth. The head of the dragon recoiled back into place, its dangerous jaws clamping shut. The sound of metal gears scraped along into a sinister steel smile.

Dagon rose and faced the dragon. In a show of honor, Dagon wielded his sword in a large arc over his head. An optical illusion made the engraved branches on his sword appear to break the plane of the blade, only to rejoin the blade when his sword came to rest in front of his face. The dragon shook, blurring and obscuring itself until finally, a woman emerged from the haze. Steam sizzled in the air. A tornado-like vapor rotated toward the woman's back, pulling the steam back inside of her.

Unlike the beastly dragon, she was drop-dead gorgeous. She walked methodically like a chess piece. Not a knight or a rook but a queen. Her knee-high boots crossed over each other as her hips swayed tantalizingly. Her black dress combined fashion elements of a mini skirt and long dress. A long swooping piece of fabric slithered down her side clinging tightly to her hips, accentuating her voluptuous body. The piece of fabric wickedly flapping and slithering behind her like a snake.

Her collar slanted to the left with feathery threads rippling in the wind along the edge. Her long sleeves had the same feathery edging, accentuating her red, manicured fingernails. Shards of glass held her golden hair in place. Her midnight blue eyes set like steel. Scintillating light shot out from the top of a massive round diamond ring, and light ricocheted off every fine cut angle.

Brazenly, she flaunted her bauble in the face of its creators, Dorian and Magethna. With diamond-hard will, she prepared to crush them while the gleam of her ring reflected in their eyes. This, Dagon couldn't wait to see. The memories of his creation, clouded by Savila's doctrine and charismatic lust for power, left him anticipating someone's destruction.

She made her way to Dagon and stood in front of him.

"Lady Savila, your presence has been expected." He pointed the tip of his sword to the ground, submitting to her authority.

Her nails subtly stroked the fabric on her hip. A wicked grin hardened on her mouth, her tongue dragging over her parched blood-stained lips, seeking moisture.

Savila was thirsty and shot a glance in the direction of Mary's house.

Dagon's heart raced. He needed to draw Savila's thirst toward himself to shield Mary, but how?

Savila raised her arms over her head, then flicked her fingers toward the sky. The fog drifted past a cloud which fluttered and floated to the earth, resembling a sheet. The sheet picked up speed as it fell toward the ground. Halfway down, the sheet ripped into three pieces, each one falling together at the same pace. The three pieces twisted and thickened. Three snakes appeared to slither and coil as they made their descent. Amber slit eyes never lost sight of their destination. Fraying threads appeared from each snake. Their mouths opened revealing sharp silver teeth, fraying threads becoming their forked tongues.

The snakes writhed in mid-air until all three of them landed on the ground. They slithered toward their appointed position, waiting for the command from their master.

Savila waved her hand over the three coils. "Arise, my kings."

The three coils swayed back and forth with Savila, the snake charmer. The three coils, now taller than their master, were no longer snakes but Shadow Kings. Their spiked crowns glinted with lethal sharpness. In submission to Savila, three vaporous black swords unsheathed, the tips of the swords pointing to the ground.

"We are yours, Lady Savila," said the Shadow Kings.

Dagon rolled his eyes.

"What is this? Lunion is not amongst his brothers?" Dorian's question was perfectly timed for safeguarding Mary's blood from Savila's blade.

"He's dead. I killed him." Dagon's cold, direct, and matter-of-fact revelation repulsed the Shadow Kings, but more importantly to Dagon, it hit its mark with Savila. Her posture seethed hate in his direction.

"Jealousy," said Lady Savila, slandering him.

"A casualty of war," said Dagon. "A war you fueled."

In the stagnant air, no one said anything.

Everything has its price tag. But no amount of money could replace Mary. Dagon swallowed deeply, preparing himself for the price he would soon pay. He played a scene in his mind.

"Here's your bill,'" said the voice of a waitress. Dagon took a pleasant drink from a cup. Then Mary's voice said, "No, I'll pay it." Taking another drink, Dagon swallowed the now bitter liquid. "No, I will pay it."

Lady Savila sneered, and Dagon sneered back.

"You know the law and who is bound to it." Her demeanor changed from a beautiful queen to a slick prosecuting attorney.

"*You* were created by the law and are likewise bound to it," said Magethna, serenely composed, pointing to the fence in front of them, for even if Lady Savila wanted to, she could not pass through the gate.

Barrier or no barrier, Lady Savila removed her coal-black double-edged sword. The hilt was an image of her dragon-self, while the cross bar resembled her wings. The Shadow Kings' misty drawn blades resembled her sword, but her blade was more active. Waves pulsed through her blade and seemed to bend to her mood. A presence unto its own, the sword swirled in hues of scarlet, seeking out blood to quench its angry thirst.

"The law is in place for now, but one day you will call me master, and you will bow to me. You and the pathetic Bennetts will remain on your knees and will not move," said Savila.

"Humble, isn't she?" Dagon murmured.

A muffled snarl lifted her lip. Her body readied to strike.

He said nothing, pleased to add more fuel to his sacrificial fire. From experience, he knew she enjoyed supplying the fire to all who defied her.

She sang in hissing sounds. The words and eerie melody grated and made him cringe, like those nasty lemon drops. The Shadow Kings and Dagon sheathed their swords in preparation for what was coming. No swords would be raised in homage.

"You can approach us now," said Magethna, standing in front of Mark's bedroom window.

Savila dissolved through the gate, steam hissing behind her as she moved toward Magethna.

"You cannot deny me what is mine by the law. The blood of humanity is by rights mine. You are only delaying the inevitable. My patience dwindles as my sword thirsts. You know it is by my sword that blood will spill, thus propitiating the laws of nature. I did not set these laws, but laws they remain, and laws will be obeyed."

"We know the laws and saw them set. You were not there, so do not think you can challenge us on its constitution, for you will fail. You are allowed only what the law requires," said Dorian.

"The law requires ..." Her finger shot up fast, red polish now mimicking the flow of blood, glistening in the moonlight. Her skeletal finger pointed to Mark's bedroom window, "That boy will come to me."

"You do not order time," said Magethna.

"I have re-ordered time."

The Seraphs tilted their heads as if listening to something.

"He is in your domain, but his life is to be spared," said Dorian.

To Dagon, the Seraphs danced to Savila's tune with the laws she re-ordered.

"Yes, it will be allowed and what a perfect day, a day of remembrance. Poignant, is it not? That still leaves my sword parched and the laws of nature dangling precariously. The Stone comes with the boy."

"The Stone stays," said Dorian.

"For now."

No further discussion was necessary. Lady Savila turned around, her billowing train flicked up sharply as she dissolved back through the gate. She hissed to the kings.

Dagon stood frozen in place. His mind raced, protected from eavesdroppers. His emotions were numbed. Frost bite would set in if he stayed numb too long. Pain was better, for when one is numb, they cease to care. Exposed and vulnerable, one would be easily manipulated by the desires of the devious. What he really needed was another cigarette, to take another calming drag.

Savila began to shake in a hazy blur as a tornado-like vapor surrounded her. Steam moved over the curves of her body. With one swoop of her hand, she changed back into a dragon. The piece of fabric from her dress changed into a crushing tail. The dragon wings flapped, picking up speed. Her head reared back and thrust out fast, causing fire and ash to expel from her mouth. A roar thundered from her mouth, shaking the ground. The dragon flew quickly into the air then plummeted into the gorge and was gone.

After Savila left, an intense light raced down Forest Avenue, moving through the gorge. The ground violently rocked. Gravity tore at the light, sucking it beneath the ground. Once again, Dagon's attention rested on that fleck caught in the gorge. The shaking diminished with the shrinking intensity of the light. Grinding to a halt, the ground sealed shut.

So much for that light. Just another piece of dust buried in the ground.

What a grim reminder of his own existence. He did not want to be hidden away, but to live above ground in the open with Mary. Thinking of her and what he had to do meant one thing: sacrifice.

His thoughts streamed through his mind too rapidly, making him edgy and possibly vulnerable. Taking no chances with Mary's life, he ate another lemon drop. Crunching and shivering violently, goose-bumps popped up all over his body, causing him to shiver again. The foul candy tasted worse than the one he last endured, if that could be possible. He would have eaten nails if he knew it tasted better. At least the benefits outweighed the taste, his mind closed for business.

Lighting a cigarette, he took a deep drag, letting the nicotine do its work. His tension eased, blown away with his exhale. He was now ready to do what he had to, and with this, he walked toward the Abyss. Mr. Cool and Sledge, who had flanked him at Mark's gate, halted, unable to go any further. After inhaling one last drag, he flicked its light out. Red and silver ashes floated to the ground like cursed fairy dust. The ground opened, and he walked down into the Abyss. He swallowed a lump in his throat just as the ground swallowed him into darkness.

6

Power of Blood

The light above rose over his world of night. Darkness had its good qualities; he could hide his reason to live for Mary. A man with a will is harder to kill.

Black glass, made from volcanic obsidian rocks, glowed along the path. Each step created multiple mirrored images of himself, which he didn't enjoy.

He approached the door to the Throne Room. Two shadow soldiers guarded the entrance. Each held two vaporous blades which overlapped the door. In unison, the two shadows pulled up their blades, letting Dagon enter as they bowed.

The Throne Room was expansive and rectangular. The glass floor held gruesome swirls of blood pulsing underneath it which coincided with Savila's temper. Eerie strips of partially burnt cloth hung from the rough black concrete walls and ceiling. The burnt strips were her trophies, with frayed edges subtly swaying. After she killed her victims and burnt their flesh into shadows, Savila had her prisoners hang the cloths. The oldest and most sacred to her were the burnt reminders of immortal obedience from her Seraphic kin when their bodies submitted to her will through fire, flame, and ash. The glory of the Shadow Kings' transformation hung above her throne.

Savila said nothing at Dagon's entry. Silence messed with his composure. His emotions screamed in his body. Savila enjoyed toying with her subjects like this; he knew this all too well.

Her fingernails drummed the armrest. Her jaw clenched. Her throne reflected a carved graven image of her dragon self. Wings with clawed fingers wrapped around her, curving inward to form arm rests. Her hairpiece of broken glass glistened, reflecting the blood under the floor.

He would not hang his head in shame. He would not give her the satisfaction. For Mary, for himself, he straightened his body and walked over to his throne. The scarlet color from the blood under the glass reflected and swirled on the surface of his black onyx throne. Blood in this context was a warning, submit or be destroyed. Trying his best to hide his edginess in the haunted house, he sat and occupied himself by shining his armrest.

"It is one thing when you are above, and I call you, but it is entirely another thing when you are in my dominion and yet you keep me waiting." Her acidic words cut the air around them. Her hand clenched into a fist and struck her armrest, and the swirls of red in the floor echoed her violent mood. Savila rose from her throne. Her train followed her, gliding over the red swirls beneath the glass. "They thought King Lunion still lived. Why did you inform them otherwise?"

"Where do you think that they thought he was? On holiday?"

Savila slowly moved to the side of his throne, her train barely moving, and she brought her thirsty blade to his neck. His mind escaped to Mary.

"Your existence hangs by a thread." Savila barely raised her voice. Real, unquestionable power did not need to be loud to make its point. "I gave you your power and can easily take it away. I gave you the choice of power by sealing your title over humanity, bound by the ruby of your investiture. For that reason, you and your mate will co-rule by my side, and yet, this is how you repay me? I have no master in my dominion, for I am the master."

She leaned in closer to his ear, causing him to grip his armrests. He focused on imagining the intense blue of Mary's eyes, bracing himself against Savila's cruelty. Savila may not have raised her voice, but the raised sword sliced his skin, drawing blood. He showed no outward signs of pain, though the blade burned, blistering his throat with the fire of its sharpness. Her sword drank from his wound, bringing his blood up the blade and into the hilt. The parched skin of her wrinkled hand regained its youth, which continued up her arm and rejuvenated her entire body. She flung the excess onto the floor, adding to the swirling blood underneath the glass. She took her left hand and placed it over the wound.

"You see? I can be merciful," said Savila, healing the wound.

Her mercy overshadowed by the unmistakable warning in her words. He sat struggling to hold on to his mental oasis. Quite simply, he was being punished. His high rank did not spare him the penalty of what Savila deemed as insubordination. Her back-handed attempt at mercy only made the punishment crueler. The blood loss made him more alert, but not as in control as it normally did. Yet seeing his blood on the floor gave him strength. He changed the mental image of his bloodletting to that of donating blood, making it more palatable for his mind to wrestle with. A blade at your throat makes you take stock of your life quick and think fast. Unwittingly, she helped him.

The gentle, swirling waves of his blood moved under the glass.

"They know so little. This only shows how limited the power of the Golden Land is." She smirked. "The boy's dream went well then, just as I thought it would."

He said nothing, nodded his head, and stared into space.

"You will provide a written agreement that your mate will lure him in."

This horrible command didn't completely take Dagon off guard. He half expected it. Mary did not have to be involved in Mark's capture. Savila relished in causing him deep misery and delighted in smashing all options of hope, just because she could. He squirmed in his seat. "How long do I have?"

"Four grains of sand."

"A month?"

Savila smiled. Her answer confirmed he had just one month.

"Well then, you must present your plan to me before the stroke of midnight. You have a lot at stake, Dagon: a life for lives, as it were. Before you are dismissed, I offer you one caveat, which will aid you in conjuring up a plan. The boy's family spends Memorial Day each year at their friends' house, surname Glynn."

Dagon arose from his throne and headed out. The shadow soldiers brought their swords up, saluted him as he passed, and closed the entrance behind him.

Savila remained on her throne, watching Dagon walk down the hallway. The sound of his heels echoed along the glass, emphasizing the hollowness in his soul. His mind remained blank. Closing her eyes, she watched him head to his private quarters, then *poof*, he became invisible to her.

Savila imagined herself sitting like a black widow, motionless. In the hunt, humans might think that the spider slept, but this would be folly, for her still appearance would be deathly deceiving. Her limbs felt loose and relaxed. A trap in disguise. Tightening muscles aroused her senses as prey drew closer. Without warning she would strike, taking her victims by surprise. She cared not for the outward body, which dangles, but for the life within which thrashes and squirms, fighting to live.

With this, Savila relished how humans instinctively feared creatures that hide in the dark. Her mind saw this truth in an ancient storybook, *The Princely Stone*, passed down to Henry by his father. A gift from those pesky Seraphs, Dorian and Magethna. The book, with its loud voice, now lay closed and still in Mark's room as it should.

Savila despised the book, though it had its uses. Its current function was to terrorize children with a monster humanity had tried to sanitize. Their naivety only made her evil more fun and easier to sink into the hidden recesses of their souls. "After all, they're just stories." Savila laughed.

The three Shadow Kings appeared out of the rough concrete wall. Once inside the Throne Room, they stood at attention while Savila came toward them. The train of her dress moved over the glass as waves of blood carried her toward them.

"We heard everything, Lady Savila," said Lamel.

"Blood speaks, my kin. The sands are falling into place. As the great gathering commences, we shall smite all who oppose us and bring the Golden Land to its knees."

"How many grains of sand must fall before Lunion is avenged?" All the brothers' hands touched their swords.

"The hour is upon us, and the sands will bind to the king I chose. An ancient memory reborn."

"We long for this," said the Shadow Kings.

"Dagon cannot rule without a title. You are bound to the blood, and Dagon must be made to see reason," said Lamel.

The two brothers of Lamel nodded.

"There will be a day of reckoning: a day where the blood to which I am bound will be written in stone." Savila's hands curved into the air and clenched into fists. She brought them down to her sides and continued. "I will erect a monument greater than all the pharaohs of Egypt and the emperors of Rome. My monument will seal everything that was, is, and is yet to come."

"After the Boy is taken, the Golden Land may try to aid in saving humanity."

"I have foreseen this. Their efforts will only raise me to power and nothing more. Bonds of old will be crushed and then made new. Lamel, you will assist Lord Dagon after he delivers his plan to me."

All three reached inside of their vaporous garments, pulling out three gray stones. Presenting them to her as if they were jewels, they bowed their heads.

She took the stones one by one and placed them onto Lord Dagon's throne.

"Stones from a recent earthquake ... you did well," said Savila.

"All will be as you have ordered. What do the thoughts of Dagon's blood say?" said Lamel.

"He's in love, but love has a price," said Savila.

"And what is this price you speak of?" asked Ligon. "His bonded mate has been thinking about the childhood plans she made."

"These plans have been elusive because of her insurmountable sufferings," added Listian. "The beauty is Lord Dagon will dutifully pay the price which his love requires, perpetuating deep emotional grief."

The Shadow Kings delighted at the seeds of guilt and despair, which Savila had cultivated in Mary's life. Their sprouts festering, Savila cut new furrows even deeper than before. Their root system buried deep into Mary's soul, choking out the nourishing benefits of hope.

In a blur, Savila brandished her sword and flicked another drop of Dagon's blood onto the glass floor. The Shadow Kings dissolved back through the wall. Savila sheathed her sword, watching the new addition swirl and blend with the old, the fabric of her dress caressing the glass as she moved back to her throne. She sat, eyeing the fabric trophies above her head, licking her lips.

Patting her sword, waves of blood chained to her thirst pounded the glass beneath her. Tilting her head, she smirked as she waited for the boy to be her prisoner of death. *Dorian and Magethna will be rendered helpless, seeing no option but submission.*

With this delicious thought, she pulled out one of the shards of glass from her hair, holding it up in mockery of the Seraphs. Her kin had forged all the vials of the eternal flame which hang on the White Tree in the Golden Land. The One Voice forbade anyone to pluck a vial from this tree, for fear of death. Blood from the glass floor reflected through the shard as she twisted it back and forth in her hand, allowing the memories it held to flow through her.

~

THE BATTLE OF AGINCOURT, France, 1415

"King Lunion desires your title," whispered Savila into Dagon's ear. She caressed his neck with the tip of an arrow.

Dagon didn't even flinch as she drew blood, his full attention on the battlefield before them.

Savila eased the arrow into his hand, brushing her fingertips against the fletching. "Let fly," she murmured, stepping back.

Dagon nocked the arrow and obeyed. The arrow sailed straight for King Lunion's heart. At the last moment, a cry caused him to turn. The arrow grazed Lunion's shoulder then it struck the owner of the warning cry, a soldier running toward him. In a blast of gray smoke, Lunion simply evaporated. Without a word, Dagon turned and left the battlefield. The soldier lay screaming in mortal agony, his conquest for kingship denied in this life.

In a veil of secrecy, she offered the dying soldier a chance for immortality. With his last breath, his soul entered her dominion. In her dragon form, she flew to the soldier's castle where she found his infant son sleeping.

Savila stroked the boy's curls, flowing over her fingers, turning her nails black as ebony, when the boy's mother entered the room.

"Who are you?" The woman quivered.

"You must know this day would come. You bartered your son, so your husband would be king." Savila patted the boy's head. "You have a selfish mother."

"I changed my mind. You can't have him!"

"Your husband's earthly body lies dead. Kingship, though denied in his life, will be restored in another. In my thirst, you will die. Your son will rise to be a king through paternal blood."

"No! Please ... I'll give you anything!"

"Yes, you will."

Black acid smoke moved over Savila's sword as she slashed and burned the skin at the lady's throat, killing her. The infant awoke. Silently, he stared at Savila as her sword drank from a gurgling fountain of his mother's blood. Sheathing her sword, she took out an arrow from within her cloak, dipped the arrowhead in the woman's blood, then placed it back inside the cloak.

As if the baby knew his destiny, he made no cry as Savila picked him up. At the same time, the soul of his mother fell into the Abyss. With the baby inside her dragon skin, she flew to the home of his paternal uncle. The baby's eyes widened as she flew away.

Savila said nothing as she walked into the Execution Room. The soul of the infant's mother struggled against the ropes that bound her to the stake.

"Please, please release me," the woman pleaded.

"You are in my dominion, and I can't look upon you. Leave no traces of her," said Savila to a shadow soldier.

"Burn the traitor. Burn the traitor. Let her burn," the shadow soldiers chanted.

Fire raked over the woman, burning her into shadow. Mortals, burned into shadow, are decimated in the Abyss. And now this traitor soul had been banished into oblivion.

Savila loved recounting this event. She replaced the shard of glass back in her hair with reverence to herself. Soon, Dagon's existence will be burned to ash as if he had never been created. Until then, she would dig deeper into his blistering soul. Past hurts never leave, their sorrow relived in the present, casting off hope for the future.

7

Scheduling Book

A car screeched into gear as it drove along in front of the Bennett house.

Henry sat in his office, one floor down and directly under Mark's room.

Dorian and Magethna materialized in front of his desk.

Henry's knees hit his desk. "That still startles me," he said, rubbing his sore knees.

"It is good to see you again." Dorian held out his hand. "Your hair is graying."

Henry shook his hand. "I'm surprised I'm not fully gray by now."

"Dorian, you shouldn't remind humans of their aging." Magethna smiled at Henry and held out her hand. Henry shook her hand, then ran his fingers through his hair.

"There are two more Seraphs here with us." Magethna waved her hand in the air, moving ceiling and walls.

Henry didn't move a muscle, his mouth gaping.

"It is an honor to meet you. I'm Raglen. Magethna and Dorian speak highly of you and your kin

"And I'm Mystil." She bowed her head.

"It is nice to meet ... the both of you."

Magethna waved her hand in the air again, putting the ceiling and walls back in place.

"It is always good to remember that there are no coincidences for the lives of mortals or in the existence of immortals." Magethna pointed to her and Dorian. "Dorian and I knew the family line from your fallen ancestor were chosen..."

"To die!" Henry hit the desk with his hand, then sat back in his chair. With one hand he rubbed his forehead, and with the other hand, he wiped a tear off his cheek.

"No, Henry, to live." Magethna went over to him and touched his shoulder.

"Then you're not here to guard Mark, and he's safe?"

No sooner had Henry said this, when a wing of a dove batted at a window in the office.

Dorian put his hand through the glass. The dove landed on his palm, and he brought it inside through the glass. The dove spread out its feathers on Dorian's hand and transformed into paper.

"That's Snowcap." Henry rubbed his head harder. "When you gave William the dove for his birthday, I didn't know it could do ... *that.*"

"He's a smart bird," said Dorian.

"The message on the feathers is for you, Henry," said Magethna. "Though your nephew, Mark, is being guarded by Seraphic intervention, you need to rest in hope."

Henry hung his head. "What does that mean for Mark?"

"Your family was chosen, as was Mark, for these times," answered Dorian. "Even now, after centuries of friendship with your kin, the bond is still prevalent. Like your father, Martin, and the generations before him, you have been an excellent steward of believing in and instilling hope. Do not despair now. We do not know the whole path for Mark, but we do know, not everything is meant for evil. To have

Seraphic qualities, like being able to see us, and to have some fore-knowledge of future events. You can also cast your thoughts and feelings onto others." Dorian pointed his finger up toward Mark's room.

"These are generous gifts the One Voice bestowed on your family," said Magethna.

"I guess I can remain hopeful, even though...Mark." His doubts and quivering arms proved he was fully human.

"Do you think strength comes from what you see or in the knowledge you know?" asked Dorian.

"The world can't see all of you, but ..." said Henry.

"You can!" Magethna pointed at Henry and smiled. "I'm not making light of this, but the fact remains, if Savila only needed Mark, we wouldn't be here."

"Can I make Mark believe what I want him to believe?"

"No more than we can make you believe that evil is *not* the only influence." Dorian crossed his arms.

Henry nodded.

Little chirps caused the paper on Dorian's hand to flutter. "There is another message." Dorian rubbed the paper with his hand, silencing the dove. "All the hot action is back at home ..."

"Even for the mind of an immortal analyst, these modern words sound cryptic," said Dorian.

Bewildered, the Seraphs looked at Henry.

"It means William is coming home and not to start the party without him."

"Party? Oh, I love parties! I will create a dress for this lovely occasion." Magethna beamed. "And ..." She nipped at her lip, thinking. "Wait now, I will wear what I wore four years ago, for it is a classic."

"But to wear that again and with friends you rarely see ... I'm not sure ..." said Mystil.

"I'm sure Dorian would wear something different." Raglen firmly crossed his arms.

"Wait, wait," said Dorian. "There are other matters at hand—"

Magethna stood firm, hands on her hips. "Mystil is right, even in the Seraphic world, one would never wear the clothes of humanity several times over. It may be a classic but to wear it again? No, you will do no such thing. I will tailor yours myself if I have to." Her mental scissors snipped at the fabric for her own dress.

"You can design a new jacket for me," Dorian conceded, "but my white shirt, brown trousers, waistcoat, and bow tie stay!"

Magethna seemed to think it through and agreed to the compromise. She eyed him head to toe as if to ascertain his measurements, beaming at the creations she would soon reveal. "I feel like the fairy godmother in Cinderella, and you will have a grand blazer."

Dorian did not say a word while the designer-fairy-godmother created away in her mental studio.

"I wonder if it should be white?" she mumbled and squinted while pulling thread through the eye of a needle.

"White? You didn't wear white four years ago. Besides, this isn't a wedding, it's a war!" Dorian looked to Henry for help.

"Are you referring to the veil?" said Magethna. "I simply wondered if my dress should be white. Of all the things to bring up."

"Yes, that's bad form," said Mystil to Dorian.

"Magethna knows, I had no intention in bringing that up," Dorian said while still looking at Henry.

Bemused, Henry just shrugged. "I just feel so much better about things now that you're all here, and William's coming home."

"I do know," said Magethna, "but if I had a scheduling book, I could write down memories like this." She waved her hand, transforming the room.

Four years earlier

TRIUMPH AND VICTORY waited on the driveway of the boarding school Mark attended in London while Dorian and Magethna stood at the door, unsure of what to do. With the constant rain, the ancient castle structure stood soggy and gloomy, the stone gargoyles upon their perches the only signs of life.

"Maybe the door opens by itself when it's ready," said Magethna.

"How do humans usually announce their presence?" Dorian searched the intimidating wood panels.

"Like that lovely gentleman is doing across the street."

"He doesn't look very gentle." Dorian scowled at the distance. "He looks upset."

"Nonsense! The doors are just too thick for the humans to hear, that's all."

"Very well, I will do the honors." Dorian banged on the door. "We're here, Henry!"

The man who opened the door stared at them, mouth hung open. "Are you ... um ... Mr. Bennett's friends? Mr. Dorian and the Lady Magethna?"

"Most certainly," answered Dorian with a flourished bow.

"Is anything amiss, sir?" Magethna asked as the man continued to gawk. "You were expecting us, yes?"

"No! I mean yes."

Magethna looked down at her outfit and across to Dorian's, following the man's gaze. She had chosen a long flouncy embroidered pink chiffon dress with eye-dazzling silver shoes. Dorian had on a waistcoat with loud, yellow squares.

"Too much sparkle?" Magethna closed her lacey parasol. "This wouldn't be the first time I missed the current fashion trends by a century or so."

Um, no ... the both of you look fine ... just fine." The man stepped back, opening the door fully. "My apologies. I am Mr. Dawson, Mr. Bennett's assistant. Please, come in. The Bennetts await you in the office of the headmistress."

Mr. Dawson brought Dorian and Magethna into a room with an enormous picture window. Three crystal chandeliers hung over a cherry wood table with a delicate piece of fabric draped over it.

The man knocked twice upon a mahogany door at the back of the room then left.

Henry walked out of the door, closing it behind him. His eyes, swollen, he reached out to clasp their hands. "Magethna, Dorian, it's good to see you both. How I have longed for this moment. I just wish the circumstances were different. Thank you for coming when I called. The sudden loss of Arthur has left us all in grief."

"Your brother was a great man," said Dorian, placing a hand on Henry's shoulder.

"Though it remains a difficult time for you," added Magethna, "know that he now resides in the Golden Land."

Henry nodded. "I know this, and Frances knows this. But our focus is on Mark. It's been quite a blow to him."

"We will veil ourselves for now so as not to complicate matters even further," said Magethna. "You alone will see us."

Inside the door, the office showcased a massive, mahogany desk before which Frances knelt in front of Mark, who was hunched over and dwarfed within a high-backed, leather chair. Mark's crisp school uniform creased in contrast to his crest-fallen demeaner. The headmistress stood by the desk, stiff, yet patient.

The seraphs shadowed Henry, who sat next to Mark and placed a reassuring hand on the boy's shoulder.

"For the most part, Mark is a gentle, kind student," said the head-mistress. "He is inclined to curiosity which reflects his tardiness, and—"

"I like adventures," Mark whispered.

"Speaking when not spoken to," continued the headmistress with a sharp tap of her foot. "Scuffling in the courtyard—"

"They were trying to rob me, but I wouldn't let them."

"Rob you! That's ridiculous."

"Rob you?" said Frances, her tone gentle. "Of what, honey?"

"Of this." Mark pulled a chain from around his neck and placed its pendant in Henry's hand. A silver key.

Henry knelt in front of Mark "Your dad gave you this?"

Mark nodded. "The last time he came to visit."

"Do you know what it opens?"

"His writing desk. But it doesn't work. He said to give it to you, and you would know what to do with it."

"None of our students steal," the headmistress insisted. "Ever. Mark, I am simply warning your aunt and uncle of your behavior."

"Madam," Henry said, standing. "I think we can re-acquaint ourselves with Mark in due time."

"Yes," said Frances. "We will be taking him back to the States with us. There's no question."

"His father's endowment ensures his place with us for his entire educational career," the headmistress countered.

"Ah, I see your hesitation in seeing him go." Henry looked down at Mark who stared at him with huge, somber eyes.

"I beg your pardon! I only want what's best for Mark."

"What's best for him is to be with family," said Frances.

All three began to speak at the same time.

"Do I get a choice?" said Mark, breaking through the rising voices.

"Of course, dear boy," said Henry.

Mark turned and stared at Magethna. Taken aback, Magethna stepped toward Dorian, with whom she exchanged startled glances. Their veils were drawn, she was certain. He could not see them, and yet, his sad eyes pinned her where she stood. "I want to go with you to America. There's nothing for me here now."

Shocked silence thundered the room. All eyes followed Mark's to Magethna, but Frances and the headmistress only shook their heads, brows furrowed, their confusion evident. Henry inspected his shoes, a slight smile playing at the corners of his mouth.

The headmistress cleared her throat, rubbing her arms and shivering at what appeared to be a sudden rash of goosebumps. "I will have Mark's things collected."

"Please be assured," said Henry, "the rest of the term's tuition and boarding is paid."

"No, no, it will be refunded to his account." The headmistress crossed the room to the door. "I will not take money from the dead."

∾

MAGETHNA FLOURISHED HER IMAGINARY QUILL. "Ah, we ended the memory just in time. Henry, do you remember what I told you after you brought Mark home?"

"You said Savila used the timing of a terrorist attack to get Arthur killed." Henry's shoulders drooped.

Magethna gently lifted Henry's chin. "Many humans lost their lives. This is Savila's aim. The ruby invested to Dagon was a gift, an *entente cordiale* to humanity. Dorian split the ruby in half on a battlefield in France where Nuvila handed one half to the English king. That half remains with the current rulers of England. The other half …"

"Savila gave to my ancestors," Henry continued, easing back into his chair. "And Arthur gave it to Mark, which means Arthur must have known he was going to die. My question is, what is Dagon's role in all this?"

"Balance of power," said Dorian. "Savila can't rule the Second Land without Dagon, or at least without his title. Dagon can't rule the Second Land as long as the Ruby remains in the custody of humanity. His investiture as Guardian ensures nothing is all bad or all good."

"Up until this point, your ancestors have inherited the writing desk in Mark's room and owned the key," said Magethna.

"And the desk houses the Ruby," said Henry.

"But the key has another destiny of great significance."

"Arthur would never let me touch the key, but when he wasn't looking, I tried opening the desk. The key never worked." Henry reached into his pocket and pulled out the key. It lay in his palm, dangerous and innocuous at the same time.

"The key is no ordinary key. This is the key to life and death and can only be used by the bearer for a particular purpose. Do you know the origin?"

"No."

"It was Savila's house key in the Golden Land."

"How did it get here, and why doesn't she have it?"

"It was confiscated from Savila when she fell, along with the legions that followed her. But she has plans for it, you can be sure. The key's path is linked to Mark and William—"

"William, too?"

"Yes. For now. Mark is the bearer of the Stone, and the writing desk was specifically crafted to house the Stone. But without the key, the desk will not open for him. The Stone is linked to the book we gave you."

"*The Princely Stone,*" said Henry.

"Indeed," said Dorian. "The Ruby cannot be removed from your house until the appointed time. And now the time draws near."

"But Mark's not ready. He's just a boy! Can't we stall?"

Dorian and Magethna exchanged glances. "Send the key to William."

"But that's not much better! William is coming home."

"Balance of power," said Dorian. "It may only be a few hours or a few days, but it may be just enough to temper the coming storm."

After a moment's hesitation, Henry placed the key on William's letter and folded it.

Magethna whispered into the feathers causing them to ruffle. Chirping and hopping onto Dorian's hand, the bird flapped its wings. Dorian reached his hands through the glass while Magethna hummed, guiding Snowcap back to William.

Impromptu tweeting erupted from other nearby birds. Snowcap's wings flapped in the wind as the dove soared higher heading east.

"Is that smoke above those trees?" Mystil asked.

"Indeed, it is," said Dorian.

"No one seems to be hurt," said Raglen.

"Does anyone hear anything?" said Magethna.

Mystil at first shook her head then stopped. "Wait. Yes, a faint voice, but I can't understand anything."

"Perhaps, we are hearing only what is necessary," said Dorian.

"It's a cry for help ... from Dagon." Magethna looked at Dorian.

"Maybe that is what we are meant to think. Maybe, he is toying with a connection you are trying to rekindle. He is fallen, Magethna. Only a shadow of his former existence remains."

"He is not a shadow. He is half-human. If anything of his former existence clings to him, then I will continue to believe he can change." Magethna placed both of her hands over her heart.

"I know he is not a shadow." Dorian placed his hands behind his back.

"Then all is not lost," said Magethna while staring out the window.

Chains of broken incoherent thoughts moved further apart as the fumes rose higher, carrying the garbled voice away.

"Maybe what we are seeing and hearing, comes not from the mouth, but the heart," said Magethna. "This is the sort of information I would put in my scheduling book."

8

Private Blood

L ight is always brighter in the dark.

Out of the Throne Room, Dagon inhaled deeply from his cigarette, controlling the flow of nicotine going into his lungs. Holding the smoke in his mouth, he stood there enjoying the pageantry of the soldiers dramatically closing the door. Nodding his head towards the soldiers, he acknowledged their performance while releasing the smoke from his mouth. Heels clacking along and silver ashes falling around him, he headed down the darkened hall to his private quarters.

Out of habit, he scanned his room, satisfied. In his room, he could freely be himself, but it tasted bitter-sweet. His cigarette created a smoke screen around him, while his reason for living was being used as a pawn.

On his ebony chair, he stared at the ground. He covered his face and wished he could remove every ounce of pain from Mary. To ask her to lure Mark ... he had no words for this grief. He loved her more than his own existence, and to ask her to do this was unthinkable. But unavoidable. No amount of pain he inflicted on himself would be justified. In the end, Savila owned his sword, his life, and the life of his bonded mate in exchange for power.

Not bothering to remove any of his clothes, he sat like a warrior on a battlefield. He unsheathed his dagger and, with a cry through gritted teeth, sliced his arm. The pain ripped through him. Blood flowed into the crook of his elbow, saturating his shirt. His shame and guilt flowed with his blood, making him feel alive and in control.

He gripped the dagger's hilt as a surge of blood moved down both sides of his arm. *Here's your bill.* A bill he would willingly pay for Mary, indefinitely if need be. A gaping wound now burned under the sleeve of his shirt. Fraying fibers raked his raw flesh. Methodically, he cleaned his dagger. From his coat, he removed a crystal lighter.

Once the bleeding stopped, he eased out of his shirt. He ignited the lighter and waved the fire under the shirt. White flames raced upward, the fire engulfing every fiber.

Wincing, he walked across his spacious room and into the closet. Out of the corner of his eye, he saw something black scurrying behind rows of shoes. Cautiously, he went to investigate when a spider shot out. He brought his boot down onto it, squishing it dead. He had no fear of spiders, but they still grossed him out, for he did not like anything in his quarters that he did not place or invite in. "Nice try."

Years of living on the edge and under the ground made him slightly paranoid. These unwanted creatures were spies. He cleaned the remnants of the spider from the floor and torched it out of existence.

Pulling off his boots and remaining clothes, he placed them into a duffel bag and eased his aching, lonely body into the mineral waters.

If this tub were anywhere else, this would be the life. Maybe I can put one in Mary's house, smaller of course.

With a chill in the air, he dried off and dressed. He went over to the side of his bed and stood in front of a floor length curtain. With a firm yank, he opened the curtain to reveal blackness. In most ways, it was odd for him to have a window below the earth, for there was nothing to see except varying shades of black mountains, which formed when Savila smashed one of the vials of the eternal flame, creating the Abyss. This shameful thought made his wounds throb.

"Unbelievable." he said out loud, looking through the window. Set upon a rocky ledge, the small speck he had seen earlier grew brighter being underground. He yanked the curtains closed, extinguishing the light.

Going over to the bed, he grabbed a bottle of shampoo and a book, *The Iliad*, his favorite. He pondered the book, its old pages worn from hours of reading. This book had been Alexander the Great's favorite, too, his written guide on warfare. Dagon admired him for how he had lived his life out in the open, risking everything, giving it his all. Out in the blackened hallway, a light in his heart moved him on, encouraging him to live his life out in the open.

A SMILE CAME over Savila as she sensed Dagon's blood awaken. His blood called to her from his weakened mind, making her thirsty again even though her lips were still moist and supple from the recent drink. In a moment, his thoughts quieted. Tasting victory, she lingered on the stones her kin delivered. Stones she will fashion into an altar of death. *Poetic justice.* She gloated over her former conquests, the strips of cloth which hung subservient to her will. A hint of their former military glory remained in the twisted lapels and crushed medals. These uniforms bowed to their new general, their new master. On the battlefield, before the soldiers' last mortal breaths expelled, Savila had come like an angel of mercy. She offered her hand and the gift of immortality to those fallen soldiers. The soldiers had only seconds to decide if they wanted to live in immortal glory or die in mortal agony.

In the light of day, Dagon made his ascent out of the Abyss. With pleasure, the spider watched and waited for her victim to make his way into her invisible web.

9

Hopeful Romantic

A door opened in the hallway above Henry's study. The Seraphs and Henry turned toward the sound. Mark rumbled down the stairs past Henry's study door.

"He, too, could use a scheduling book to know the time of meals, thus additional chores," said Magethna.

Dorian's eyebrows rose.

"Are my notions for a scheduling book grandiose? Perhaps. They are my notions, and I would love one. I can see your mind spinning around every correlation, trying to validate all this." She twirled a finger in the air.

"I don't understand it. I just don't." Dorian squinted.

"Most things are not understood." Magethna beamed.

"Analysis clarifies," said Dorian.

"Yes, I know, but ..."

Dorian touched her arm. "Do all of you hear that?"

All the Seraphs detected whistling, growing louder by the

moment. They looked out the window. A light clicking of heels moved to the rhythm of the whistled tune as Lord Dagon stepped through a watery veil, now standing openly in the light of day. Dagon saluted them, but they did not return the gesture. Dagon's mood seemed light and fresh, as if he had forgotten what happened the day before. To the Seraphs, he acted like any normal man walking down the street. Right on cue, a light breeze caught under his trench coat, which was draped over his arm looking quite earthly but expensive.

"WHAT A NIGHT," said Dagon.

He lit a cigarette. Thin tendrils of smoke began escaping from of his mouth.

"Dagon, is there anything else you like to do besides smoke?" said Dorian.

Magethna exaggeratedly waved her arms, coughing.

"I like to eat and listen to rock and roll, not necessarily in that order."

"Don't you look nice today. What is that jacket called, and what kind of pants are those?" said Magethna, smiling cheerfully.

"Oh ... um ... thank you. The jacket is called a blazer, and the pants are blue jeans." Dagon was flabbergasted, not by the question but by the compliment.

"You see, Dorian, even Dagon wears a blazer."

Mystil's eyebrow rose.

Dagon closed his jacket and wanted to crawl into a hole. *Maybe they won't even notice my t-shirt.*

No such luck, for Magethna asked him about it.

"That is private. Anyway, I've got to go now." Not waiting around, Dagon walked down the sidewalk, making his way over to Mary's house. At her front door, Dagon stopped cold, the air punched out of his lungs.

"How long has it been since you saw him?" The voice on the other side of the door sounded like Mary's friend.

"It's been two weeks, Caroline." Mary's voice was hollow.

"You don't even know him ... he's probably married. You need to get out, have some fun."

"Maybe it would be good to get out." Mary sounded more defeated than convinced.

"What were you doing earlier when you asked me to come over?"

"Just looking at wedding plans that I wrote down when I was twelve."

"Okay. That's it ... we're going out."

"Okay."

Dejected, he turned around, his zombie body lumbering back, coming to the spot where the battle lines had been drawn. *If I only arrived sooner, I could have asked her out first.* In anger, he fired at the cause of his catastrophic delay: the Seraphs.

Quicker than a blink, he tore his sword out of its sheath with such force the friction ignited flames around the edges.

With the same quick stroke, Dorian reached for his sword, but Magethna stopped him. "He has been wounded in the heart by something more powerful than a sword, but at least he retains his sense of humor.

Dorian eased his hand off his sword but glared at Dagon. "You are a hopeful romantic."

"Hopeless romantic," Dagon corrected. "Humans would not say 'hopeful romantic.'"

WITH THAT COMMENT, Dagon put his trench coat on, and in a hazy blur, he manifested into a dragon and shot up like a rocket. Magethna and the other Seraphs continued to watch from Henry's window. The dragon's legs propelled like boosters higher into the atmosphere. Its serpent snout narrowed like an arrow, leading the way into the thinning air. The wind forced its thick black whiskers to its scales. Rows of sharp silver teeth peeked through a wide clenched mouth, lips vibrating in a thin line. The wings looked harmless compared to the rest of the body.

Silver scales folded inward from the shearing of the wind, making the dragon aerodynamic as it flew east. An awful cacophony of yells and screams came from the throat of the sharp whiskered dragon. High pitched, heavy metallic words came from its mouth, followed by guttural non-verbal sounds. "Highway to hell!"

The words were not pleasing to Magethna, though she understood where they came from. The dragon flew further east on wings which began resembling a bird.

"With a scheduling book, he could have been there in time. What if he does not have a way of knowing Mary's schedule?" said Magethna.

"We cannot give Dagon her schedule, and we are not here to alter days. You are not a fairy godmother, and ..." Dorian trailed off when Magethna shooed him with her hand.

"I know. Matters of the heart are obvious to me, surely your scientific mind can see this."

"Matters of the heart are not quantifiable."

"Perhaps, but the explanation is plain as night."

Then, as if a sudden realization hit him, Dorian said, "He cannot read her mind?"

"Cannot or will not?"

"But why?"

"Love." Magethna's reply may be naïve, possibly cliché, but it cut to the heart of the matter.

"Love is plausible, but we know not his intentions for Mary," said Dorian.

"In his anger, he only heard the human response of hopelessness, for his notion of love has been swallowed in darkness, yet a faint light lives in him."

"One can live in the light and yet remain in darkness, hidden."

"All decisions are not made for darkness, for even the hidden want to live in the light, flying free like the dove."

Dorian merely shook his head, their partnership running smooth as it always had. He furrowed his eyebrows, concentrating on some unfathomable concept. "About Dagon's blazer, I don't know if I want you to create that."

"I thought he looked smart. It will all work out just fine." The seamstress was going over her creations in her mind. "There, all done."

"Well, show me what it looks like."

"You will see when it is time and not before. Now you will look dapper, and you will love it! Have I ever dressed you wrong?"

"Well no, but you also have never sewn for me before."

"You remember how my frock looked four years ago? Mr. Dawson could not help but admire our stylish ways."

Dorian couldn't argue with that.

10

Under the Veil

The exchange with the Seraphs gave Dagon an idea that could wind up saving Mary. He decided to go to Rome. Blood was the answer to rescue her, and since blood loss gave Dagon a sense of being alive, he was sure of it. Putting all this together, he set a plan in motion to redeem Mary, a plan which involved Mark. Capitalizing on his emotions being in check, he ran over the details for his European excursion.

No customers stood inside the bank in Rome or outside, so he removed all his Seraphic veils. The clerk practically fell over a chair when Dagon appeared out of nowhere. This bank was not open to the general public, but then, he wasn't exactly the general public. The fun really began when he told the banker he wished to obtain a safe deposit box.

Pen and ink flew, the man writing Mary's and his name on an official document. The banker offered his pen to Dagon for his signature. Dagon waved the pen away. After seeing how Dagon signed his name, the banker shakily reached for the key on his desk and gave it to Dagon, which he again waved away. The banker began sweating profusely while checking the paperwork over. Out of Dagon's coat came two suitcases with large sums of money in them. The clerk passed out cold.

Dagon transferred the money from the suitcases to the lockbox.

Making his way to the vault, he came to two thick Gothic wooden doors, which he dissolved through. The vault was a spacious, almost sterile room, with the exception of one office-style desk and two chairs placed stiffly around it. Before returning the lockbox, he pulled money out and placed some in a wallet and some more in his coat.

Then came the moment he had been waiting for: to see if his old house key from the Golden Land worked here. Made from immortal metal, it should. The lockbox was in the slot when Dagon put the key in the keyhole. With a sigh of relief, it fit, and the contents were safely locked away.

Mission accomplished, he bragged to himself, placing his good old key back into his coat.

FROM SOMEWHERE IN the stratosphere came loud, crunching sounds. The dragon ate its pre-landing snack with gusto, savoring the last morsel before it descended. The Seraphs watched the air show. Gradually descending, its wings spread out like an airplane. It seemed a pilot flew this craft, not the dragon. The wings tilted back and forth as the air caught underneath it. Even its tail flapped side to side, trying to counterbalance the erratic movements of the wings.

"Whoa, Searcher. Steady there." The dragon's voice rasped out between silver clenched teeth. "Steady, girl, steady."

The commands kept rolling as the dragon flicked out claws ready to land.

"His dragon is female and has a name?" said Magethna, turning to Dorian.

"Apparently so."

The dragon's landing was rocky at best, its wings shook at the jolt of the impact. Its legs skidded along the concrete with a grating screech as its claws dug into the firm surface before coming to a complete stop. The pilot, or dragon, needed more flight training. Magethna wondered how this could be the same dragon which had taken off hours earlier, soaring high into the air with flare and force. In a blurry haze, the dragon dissolved away revealing Dagon. He smoothed the scales of his trench coat. He did not acknowledge the Seraphs.

"It was hours, not weeks, since I saw Mary last," Dagon mumbled out loud to himself. "She seemed so happy. At least I thought she was."

"Dragon transformation," said Dorian. "Nice feature, that coat."

Dagon stopped then turned sharply toward the Seraphs. After making eye contact, his body shook, and his mouth and eyes contorted. Then in a blink, he veiled himself. Magethna looked at the other Seraphs, noting their bewildered expressions reflected her own.

DAGON HADN'T WANTED the Seraphs to witness his blunder of audible mumbling. Like a sick joke, he found the same bench Mary had recently occupied, the scene of their first date, now surrounded by nothing but lonely darkness.

Drained and numb, he stared into the night sky, another lonely Abyss. He did not want to go back down to his private quarters. Suddenly, it struck him: He was, for all intents and purposes, a man caught in between two worlds, homeless. Stopping himself from lighting up a cigarette, he filled his lungs with the air of the night. He inhaled deeply, exhaled slowly, the stars bright this night.

The skeptical look that Dorian had given him when he walked past still stung. Trust was not a concept he understood, and he saw very little of it. Although Magethna, he wondered about her. Darkness in contrast to light. Eureka! He was meant to live life outside the Abyss, but how?

Relaxation still eluded him. More than ever, he needed to remain in control. Safe behind his veil, he leaned down, removing the dagger. Fire raced over his already raw emotions. *Is she sick of me? Did she find someone else? But we are bonded. I can't control her feelings, but I can sure control mine.*

Twirling the dagger which felt like a piece of flint, he placed the blade on his coat sleeve, paused, then slashed with exacting precision. Waves of painful rejection pushed his warm blood to meet the air, and it dripped down his right arm from inside his undamaged coat. Dagon groaned, "She loves me; she loves me not."

After meeting Mary, everything had fallen into place. She was the reason he carried on, why he clung to life. She was like the heart which pumped blood into his veins, giving him warmth and a will to live.

His gash burned something fierce. Gingerly, he took the shampoo bottle from his coat and poured the silver watery substance over his blade and his wound. He winced at a frightening thought. *What would Mary think of me with all of these scars? I'll tell her battles and swords are an occupational hazard. Wait, how will I tell her about the battles and swords without freaking her out in a day when none are used?*

To try to break the bonds he had agreed to by refusing or otherwise would be suicide. If Mary would not sign the agreement to lure Mark in, Savila would waste no time and call Dagon to the terms, sealing their deaths.

He began to trust that Magethna's exuberant ways might be catchy, for he was less hopeless, indeed, more hopeful. Maybe he could halfway live in the light.

He took a deep breath and removed one of his veils, leaving him exposed to the Seraphs and Savila. Then he mentally slapped himself. Weighing the dangers of exposure, he conceded this was the path toward living partially in the light.

After eating a lemon drop, he took off his coat, folded it several times, and placed it on the wrought iron armrest, a sort of makeshift pillow. The bench would be his bed. It wasn't quite long enough for him. It didn't take a brilliant mind to figure out that a bench doesn't grow, so he made the best out of a bad predicament. He lay down on the bench as he eased his head onto his coat. It took him several times of shifting it until he finally had his pillow at least somewhat comfortable. But his legs. *If I could chop them off just for the night.* Clearly, his height was not an asset in that moment.

Maybe if I could find a way back into the Abyss long enough to retrieve my bed and then ... Nope, I do love comfort but not that much.

Dagon dangled his legs over the end of the bench. His legs twitched, trying to somehow make the wrought iron less wrought. With his precautionary measures, he would sleep tonight. Despite the cold hard bench, he began to relax. This "homeless man" began to whistle a lamenting tune.

BACK IN THE ABYSS, the Shadow Kings and other shadow soldiers stood before Savila.

"What news do you have to report?" she shifted upon her throne.

"For a while we could not perceive Dagon's presence, but then our bodies were drawn to him. We saw him come out of a bank," said several shadow soldiers in unison.

"What was the name of this bank?"

"We know not, Lady Savila, for the title hurt our eyes to look upon it."

"You did well, but when you are with Lord Dagon, you are to keep a watch on him and report everything to me no matter how infinitesimal the information may seem to you."

The shadow soldiers were aware of the punishment for failure: they would be consumed in eternal fire like shadows whose old life lingered in them to the point of rebellion.

She dismissed the shadow soldiers with a nod, leaving the Shadow Kings alone with her.

"So, he was at the Bank of the Holy Spirit in Rome," said Lamel.

"We can't see in or get in, but he can. I believe it is his title which gives him entry. His title is not fully sealed yet until the ruby with blood is in our possession. Now he seeks an opportunity to save his bonded mate."

"With blood, love begins," said Savila.

"Whatever love means."

"It means power in brokenness. It is time, my kin, to pour some salt on the wound. Let their agony remember as they climb on shattered glass." Her head tilted as she breathed fire into the air. Spiraling coils of smoke crawled out of the Abyss on to the streets above, rising into the wind, moving through the thoughts of the night, whispering evil to anyone who would listen.

IN A WATERY BLINK, the four Seraphs saw Lord Dagon materialize. He neatly folded his blazer and hung it over the arm of the bench along with his dragon coat. Magethna smiled at the sight of the blazer and the thought of the one that she had created for Dorian, which he would be seeing soon. She looked forward to the unveiling of her masterpiece.

In this state of open exposure, Dagon looked more human. They drew their swords as a vaporous pestilence passed by him before tunneling into the ground.

It was not their duty to protect Dagon, yet they had drawn swords as one by instinct. By compassion.

Magethna wondered why Dagon would remove his immortal veil, thus rendering him visible. Why was he on the bench instead of in the Abyss? Then Magethna froze, saddened. For she saw fresh lacerations on both of Dagon's forearms. Similar marks were covered over by the hairs of his arms. These older marks looked pearly in appearance. The mark on his right arm looked very recent.

"He's been wounded in battle. They do not seem random, like wounds of war, but planned. Yet wounds of war they are," said Dorian.

11

Shattered Glass

S *lither, slither, we all come hither, agonizing over dreams which do not wither.*

Hissing shadowy serpents moved like waves over Forest Avenue. Their flapping fringes beat the asphalt, moving along in stealth. Frayed fabric scales used heat from the ground to navigate. Moving steadily, they came upon Dagon lying asleep on a bench, breathing shallowly. His long legs dangled awkwardly over the wrought iron armrests. In sleep, people have no control over what they dream and are vulnerable to an onslaught of incubus musings. But Dagon had a shield up, blocking anyone or anything from invading his thoughts. Undeterred, the shadowy serpents returned into the ground, burrowing just under the surface of the dirt toward their target. At the surface, the wind picked up, bending the grass. Bladed spikes shot up from the ground as the serpents took the shape of Shadow Kings and several shadow soldiers.

"Your pathetic blades will not protect anyone," said King Lamel to the Seraphs.

The Seraphs said nothing, their blades holding firm.

"Our fun lies elsewhere." King Ligon pointed in the direction of Mary's house. "As does the soldiers."

"We can't let them touch Mark," said Magethna, her face hard as stone.

The shadow soldiers rushed into Mark's bedroom. The Seraphs struck against blades of smoke. Dorian fought to keep acrid fumes from wrapping around his blade. Magethna yanked her sword out from a sooty vapored blade and slashed the tendrils out of her way while knocking the shadow soldier away from Mark. Dorian still fought. Mystil and Raglen's swords blocked and struck at the shadows.

Shadow after shadow tried getting to Mark.

"No!" screamed all the Seraphs as a shadowy finger touched Mark's head.

~

"RAMPART ... RAMPART ... COME IN, RAMPART! OVER," shouted Mr. Cool into Mary's shoe.

"Rampart here ... and this better be good. I'm sleeping! Over," said Dagon. The protection detail had interrupted Dagon's peaceful slumber.

Sledgehammer grabbed a banana. "Do you see shadow soldiers at Mark's house?"

"No, sleeping. Over."

"How about the creepy dream-crashing Shadow Kings approaching your lovely beloved's house? Over."

Dagon's body went rigid. "I can't help her without doing it the immortal way. Over."

"We got this, boss. Over."

"Take care of Mary, boys, and keep me posted. Over."

"Roger that, Rampart ... Mission Dream Assault is engaged. Get Ready. Over." Mr. Cool tapped the shoe.

"We were created ready. Her dream begins!" Razz grabbed a cell phone with a cracked screen and pink rhinestones on the cover. Friar found a plastic coffee mug emblazoned with *Golden Perk*.

THREE SHADOWY CREATURES *with spiked crowns walked toward a steep hill as their images morph to that of three walking men. The man on the farthest left was thin and lanky with slicked back hair. The man in the middle was portly and short, his features were ambiguous. The last man was neither thin nor portly, but muscular. He had blonde hair with deep blue eyes. Of all three men, he looked the most polished, confident. The men were sauntering in tandem toward a girl who was near the bottom of the hill. The men laughed at the crippling fear that kept her feet frozen where she stood. After a moment of paralysis, she ran up the hill, screaming for help to the only one who could help her.*

She stopped close to the top. Sweat dripped from her forehead as she tried to catch her breath. Her breathing was beginning to even out when she turned around to look back down the hill. A clothesline appeared with her white t-shirts and underclothes waving in the wind. The three men walked between the garments. The ringleader tugged on a pair of her undergarments as he roared in laughter. The other men followed suit, mocking her and making kissing sounds. Suddenly, all three of the men become nervous. The laundry continued flicking around the sides of their faces, and fear was evident, especially on the two followers. The ringleader, though, was frightened but still brass. Disgustingly, he moved his hands to the top of her undergarment, yanking them off the line. They became like a sheet of glass, streaked with blood. He flung the glass to the ground, watching in rapturous joy as it shattered.

A blinding light came up behind the girl, causing the fiendish men to run. The glass remained shattered and strewn on the grass.

Behind the girl was safe and comforting warmth. She turned around to see a man dressed in white run toward her, and she too ran toward him.

The scene shifted.

A man and a little girl sat in a parked car. The girl was looking out the rear passenger window amazed at the beautiful, blooming trees. The man excitedly showed her the diverse types of trees, and both marveled at the numerous species they saw. The man now was still, quiet, while the girl kept pointing. The man frantically tried to read the girl's lips, for he could hear nothing from her. The car began to shake violently, but the girl only became more animated. In horror, the man shouted as he pointed out the back window, still trying to get the girl's attention.

Mary watched from across the street. She looked to where he was pointing and saw why this man was so frantic. Out of nowhere, two shadows flew toward the car, armed with black lethal spikes drawn from crowns worn on their heads. Long tattered strips of cloth swung ominously along their ghoulish arms as they approached the car. The man turned around in his seat and faced Mary.

Mary panicked, for the man was Dagon, and he and the little girl were trapped. Dagon pounded the window, pointing at the girl, who continued to list all the flowering trees. Meanwhile, the shadows pulled their bladed spikes close to their chests in the shape of an X. In a violent gust of wind, they scraped the sides of the car as they flew by, producing a spine-chilling sound and shattering the paint, which fell in gritty flakes. They thrusted their faces up against the car window where the girl sat. Their breath produced no fog on the glass, as their withered, leathery, and peeling faces stared into the window. Clots of blood and rotting flesh from recent kills oozed from open wounds in their undead open mouths. The villainous creatures pointed at Dagon, the girl, and then to Mary's terror, herself. Screams of wailing gushed from their mouths, like thousands of trapped voices trying to get out. With a satisfactory snap, their mouths closed, and then they vanished.

Dagon was beyond frantic when four more shadows appeared, two black and two red. All four of them removed bladed spikes. In exasperation, Dagon attempted to get the girl's attention.

"Mary, open the door, help me ... open the door!" Dagon pounded wildly on the glass window with one hand while yanking on the door handle with his other hand. "Use your key, luv!"

Mary opened her purse in haste. Her fingers clumsily fumbled over everything in there except her keys. Finding the key, she inserted it in the lock, trying to open the door from the outside. Dagon started kicking the door. *All four of the shadows had their spiked blades crossed against their chest in the shape of an X as they began to charge the car. In their rapid descent, the two red shadows uncrossed their blades and placed their spikes one on top of the other, creating one thick blade. The four shadows scraped their spikes over the side of the car door, sending sparks from the grinding metal. Moving at a blinding speed, their gruesome faces stared into their prey like death. More paint chips flew off the car like falling debris.*

"Of all the cars to be stuck in!" Furiously Dagon pulled on the car door. "I'm in this sorry tin can. Ah, help me please." He continued to rant and rave while he wildly shook the handle. "Oh, come on!"

The car was Mary's to be exact, which she had purchased with her own money.

Yes, it is used, but it's hers. Good-looking or not, she planned to have words with him. He was a captive and was going nowhere, so she began unleashing her pent-up frustration.

"Listen here, Dagon! I haven't seen you in weeks, and now you're back ... which I'm glad ... really glad, but then you insult my car? Why, I ought to ... I ought to ... I ought to hug you ... no, I didn't mean that ... and another thing ... are you, or are you not, my boyfriend?"

Vigorously he nodded his head to say yes, while he continued trying to open the door. The four mangled shadows pushed their faces against the window next to the girl who was singing in a cute mousey voice, oblivious to their rampage.

"Do you know the muffin man, the muffin man, the muffin man?"

Humming the rest, she pulled a sticker from inside a sticker book in her lap. She placed a crescent moon sticker upside down over one of the ghoul's faces, giving it a whacky mustache.

"Look at those four scraggly trees. Someone should pull their roots out!" said the girl.

Dagon did not appear to hear her.

"Get the boy ... it's the boy!" said Dagon at the top of his lungs, while pointing and motioning to Mary to look behind her. *The boy was on a hill reading a book, oblivious just like the carefree girl.*

The scene shifted.

Mary was then in a walled courtyard with scraggly ivy climbing up all along the walls. Piles of leaves blew in circles, caught up in a wind tunnel. This place was lonely, as if no one had lived there for years. As she moved through the courtyard, Dagon jumped down from the wall, startling her slightly, then disappeared.

Two oak doors with Gothic brass hinges creaked open, pushed by an invisible hand. With trepidation, Mary walked in on new and polished floors, suggesting someone lived here. Hollow, mournful singing rang through the air as if the singer was aged, leaving only a hint of its former sound. Chills quickly ran through her. She tried to go out the door, only the door disappeared. A thunderous rush of wind came from the wall, materializing into one of the black shadows. The shadow flew at her, with its putrid mouth open, revealing a cavern of fire. In an instant, a man appeared in front of her, facing the monster. Light poured from him, rippling down his white garments. She recognized Dagon, though his head was wrapped up in blinding light and he walked barefoot. The shadow instantly left. She found herself turned around, looking down a long hall, and shaking when an eerie singing began. She moved slowly over the same floorboards, which seemed to become more beautiful with every step, as did the singing.

Cautiously, Mary walked down the hall, turning the corner and entering her parents' bedroom without fear, for the singing soothed her. Mary saw her parents lying on their bed. As her mother stopped singing, her head turned with the creak of an old hinge. Her parents' fingernails were blood red. Mary shook, trying to speak, scream, or do anything. Her parents sat up facing her with leathery, decayed, mummified skin, extending their bony fingers toward her. Acting like they wanted to grab her instead of embracing her. Parental words of kindness were replaced by blood-curdling screams when Dagon came behind Mary, a sword in his hand.

"No, Dagon, they're my parents!" screamed Mary.

Dagon seemed not to hear her when he moved in front of her, spinning his sword.

"I'm going to kill them!" said Dagon.

Her parents' nails reflected off his sword like drops of blood on his blade. Loud, venomous screams shook from the mouths of both parents. In one quick stroke, Dagon did the impossible, he simultaneously plunged the blade into the hearts of her parents.

"I love you, Mom and Dad," said Mary.

Dagon withdrew his sword from their chests, but not a trace of blood stained his sword.

Instantly, the faces of Mary's parents changed. They lay down on their pillows, youthful and peaceful.

MARY WOKE up in her bed but did not move. The blades of her white ceiling fan gently oscillated the air around her, giving her a slight chill. She pulled her covers tightly under her chin, imagining Dagon's arms embracing her. Glancing over her shoulder, she caught a hold of her old stuffed cat's glassy eyes. Mary felt guilty for her switch in loyalty, but then she saw a twinkle in one of the irises of her old protector. The toy seemed to give her a wink of approval.

Her last dream made her happy and sad all at once. All she needed was to love and protect what was hers. Dagon, whom she only recently met and became a girlfriend to, had been her Angel Dream for as long as she could remember. These protective dreams safeguarded the deepest parts of her heart. She couldn't have imagined him into her waking life. Even her friend Caroline saw him. It's funny what the mind will tell a person to validate or refute gut instinct. Even though she had been dreaming of him, she had always known in her heart that he really existed in the flesh. She hadn't imagined him putting himself in front of her, standing up for her when no one else would. Still lying in bed, she clenched the edge of her blanket.

All these images of Dagon only made Mary's heart sink, for it had been two weeks since they were together. Halfheartedly, she had gone out with Caroline, though her mind, body, and soul were elsewhere.

With this ache, she blankly watched the circulating ceiling fan. Blade after blade whizzed by, but she focused on one of them. *Why that blade? They're all the same, aren't they?* The fan blade reminded her of the massive sword in the dream. The chill was back after envisioning the hideous faces of what looked like her parents before Dagon plunged a sword into them.

Dagon, was out there somewhere, but where? Where do you start looking when you only know someone's first name and nothing else? It's not like he's the only blond guy in Oak Park. But still, there was no one like him.

She pushed the covers off and got out of bed. Downstairs in the kitchen she started a pot of coffee.

Through the kitchen window, she saw an overcast day, and she remembered that there was a chance of rain.

While the coffee brewed, Mary went upstairs to let the warm rain of a shower nourish her skin. The smart tablet on her vanity played her favorite Chicago radio station through a portable, wireless speaker. She poured shampoo into the palm of her hand and sang along until suddenly chills ran up her spine. She remembered the part of her dream where her undergarments had turned to glass. As a girl, without her parents noticing, she had burned her underwear out of shame after being abused. As the ashes built up around her, they were shoveled under and tossed out as if they had never been there at all.

This kind of flashback would have normally sent her into a tailspin, checking every window and door to make sure that they were locked. She relaxed as the warm water ran down her body. The chill left, and her body became warm, making her eager for a cup of her special blend of coffee. Nothing could dampen her happiness. Dagon, her Angel Dream come to life, infused her with the courage to leave her past behind. Because of him, she had come to life, her old chains of captivity loosening and falling to the ground. If Dagon was trapped somewhere, she would help him.

"Rampart ... Rampart ... come in, Rampart! Over," said Mr. Cool.

"Is Mary safe? Is the situation under control now? Over."

"Roger that. Safe and sound. The situation is neutralized, sanitized, deodorized." Sledgehammer sniffed his banana. "Yeah, deodorized. Over."

"So ... what happened?

"Um ... we need a powwow first," said Mr. Cool.

The guys began discussing in heated whispers amongst themselves.

"Excuse me ... this is your boss speaking, and I'm going to give you a pow on your wow, if you don't put a sock in it. Otherwise, I'll put my foot in it."

"That's gross!" Razz looked at his reflection in one of the rhinestones.

"What happened in the dream? Out with it or it will be in with it."

"We only know tidbits about Mary's dream, though we had to stun the dream crasher with Friar's laser beam ... which was seriously awesome possum!" said Sledgehammer.

"Back up ... what laser beam?"

"Well, he flashed his silver belt buckle at them, whoever it was, blinding them momentarily. Then they left like possums. We're glad that you had used such kind words in suggesting that we might, when we get around to it, move our bottoms and spit shine all our weapons, and Friar did it. Now everything is shining like a mirror. He should probably be careful. We're assuming you want this house left standing and not burned to cinders."

"He used his belt buckle?" Dagon chuckled. "What else did you guys use?"

Sledgehammer rattled off all the communication gizmos each of them used. "Do you remember the spy on the television show that talked into a shoe?"

"Yeah, I do."

"If humans can talk into those little screens they carry, anything should work."

"That's true. Could living in the light be this simple?" asked Dagon.

"In your case, probably not," said Mr. Cool.

"Not very encouraging." Dagon's light mood soured.

"Just keeping it real."

Dagon's mood went from sour to rotten. "A lot of years have passed since I first saw this house, and it better remain standing and in one piece!"

"And stand it shall. You can better see the light without the dirt, boss. Clever ... he was like a superhero with his belt buckle weapon ... *zizz* ... take that and that ... *blamo!*"

"You know, boss, necessity is the mother of invention ... and what a great mother she is. Sort of gets you ... right here," bragged all the guys, tapping their fists to their hearts.

"Well, nothing comes back void, does it, boys? Is there anything else worth reporting? Get on with it; I'm still sleeping."

"Yeah, there was one teensy weensy minor thing which happened ..." said Mr. Cool. A barefoot man with long white garments put himself in front of a dream crasher, and Mary ... we—"

"What? Are you sure it was a man?"

"Pretty sure, though we couldn't see his head. It seemed like Mary felt safe."

Dagon felt a sudden rage well within him.

"Um ... um ... then not too long after that the dream, um ... you ... um—"

"Spill it!"

Sledgehammer clenched his fist. "Boss, you killed Mary's parents in her dream."

"I what?"

"Actually, it looked like they were—Ahh! Um, were already dead."

"What's wrong, Razz?"

"Nothing, boss, just a little banana trouble," Razz answered. "You better hope *you* can clean this off my blazer, Sledge. No, not like that, now it's wet and gooey."

"What's going on in there?" Dagon said.

"Sledge tried cleaning my blazer with a wet paper handkerchief thing."

"Forget about that. What happened!"

Mr. Cool snorted into the shoe. "There was no blood when you withdrew your sword, and there wouldn't be if they were already dead ... right, boss?"

"I did not kill Mary's parents! Whoever is listening, that was not me. This must be a plot. Mary is going to think I killed her parents." Dagon's mind whizzed, landing on several key components. "Mary's parents were dead. In the dream, my sword had no blood on it. These are not 'tidbits'! The next time all of you are on high alert, you best report back immediately. Understood?"

"Yeah, we understand," said Mr. Cool. "Oh, you owe us big time. Especially with this high alert black ops mission and all ... and look at the informational nuggets that we brought back. You know, you really can't put a price tag on this, can you? Why are we doing the dirty work here, picking up what the boss can't do or chooses not to do? Our skills, our improvisation, and digging up juicy dirt ... it all adds up to wads of cold, hard cash. Pay as you go, and you will never owe."

"You will get paid today, you scurvy rats!"

"Ah, there he goes again, with those nice kind words ... just stabs you in the heart, doesn't it?"

"What happened over at Mark's house?" asked Dagon.

"Don't know, don't care," said Mr. Cool.

Dagon raised his eyebrows but said nothing.

"Sledge, you're going to need a new walkie talkie." Friar said.

"Yeah, something that doesn't explode," said Razz, still trying to mop up, brush off, or scrape off the slimy banana guts.

Friar opened and shut the kitchen drawers.

"Get out of Mary's house!" said Dagon.

"Wait ... here it is. I remember seeing something like these before. You can send smoke signals—"

"No smoke! No fire! Get out now!"

One by one, the guys came out the front door. "We'll find something for you, Sledgehammer." The guys said while patting Sledgehammer on the back.

Keeping a close watch on his Cherbs, Dagon planned to step out in boldness, like that shining cement fleck which continued to glow brightly in darkness.

OUT OF THE SHOWER, Mary dried off. The awaiting coffee perked her up even more. A shattering sound jolted her. Frozen in her tracks, her heart pounded in her chest as she tried to figure out where the sound came from and what fell. Afraid, she locked the bathroom door. She didn't know what she would do if an intruder came in. It sounded hollow, as if it were a sound effect, a remnant of something that had already happened. With this thought, she put her robe on and warily unlocked the door. Except for the basement, Mary checked the whole house and saw no explanation for the shattering noise she had heard, though she noticed a smashed banana on the kitchen floor. She didn't remember doing that. After cleaning it up, she felt foolish for letting her mind run away like it had. As she drank her coffee, her mind ran away with warm thoughts of Dagon instead.

THE TRAIN of Savila's black dress thrashed the glass floor beneath her as blood swirled underneath with hurricane force. Pacing, she breathed streams of fire, recalling Shadow Kings and shadows. All of them bowed and stood at attention.

"You did well my shadow soldiers by giving the boy a bad night." Savila said, then addressed the Shadow Kings. "My eyes saw through yours, my kin, and I saw the arrogance in a feeble attempt to deny me what is rightfully mine. No mere blade can remove this truth, for we saw it in the dead. His blade ran clean, being already claimed by me. Now he assists in the breaking of laws and what, my kin, is the punishment for law-breaking?"

"Death!" shouted the Shadow Kings in rapturous unison.

"In the end, the punishment of lawbreakers is death. Blood from the Golden Land will try and reclaim what is mine. This blood will bind the light over the stones, breaking the bonds of old. As I mentioned before, this will raise me to power, by which death will be sealed." Savila snickered at this, her mind seeing the proverbial fly being snared into her web, trapped.

"Dagon's decisions must still run with the will. Even a co-ruler needs a title to stand upon. No title, no co-rule. It's not a matter of him being made to see reason to abdicate his title, he must be shown," said King Lamel.

12

The Big Day

The morning started completely overcast and threatening rain. Some of the plants in the neighboring yards appeared desperately in need of care, the yards whose owners moved from car to house and house to car at chaotic speeds.

A water-filled sea of clouds billowed. The Seraphs' senses pricked as the air around them shifted. The Shadow Kings may be gone, but the memory of their fight and loss of not being able to stop a shadow from casting fear into Mark.

"If you and Mystil did not act promptly by crossing your blades when you did, the shadow could have transformed Mark's room into a vision of the Abyss for all of us to see, and Mark's dream would have been much worse. It could have been real." Dorian bowed to Raglen and Mystil.

Magethna thanked them with rounds of hugs. "Thankfully, Mark is fine," she said. All the Seraphs were relieved. The shadow soldiers gawking at Dagon bothered Magethna. Maybe Dagon's present state of vulnerability or his recent wounds gave Magethna desire to protect him. Even stoic Dorian voiced a concern.

In one sense, Dagon appeared to be dead, his limbs, listless, cold as if rigor mortis set in. The only hint of life the Seraphs could hear came from his mouth, which hung open and emitted snores.

From the vantage point of the Seraphs, Dagon resembled a marionette. One leg hung over the back of the bench while the other hung over the wrought iron armrest. His left arm slumped over the back of the bench, and his right arm dangled over the front edge of the seat, his onyx ring gently swaying like a pendulum through the blades of grass. With the light of the new day, they saw his wounds clearly, and even for them, they were hard to look upon. Dried beads of blood clung to the wound on his arm. His black stone ring, a spoil of war, lay hidden among the shoots of grass, gleaming yet tarnished. A new power consumed its once radiant glory, causing the memory of its past to be shattered into oblivion. No more than a lingering myth or legend perhaps of what once was. No detail was too trivial. Still, Magethna could not let go of Dagon's uncomfortable state. His arms and legs looked bizarrely twisted, not comfortable at all. Magethna almost had the mind to go down there and make him comfortable. He slept like any normal man would, except Dagon sprawled on the bench with his mind blocked.

Magethna diverted her attention, composing herself. The Seraphs turned their thoughts to other things. They were not dismissing Dagon but studying every aspect in the knowledge of what was to come as blood flowed in the shadow of the bladed spring grass.

Mark stirred. Dorian and Magethna turned to face the boy, who looked like a miniature version of Dagon, as he lay sprawled out on his mattress. Sound asleep, he snored quietly with his arms and legs poking out awkwardly from beneath his patchwork quilt. Both sleepers should be awake, for it was well into the morning. Perhaps the overcast sky played tricks on their body clocks, keeping them unconscious. Magethna reminded Dorian of the late hour when Mark came to bed, weary from hours of chores.

Mark was half awake. His eyes moved between the rippling waves of his curtains and the nightstand with the book he wanted to read. He yawned and propped himself with an elbow, turning around to stretch his arm up over his head. He grasped an object from the shelf on the wall above his headboard. Magethna heard clinking metal, the winding of gears. When the key would not budge any further, Mark hastily and haphazardly pushed the alarm clock back into its approximate location.

As it rocked back and forth, the clock face opened, startling Magethna.

As Mark settled back to sleep, Magethna gazed at Dagon again, and her mind latched onto a new theory. Dagon and Mark lay within proximity of each other, each unaware of the other's presence. Although the Seraphs did not know Dagon's fate, they did know that for better or for worse, he had a part to play, just like Mark, whose snoring now seemed synchronized to Dagon's. The pair seemed charming to Magethna. The sleeping giant was harmless or at least defenseless as his wounds proved.

"A trapped person will fight, Magethna, and more so if they are wounded," said Dorian, sensing her thoughts. "Recent events may have woken the sleeping giant. We cannot assume that all is as it appears. If I knew you not, I would wonder if your eyes were being colored by roses."

"I love roses. Even the trapped can smell them."

The bizarre became even more so when Mark and Dagon arose at the same moment, yawning and stretching. In one last synchronized movement, they both brought their arms up over their heads, grunting slightly as they arched their backs trying to work out the kinks of sleep.

Mark left his bedroom and went down the stairs into the kitchen where breakfast waited. His Aunt Frances said nothing about the late hour of his approach.

Now standing, Dagon reached down into the folds of his coat. To the Seraph's dismay, he took out a cigarette. He re-folded his coat, patting it and smoothing it several times. Then he tossed a lemon drop in the air and held his mouth open like it had been in his sleep, waiting for the fast-falling sugary treat. It landed in his mouth with a plunk and a shudder. Then he lit the cigarette and placed it between his lips. He turned and looked at the Seraphs, who stood stationary at the window. His hand lifted as if he were about to salute, then it dropped. He looked rattled, but Magethna did not know why. His cigarette quivered in his mouth. He quickly put the blazer on with his back to the Seraphs, followed by his coat, firmly tugging and pulling on its fabric. Composed and with panache, he turned around.

"These are wounds inflicted in war," said Dagon.

DAGON SHOOK his hands in front of his face. *Why did I say that? Now they will know about my cutting. Am I in a perpetual nightmare? Yes, a nightmare of my own making. Silence in this case probably would have been 18 karat white gold.*

These are wounds of war, my own personal war. Yeah, get a good look at what Savila has brought onto me.

All actions have consequences even if made with good intentions, like living in the light by removing one of his veils. He then slumped in failure, for he ate a lemon drop to block his mind. Even power has limits. And a price tag. It's better to let people believe you are weak than to show it outright. There is dignity in silence.

Dagon sat back on the bench, deciding to let it go. Today started scene one, take two, for he was going back to Mary's house.

He would do anything to dull the blinking "vulnerable" sign that haunted his thoughts. Like smoking for instance, once a classy and chic action. Years later, he had found the dangers, but by that point he was beyond hooked.

He needed some time to adjust to thinking in the light, even if partially. Nothing in his existence seemed coincidental. He assumed where Mark was. And where Mary as his bonded mate would have to be due to the binding nature of his title.

His fingers cradled the cigarette while he blankly stared straight ahead. *If nothing has been an accident ... then ... that's it! I'm going to quit cold salmon!* He didn't like turkey all that much. In his quest to be normal, he longed for a normal relationship. Not sure what that really was, he needed to learn, for he never even had a friend. Logic would suggest that if you were bonded mates, then all would work out. But it didn't work this way, for a person can't be forced to feel something for someone else. To boost his chances with romance, he had planned everything. Down to his smoking and fashion, just to prove his worth.

He had so much that he wanted to share with Mary, but those conversations would naturally occur in time. Passing the time away, he sat back savoring this one, final cigarette. O*kay, maybe two.*

THE SERAPHS WATCHED Dagon smoke one cigarette after the other. They could not read his mind, but by his face they could tell that he was deep in thought. The Seraphs saw Mark's clock on the shelf, which now read eleven o'clock. They didn't need a human device to tell time, but people did. Time really meant nothing to their immortal minds, but they did enjoy the finer aspects of humanity, and since time was crucial to life in the Second Land, they tried to embrace it.

"We need to get ready now, for the hour soon approaches." said Magethna. "Are you ready to see your charming blazer?"

"Well ..."

"I told you, it will be very refined. I do believe that this may be another talent that I was created with. Okay, on the count of three. One, two, three!"

Her creation went into the mind of Dorian. He tilted his head back and forth, his mind seeing the potential in her creation, as his true analytical personality became woven into its fabric.

"Well?"

"You know, Magethna, I like it. Why, it suits the other elements of my clothing just fine. This may be one of your finest, created gifts."

From Dorian, the praise equaled a standing ovation.

"Thank you. Oh, yes. I told you that it would work out."

"You are most welcome. Now, what did you design for yourself?"

"Oh, it is truly enchanting, and it is time for us to now get ready, but I want you to go first, so I can adjust, fix or alter whatever is needed on your blazer. It is customary to do this while you are wearing it."

Dorian donned his blazer. Modern, it showcased his strength of character. The slim fitting silhouette outlined his athletic build. It even had black satin elbow patches.

"Oh, Magethna, you did a wonderful job," said Mystil. "The blazer looks nice on you, Dorian."

"And it compliments everything else," said Raglen.

Magethna said nothing at first. Coming over to Dorian, she straightened, pulled, and studied his blazer. She backed up, scrutinizing her creation closely. She waved her hands over some stray threads, and then declared it to be perfect.

"Would you let me create you a new waist coat, perhaps?"

"No, we agreed to this. Raglen is right, the blazer offsets the classic components in this ensemble remarkably well."

"Thank you for the compliment, but my offer still stands to change the other items of your ensemble."

"Thank you indeed, but I am quite satisfied. A classic never really dies, does it? I believe it is your turn, Magethna."

Magethna smiled but wished that his choice in clothing would bend. She twirled, and the dress she created appeared onto her body in a true Cinderella moment.

The delicate white chiffon fabric loosely draped her in layers. A slim bodice with a lighter silhouetted line gave her a natural but modern look. She even had a new hair style, an up-do with a rhinestone headband. As a finishing touch, she revealed the white chiffon parasol, which she loved so much.

"You look stunning," said Mystil.

Dorian reflexively ran his hands through his hair, as if trying to fix what he could.

Magethna approved of Dorian's silence, his self-conscious grooming speaking volumes.

Dorian and Magethna lithely and invisibly went down the Bennett stairs. They dissolved through the front door and made their way to the front of the gate. They waved to Raglen and Mystil, who were stationed at the window, then reversed one of their veils, making them visible to the one they awaited.

Magethna opened her parasol, twirled it three times behind her and then brought it to a graceful stop.

Their keen ears detected a rumble and the sound purred closer and closer toward them. William drove up in a black car. He pulled up next to them and got out. He wore faded jeans with a gray argyle sweater over a white dress shirt.

"Hey, my favorite Seraphs." William shook Dorian's hand and hugged Magethna. "What do you think of my wheels? Aren't they bad?"

Magethna wondered why he concerned himself with the wheels, and why he said that they were unsatisfactory. He looked like he enjoyed the car, for he beamed from ear to ear. He even buffed it slightly here and there with his sweater sleeve. His words seemed more like a mathematical algorithm, but an actual algorithm would have been easier for her to solve.

"What kind of car is it?" asked Dorian. Magethna nodded slightly at Dorian, for she liked his redirection very well.

"It's a hot 55 Chevy muscle car ... and, man, can it book!"

Magethna looked at Dorian, more confused than ever.

"I've been psyched all day, waiting to see ya both. It's been too long since we were all together. I've missed ya very much."

"It is joyous to see you too, dear William," said Magethna.

"Dad will love the sweet ride that I purchased. I was just flying by the seat of my pants, booking my flight at the last minute. I've been here for two days staying at a friend's house, waiting to make my grand entrance today with you. The car deal went down quickly, and here I am. What a ride! It's wicked fast."

The Seraphs said nothing, for what could they say? Thankfully, William moved on by complimenting her dress and Dorian's fine blazer, but he stopped cold, his eyes on Dagon, who sat on the bench and did not acknowledge their presence.

"Why doesn't he go back down into the hole that he crawled out of?"

"William Henry Bennett!" Dorian chastised.

"Dagon could have heard that. "I believe he is changing." Magethna said.

"He's a waste of time and space." William spat.

Magethna was about to speak but cut off.

"Do you believe he can change?" William rolled his eyes.

"I'm very skeptical." Dorian touched William's shoulder. "Let me finish. Yes, I'm skeptical, but I will not pass judgement on him or say no change could never occur, even as remote as it may be for Dagon."

William smacked the steering wheel with his hand. "He has been judged. He got his ... he got kicked out."

"Then why is he still half human? Savila could have turned him into a shadow or worse, but she didn't or couldn't," said Magethna. "And might I add, your outburst proves the bitterness of the heart which invades all humanity."

"Hey, I didn't side with Savila or doom humanity, like *he* did!"

"True, but if there is hope for humanity, then I must believe there is hope for Dagon as well." Magethna adjusted her dress.

"We can just disagree on that." William looked over his shoulder briefly, his mouth twitching. "Um ... thank you for the key, by the way," said William, ignoring their censor. "Snowcap delivered it, no problem. What's it for?"

"You will know when the time is right." Dorian and Magethna replied in unison.

They walked to the front of the house where Mr. Dawson smiled to William while quietly escorting Dorian and Magethna into the house, his reaction drastically different than before.

Magethna felt a natural informality to an otherwise formal occasion.

Informality aside, Frances and Henry welcomed William, who was beyond under-dressed. William promptly scurried off, but the rebel (with a cause or without) returned in evening wear similar to that of his father, except with a slightly opened white shirt.

"Mark is still at school, but he'll be thrilled to see you," said Frances.

Teatime with the Bennetts was right downright amazing. Magethna stared at the delectable sandwiches which sat on her plate of fine china before eating them. She carefully placed the delicate teacup onto its matching saucer.

After tea finished, the conversation warmed up.

"Dad, I bought a black 55," said William.

"Really? When?"

"Yesterday. Let's go see it." Nodding his head in the direction of the door. They both dismissed themselves with forced pleasantries.

They were gone for a while. When Henry came back in, he was flushed and slightly disheveled. He winked at Frances, and then whispered into her ear. "I took the car out for a spin. Several spins, actually."

"You what?"

"Yes, and I drove with my coat off."

"You drove with only your shirt on?"

"Yes, and it was fun, or as William keeps saying, wicked."

"What on earth?" whispered France, as she leaned away from her husband slightly; her husband and William sat as antsy as boys.

Henry reached behind him then placed a square, flexible package into Magethna's hands. "You've given us so much, so we decided to give you something in return. You can open it. This is from the whole family."

Delicately, she unwrapped the package, careful not to damage it in any way. She was glad that Dorian said nothing about ripping the paper. Amazed, she held a pink, leather-bound scheduling book. She hugged it against her chest. "How did you know? I love it so much!"

"Dorian mentioned it," said Henry.

"Dorian, thank you! I will place all of our important times and dates in these fragile pages with love and care."

"I thought you would like your daily planner to be pink," said Frances.

"Oh ... a daily planner ... how nice! And yes, I do love pink."

"And now, for you," William said to Dorian. He handed Dorian a silver pocket watch attached to a matching, heavy-looking chain. "Sorry, I didn't wrap it. Dad has its twin. I figured you could use it more than I ever could."

Eyes wide, Dorian opened the watch. Everyone listened to the subtle ticking of the second hand.

"Thank you," Dorian murmured.

"Why is it ticking backwards?" said Frances.

"Mine is doing the same thing," said Henry. "It started the night of the storm."

Dorian wrapped the chain around one hand and held the watch fisted in the other. "It's a Doomsday Clock. It's counting down to a significant event that will affect all of mankind."

"Mark," said Magethna.

"What can we do to stop it?" said William.

"Everything we can," said Dorian.

Seraphs do not shed tears, but if they could, Magethna would have. The skies opened above them, right on cue. Light drips tinkled on the glass windows and the roof. The rain performed a symphony against the windows and the roof. Its pace quickened and slowed and quickened again with the wind.

"I'm leaving Oxford," said William. "I feel I should be home now."

Frances leaned forward.

"Mom, I will go back and finish my degree, but for now I just need to be here. Besides, the action is here, not in England." He told his parents of his desire to help in the jewelry store.

"Son, I'm glad to have you home now. I know your mom is happy, too." Henry winked at Frances.

The rain began to let up as the sun peeked through the clouds.

Magethna cherished this joyful time, but Dorian stared at his newly-acquired clock, a bittersweet expression on his face. His eyes met hers, and he smiled. They both dreaded the time fast approaching, but for now, they laughed and talked as if nothing could ever go wrong.

13

The Unexpected Visitor

"Our tulips! Someone took our tulips! Josephine, come quick. Someone took our—" the man stopped mid-sentence and looked wildly up and down the street. "Thief!"

"The thief is over here." The Cherbs pointed to Dagon.

Dagon shot them an angry look, but they ignored him as they continued counting the money that he had thrown to them from his new wallet.

"In the future, can you limit or omit ones and fives? Just stick primarily to tens, twenties, and higher. It makes the counting a lot easier," said Mr. Cool. The others agreed with loud cheers.

The Cherbs zeroed in on the clumps of dirt which still hung onto the exposed roots, brushing them off and straightening the bouquet. Dagon saw that the man who had inspired this gift of flowers wasn't faring much better. He stood like a stooge at a door across the street, just like Dagon did in front of Mary's door. Their prospective girlfriends stared out the peepholes. Seeing no clumps of dirt on the stems of the other man, Dagon began to shake the remaining dirt from his roots, until to his horror he realized that Mary was watching.

Now she's going to think that I have some kind of spastic disorder or something of greater magnitude.

Between hoots of laughter from Dagon's rowdy imps, the woman across the street yelled at the man, "Now you come? Why now? You haven't called, and now you just show up unannounced and think that I will take you back?"

Wasn't Dagon coming unannounced? Just showing up? Expecting Mary to welcome him? What a self-esteem crasher. If the school of hard knocks existed, he would get a capital F. *Go back to your hole!* Laughter only diminished the memory of William's jeers to merely an insulting echo.

Shouldn't the light protect me? What was this light anyway? It was hope. This light permeated the Golden Land. Savila did not want humans to have this light. Savila knew the light, for she was created in it, but in her pride, she abandoned it, in favor of herself. Now she couldn't even look at it. *Perhaps, she's not as powerful as she believes, but powerful enough to not get cocky.* Hiding everything in the light could be the best kept secret from that evil, sulfuric witch.

Well the light had not protected the other man. It would have been better to have a problem, so that maybe Mary would take pity on him. None of this mattered anymore when, to his delight, Mary opened the door and hugged him.

She looked around. "Why is my neighbor screaming?"

Dagon shrugged his shoulders and carefully kept the flowers behind his back.

"Oh, what a tangled web we weave, when first we practice to deceive," came the ominous warning from Mr. Cool.

Mary stepped back, "Why were you gone for two weeks?"

Dagon breathed a sigh of relief, for her expression was calm, not like the other man's girlfriend. "It was more like two seconds than two weeks." He winked. Whatever calm Mary had was gone.

"Do you know how many seconds are in a day, a week, or two weeks?"

"Of course, I do, there are one million, two hundred and nine thousand, and six hundred in two weeks, and I used two of yours." Again, he winked.

His mathematical wit did not help him but seemed to make things worse. Dagon opened his mouth—

"Did you miss me at all?"

"How absurd, of course I missed you."

Mary puffed her chest and let out a deep sigh, then rolled her eyes. "You missed me so badly, but you didn't come by? You know where I live, but you haven't told me where you live or even your last name. I have been going out of my mind. Why didn't you come by?"

"I'll explain everything to you, baby. I will."

Mary seemed somewhat satisfied with this when she threw out a zinger. "Is this how you treated past girlfriends?"

"I never had a girlfriend before."

"How is that possible? I was so worried about you; I wanted to put up missing person posters."

With a stifling pause in the air, Dagon presented Mary with the flowers that he held behind his back, hoping that they would smooth everything over.

She smiled sweetly and thanked him. To his dismay, Mary kicked some of the clumps of dirt which fell onto her hardwood floors to the side.

She scrutinized the roots. "Did you pull these tulips from the ground?"

"I did not pull these tulips from the ground."

"Did you cut them with a knife?"

"Not exactly." With flair, Dagon showed her the dagger he used to loosen the dirt. *This had to be better than if I told her I flat out hacked the roots.* Apparently, it didn't help, for she only wanted to know why he had a dagger in the first place, and again he assured her that he would explain everything.

With a weak smile, she went to get a vase, and she brought it back out, half full of water.

"I shouldn't have yelled at you. I really did miss you. This was my great-grandmother's vase from Sweden. It's very special to me. You can put the flowers in here."

Touched, he put the flowers in the vase like she asked.

"That's sweet," she said and smiled. "Is this why my neighbor was screaming?"

Dagon coyly shrugged.

She let it go and went to put the vase by a window. "I've never had a bad memory, but I can't find one of my gym shoes and a coffee mug is gone."

"Really, you don't say, That's, um ... that's too bad." Dagon wrung his hands, trying to calm his nerves before she came back. *It's a good thing I didn't mention the portable phone and ...*

"Oh, and another strange thing, I cleaned up a banana mess in the kitchen, but I don't remember eating or spilling it."

"Huh ... isn't that something. You know, it's often the mind that goes first."

"Very funny. So funny I forgot to laugh."

"You see?"

Mary shook her head.

"We're keeping our walkie talkies, boss. It would seem even more strange to return them," rationalized Mr. Cool.

"Ok, but don't take, steal, borrow, or remove anything else from her house," whispered Dagon. "Now, get out."

Mary walked back to where Dagon stood.

"You can come in, you know. Mary looked around her porch. "Were you talking to someone?"

"Mary, I think I've been here before." He walked into the open door and glanced around the room. He took a leap of faith, gulped, and cleared his throat. "In fact, I know I have. This house was built in 1903, but I wasn't in this house until 1951."

Her smile faltered. "Did you know someone who used to live here?"

"Kind of."

Mary led him on a tour of her house, for she wanted to know how her house had changed over the years.

He eagerly followed her, but soon he saw rooms filled with dust and clutter. His mind couldn't get over it. Dusty knickknacks sat on dusty shelves while piles and piles of stuff sat everywhere with magazines haphazardly strewn around. Even a stylish brown suede couch sat as if it screamed for air, and the curtains were peppered with dust. The kitchen, though messy, looked promising to his culinary mind. *Well, this is just the downstairs ... it's probably better upstairs.*

The upstairs completely overwhelmed him; it was far worse than the downstairs. Spare rooms, her master bedroom, and the bathroom were filthy. After all the centuries of longing to be with his beloved, he had never thought of what she would be like. With a gulp, though he loved her, he saw their differences and many hours of cleaning ahead.

Her walk-in closet appeared to be neat with one whole side cleared. Still though, it needed some work. Her bed, though made, wouldn't win any awards. A rag doll with yellow yarn hair lay by the headboard and an old gray stuffed cat sat crouched and slouched on her window ledge.

"Do you like the doll and the cat? What's the story about these?"

"Christmas gifts from my parents. The cat is a guardian knight, my protector." Taking the cat off the ledge, Mary showed Dagon the cat's heart-shaped tag on a red collar. The front of the tag was written in black crayon. Her sweet childish penmanship still looked crisp for its age and read, "Frosty." The back side read, "Loved by Mary."

One quick hug later, Frosty was back to guarding her room. Dagon thanked the noble cat for watching over Mary by patting its head. Even though Dagon was here now, Frosty's protection was still appreciated.

Curiously, Mary glanced at Dagon's t-shirt. The orange letters were slightly covered by his blazer. Mary opened his blazer just wide enough to read it. Dagon liked this, though it made him nervous. His heart raced.

"Do you think I have my groove on?"

"We'll have to go dancing again for me to find that out," she giggled.

"I would love that. I bought the t-shirt back in the 70's at a concert in this city."

"Why haven't I seen you before?"

"I'm not sure, I've been around since the 50s."

"You don't look old enough. How old *are* you?"

He never answered her question but led her downstairs. Nonchalantly, he stretched his hand up and swept some of the webs down. Now he had a sticky mess on his hand. He tried to shake them off, but they wouldn't budge.

"Are you all right?"

"Yes ... fine, luv, just fine," said Dagon through a forced smile. He shook his hand more violently.

"Are you sure you're all right? You seem nervous."

"Yeah, that's it. I'm nervous. Very nervous." He shook his hand again.

"You should have told me that the first time. I'm kind of nervous, too. We can be nervous together."

Dagon liked the word "together" though he wondered if she was nervous about being stuck with a man who had a shaking problem. Thankfully, she led him the rest of the way downstairs.

Dagon wiped the couch and sat down with a dust-releasing plop. He paid more attention to the dust than to Mary. Making up for it, he told her how beautiful she looked. The toes of her bare feet curled in, and her cheeks blushed.

The dust settled, and Dagon began to tell her about himself in a very basic way. He told Mary that he bathes, not because he needs to, but because it relaxes him, and he has no need to brush his teeth. Dagon barely started when he saw Mary gasp. He wasn't quite sure why she reacted in that way, but he wondered. *Does she think that I have bad breath? Do I need breath mints?*

"If this is too much for you to take on, you can show me what I need to do."

"Well ... um ... ok...um what do you like to do for fun?"

So far so good.

"Listen to rock music and ... um ... what do you like to do?" Dagon twisted and wrung his hands.

"I like to read and practice ballet, though, I don't dance as much anymore."

"You are a great dancer. How did you learn?"

Mary blushed. "Thank you. I took lessons since I was four, until I was eighteen. Many instructors told me I was a prodigy...whatever." Mary brushed this last part off. "Catherine took lessons, but not as long. It just wasn't her thing. I guess like baths, dancing has always relaxed me."

Dagon adjusted his collar, causing a blazer sleeve to ride up his arm.

"Dagon, woah, that's a bad cut on your arm. I'm going to clean it for you."

"What? No thanks, baby. It's almost healed. It's fine ... just leave it."

Mary shot up from the couch. "I am not going to leave it. It looks like it may be infected. I'll treat it in my bathroom." She held out her hand, which Dagon reluctantly took.

Back upstairs they went. Seeing more cobwebs, he fought the urge to remove them.

"You can sit there." Mary pointed to the toilet.

"You want me to sit ... there?"

"Yes, now sit." She nudged him down on the toilet seat. "First, let's take off your blazer."

"No, Mary! Please, no, just leave it. Please?"

"It's ok, I took a class in first aid."

Mary helped him take his blazer off.

"Honey, it must be cleaned. I will take care of you."

Dagon sat quietly as he waited for the pain of rejection to come. She would see his scars and wounds and be thoroughly repulsed. *If this is what living in the light is about ... I think I may pass.*

Mary got down under the sink and pulled out a first aid kit.

Dagon peered through the vanity and saw an awfully disorganized mess. Now he was worried that whatever she would use on him would be expired or tainted.

He tensed with the fear of rejection and old, expired medicine, for everything in the house reeked of expired dust.

Mary brushed aside the dark hair on his arms, showing some old scars and five fresh wounds. She seemed focused on her task, and she smiled at him.

"How did you get so many cuts?"

"They're dagger accidents." It was partially true.

"You need to be more careful. Some of these old scars look really deep."

She rubbed his scars tenderly, which made him flinch.

"Did that hurt?"

"No. Sorry, luv. I am just not used to anyone helping me."

"There's no need to apologize."

She opened the first aid kit, and to his surprise, the kit was neat, and the expirations, current. She took out a brown bottle. "This might sting a little, I'm sorry."

This much kindness tore through Dagon as Mary applied some bubbling liquid with a stick that had cotton on both ends. He didn't want to show how much this frothing liquid stung. Her kindness sunk in, making the sting melt away. He was guilty for his part in the doom of humanity. Yet here she was, soothing and cleaning his wounds. The kindness would probably end once he took her down his dark memory lane.

"Can I have a cigarette, luv?"

"I'm almost done."

She finished wrapping his arms in gauze and carefully avoided catching his hair with the tape. She put the first aid kit back under the sink and tenderly helped him back into his blazer.

Dagon brushed a stray hair from her face. Mary placed a hand over his and leaned into his palm.

"Thank you, luv."

"You're welcome."

"Please try not to get hurt again."

"I'll try."

They picked up right where they had left off, in the awkward string of questions and answers. Mary showed Dagon how to operate the shower, amazing him. He let the trickling water run onto his hands. Mary protected his bandages from getting wet.

"You can't get these wet for a few days. I will have to change the dressings tomorrow."

Of course this meant that she wanted to see him again, and Dagon was glad. Somehow, he had to get Mary's agreement, and he tried to think of how to ask her. He really wanted to keep her out of it, but that was impossible.

Mary showed him a toothbrush. Yes, it was a brush, but not for hair. Mary's kindness and patience were remarkable. He had revealed some strange things, and to her credit, she didn't make him feel badly about it.

Hand in hand they went back downstairs. He noticed less dirt and more of Mary, though the house still needed a good deep cleaning. Back on the couch, Dagon started explaining more of his basics.

"I have never drunk alcohol or used drugs. By and large, I use profanity sparingly. It says very little of the intellectual capacity of the one using such words. However, every so often, periodically, on occasion, and from time to time, a harmless word might just, you know, slip out."

Mary put her hand to her mouth.

"But this is not a habit by any stretch."

Mary just blinked several times. "Which word would you use?"

"You'll know it when you hear it." Dagon winked, offering no hint.

"What is your last name?"

"I don't have a last name."

"How could you not have a last name? For example, mine is Fauston. Mary Elizabeth Fauston. Everyone has one."

"Maybe, but I don't."

"How? Why not?" She leaned forward, her eyes focused on his face.

Dagon sat back, his shoulders slumped. "Because I was created and not born, I have never had parents."

Mary wobbled, almost falling off the couch.

"Are you all right?" Dagon asked.

"What kind of question is that? No, I'm not all right. Are you human? What am I saying?"

She said exactly what he expected.

"Can I just show you the rest?"

Mary nodded.

"I promise it won't hurt. Just relax, okay? Trust me, luv."

Before Mary could think of a response, Dagon placed one finger on her temple. She shook. Dagon felt anxious, too, for he was concerned about everything that he wanted to show her.

LIKE WATCHING A MOVIE, Mary saw everything. She watched his ceremony in the Golden Land. She saw Dagon's sword, but it looked even bigger than the one earlier in her dream. It looked to be as tall as Dagon, though she watched him with mind-bending speed slash the sword through the air and thrust it high above his head. *How could he do that? His arms didn't appear very muscular.* Her composure gave away nothing as she watched the next part. She saw a beautiful blonde woman put the black stone ring on his finger, a cunning expression on her face. O*kay, I'm making a note to ask him about her.*

Mary saw a woman and a man gazing at a white tree. They glowed with innocence about them. Crystal vials of brilliant flames adorned the tree, hanging from its branches. The woman gazed at the flames, drawing her closer. She took a vial and gave it to Dagon, who then handed it to the woman of cunning beauty, the blonde who had given him the ring. The innocent pair hid, and a bridge appeared in the sky. Wailing and screaming came from somewhere. Her heart raced faster than the scene.

Dagon and the cunning woman laughed and to her shock, Mary recognized herself on the bridge, despite a slightly blurry face but with the same eyes. Dagon's laughter faded away as he looked tenderly at the woman on the bridge. His expression changed to pain as veins formed within his body and the innocent pair begin walking away with their heads hanging in sorrow. They had lost their innocent glow. Forlorn, Dagon left with the spiteful woman, and his white garments turned gray. His hood split, and then she saw him fly as a dragon. Time moved quickly forward in a blur. Somewhere, there was a dark, cold, stifling place. She watched his memories of finding her, following her for a week, protecting her, and finally she watched him on her doorstep, shaking tulips behind his back.

Just like that, the images became blurry again, as he removed his finger from her temple.

Dagon was in fact a Seraph, and with a few exceptions, he was all man. Yes, all man.

"Was the partial transformation painful?"

"Yes, very."

"You said you never had a girlfriend. Who's the blonde woman? Is she your wife?"

"Her name is Savila and no, no! Definitely and emphatically not!"

"What was I watching?"

"The first scene you watched was my investiture as guardian and knighthood. At that time, Savila, the then Guardian of Wisdom, had the ceremonial honor to place the ring of investiture on my finger. Before my hood was removed, my name—"

"Beautiful. Absolutely breathtaking," said Mary.

"Before my hood was removed, my name and title were announced. I am 'Dagon, Guardian of Light and Guardian of the First Land' and—"

"What is the First Land?"

"Mary, you're sweet," said Dagon with a sigh. Every question he answered opened numerous questions. "The First Land is the home of the pair that you saw gazing at the white tree with the vials of flames. The woman was Andrana and the man was her bonded mate. This bond is stronger than an earthly bond, but it is like unto a marital bond. Savila was invested before the time of my creation as

'Savila, Guardian of Wisdom and Guardian of the First Land.' The First Land was our post of guardianship. Savila opened my mind to power, and I began to hate the humans."

Mary chewed on her lower lip. "You hate humans? But I'm human."

"Maybe hate is too strong of a word. Jealous maybe. Savila told me humans would be powerful and more highly valued than Seraphs, and since we were created first, this infuriated me. As a whole, the human race is not bad, though I've seen some really rotten examples and some okay ones. I've met one exceptionally beautiful human recently, though."

She felt heat rush to her face.

"I'm going to continue, luv. Andrana and her mate had come to the tree often. Savila opened my eyes and Andrana's. Then I placed words in her mind, whispers of power. Andrana plucked a vial from the tree—"

"Why did she do this?"

"Because I asked her to."

"She passed the vial to her mate and then to me, and I in turn gave it to Savila. Savila seeks complete domination and permanent death for humanity. At that time, I did as well, but Savila is the one who was bound to blood. Once the pair's minds opened, their blood became bound to Savila, as is mine. Savila showed me the bridge and then blew it up by closing her hand. The people on the bridge fell to their doom. Everything changed for me when I saw you. Your eyes made me sorry for what I had done, and so I hid your image deep in my heart to protect you from Savila. The no-longer-innocent pair, Savila, and I were all cast out of the First Land and into a new land. This new land is called the Second Land, or Earth."

"Dagon, my mind is hurting ..."

"I told you it wouldn't hurt and yet it did," he whispered, his eyes cast down. "I'm so sorry."

"Oh no, that's not what I meant." She leaned down closer to his face. "My mind is hurting from everything you told me, that's all."

"What do you mean, 'that's all'? I don't want you hurting at all."

"Let's see ... how to explain ..." Mary looked toward the ceiling. "It's like this, because everything you told me is new, there's just a lot to learn, that's all. Does that help?"

"Yes, I see, so it's overwhelming?"

"Yes, I guess that makes sense."

"So ... I didn't hurt you?" He placed his hand on her forehead.

"No, you didn't," Mary said, holding his hand.

"I'm glad, very glad."

She smiled and put her hands on her lap. "What did the vials do? Why did she take one? Vials seem harmless."

Dagon raised his eyebrows and shook his head. "The vials have a powerful flame, which gives the one who plucks it knowledge of good and evil. We were forbidden to take one from the tree. When she took the vial from the tree, her bonded mate also took hold of it, and his mind opened. This was the beginning of all evil, Mary, and I am so sorry."

"No, definitely not harmless," she said.

"That's putting it mildly."

Their deceptively simple remarks, lightened the moment, causing them both to laugh.

"I did not mean to brush over what you said about being sorry."

"That's ok, we needed laughter about now."

"Yes," she said in a whisper. *Now what.* "Can you turn into a dragon?"

"No, I can't. It's my coat that transforms into a dragon. I'm sorry ... it's creepy, I know."

"I don't know why, but that doesn't scare me. I'm more curious than anything."

He looked relieved.

"Can you show my mind more about how your dragon looks? Where did you go after you flew off in the image you showed me?"

"No, I will not show you this, it would profit nothing. I will not take a chance for fear that you would be scared."

"How old are you?"

"How old do you think I look?" He grinned, posing.

"I think that you look around twenty."

"Really? That's nice. So, I look twenty and you are ..." Dagon's reflection off glass from a china cabinet showed him raising his eyebrows slowly, while tilting his chin.

"Twenty-one."

"Perfect," is all Dagon said while he caught a glimpse of himself in a mirror.

"Well, how old *are* you?"

"Mary, does it matter?"

"No, it's just ..."

"The truth is, I really don't know. In the scenes you just watched, the world was newly created, before my creation."

"You would have to be over a million years old. Is that even possible?"

"Yes, give or take a day. Baby, do I look over a million years old?" Dagon posed again with his chin in the air, offering his profile for examination.

"Give or take a day? No, but—"

"Well, there we are."

"What do you mean?"

"In my homeland, time does not exist. It is said that one day is like a thousand of your human years, and a thousand of your years is like one of our days. So, another way of looking at it is that you are older than me. But that's splitting hairs, isn't it?"

"What? Oh, never mind. But when you said that you were only gone for two seconds ... did you mean two seconds or was that an exaggeration?"

"In my world, Mary, it was really two seconds. But it seemed like forever."

"Whether you call it seconds or weeks, why were you gone at all?"

"Mary, I couldn't leave. I am ... sort of between homes at the moment ... in a hotel of sorts. I do have a home, but I'm waiting on some loose ends to clear up."

Dagon said no more, got up, and went into the kitchen, opening the refrigerator without even asking. Dagon just nodded his head when Mary explained to him the reason why her refrigerator was so sparse, for she mainly ate at the restaurant when she worked. In an odd sense of familiarity, he set the table and made them sandwiches. He devoured every crumb.

AFTER DAGON WASHED the dishes and put them away, it began to rain outside. They sat back on the couch, listening to the rain. Dagon would have given anything to know Mary's thoughts. Was she thinking of him or the bizarre things he told her? On second thought, maybe ignorance was bliss.

Mary looked antsy, her toes curled in as her body stiffened.

"Are you all right? I don't think it's going to storm. Besides, I'm here for you."

Whether from what he said or from something else, her toes and body relaxed.

"I'm all right. Even as a child I was frightened by storms. I still am, but I'm all right." She smiled and held his hand again. "It's nice not to be alone now."

Is she glad I'm here because she likes me, or am I just an unexpected visitor helping to pass the time away? Well ... she looks happy. That's what counts.

She leaned back on the couch, kind of looking at nothing with a deadpan stare. "My parents died in a car accident when I was fifteen. A head on collision caused by a drunk driver. They died instantly."

Light rain pattered the house as a few tear drops fell from her eyelashes.

"I'm so sorry, luv. Can I hold you? I want you to know you are not alone."

She said nothing but scooted next to him. Dagon placed his arms around her. He smelled her hair and closed his eyes.

"I have only one sibling, a sister, Catherine. She's four years younger than me. When our parents died, we moved in with our grandmother. Then, when I was eighteen, our grandmother died. My sister moved in with my dad's only brother and his wife. She lives in Romeoville about thirty miles from here. Not that far, but I haven't seen or spoken to her in years because of ... being hurt ... well ... you know, from sadness."

Dagon said nothing but held her tight. Some things in life require a silent presence, and in many ways, this described him; silently looking for her, a presence unseen though there.

"I would encourage you to reach out to her. I believe it would help you." Dagon pushed a hair from the corner of her face.

"I know you're right. It's just ... it's been so long."

"Time is irrelevant, and I'm not just saying this because of the world I come from. Family and time move together even if separated. Does this make sense?"

"I think it does."

Even for a Seraph, it was hard to know what to say and what not to say. Maybe the language of his body holding her would speak volumes.

"My sister and I are my parents' only children, and my grand-mother only had one child, my mother, so when my parents and my grandmother died, my sister and I received equal shares of life insur-ance. That is how I purchased this house. I always loved this house. When I was little, my parents would take us on Sunday drives through old neighborhoods in the area. This house made a deep impression on me. The white color of the house looked innocent, hopeful. I wondered what family lived here or could a new family live here."

"Do you have any other grandparents that are living?"

"No. I never met my dad's parents. They died when he was young, and I never knew my mom's dad."

In a brief time, Mary shared deep parts of her heart. Losing her parents and her only grandparent three years apart broke his heart. All this suffering for what, power? So not worth it. His love for her? Worth everything. Now the deadpan stare made sense. Still, some-thing felt off. Maybe being new to relationships caused him to read into something which wasn't there.

"You know, I have a thought," Dagon said.

"What is it?"

"I know the hour is late, but would you mind if I share a memory of my past?"

"I would love that." Mary perked up.

"I believe this will help soften what you shared, and, baby, you have never been alone."

Whether from what he said or from something else, her body and mood changed, so he began telling her one of his memories from his vast existence. Time is irrelevant. Both of them moving as one.

14

The Well of Souls Desire

"I was in Delphi, Greece, in 328 B.C. though we didn't call it that back then. The very place where, legend has it, that the Golden Land and the Second Land, or Earth, would meet ..."

"328 B.C.? How can that ... in Greece?"

"I know, it's ancient."

"Well yes, but you were there?"

"So, antiquity aside, the issue for you is how can I be here yet had been alive that long ago. Is this it?"

"It's hard to believe ... it's hard to take in." Mary scooted to the edge of the couch and placed her hands under her thighs. Her eyes narrowed and focused in the middle of the room.

"You said you would love to hear a memory ..."

"No, it's not that. I don't know ... all this still is ... well ..." In a flash, Mary adjusted her position on the couch and stared point blank at Dagon. She slapped her thighs. "Seriously, 328 B.C.?"

"Mary, you know I'm half Seraph, and I've existed ..."

Mary waved her hands back and forth in front of her shoulders. "Yes, I know, but processing this supernatural stuff is hard."

Dagon opened his mouth and Mary held up her hand. "And for the record, I want to hear your memories."

Dagon smiled. "I understand. This human stuff isn't exactly a cake walk."

"I guess it wouldn't be." Mary put a hand on his lap. "So, what happened in Greece in 328 B.C.?"

Dagon kissed her cheek. "My goal was to visit the Oracle of Delphi, whom I believed to be a fraud, but I hoped would offer me information on when I would meet my beloved. That is you, Mary."

A stray tear streaked her cheek, which she wiped away.

"So, in a long line, in the hot baking sun, I waited to ask the Pythia ..."

"Who's that?" Mary asked.

"After answering this, let me continue, ok?"

Mary nodded.

"The Oracle of Delphi was a shrine dedicated to the Greek god Apollo, and the Pythia was his earthly mouthpiece to impart divinely-inspired answers to patron's questions regarding their fortunes."

"Interesting."

Dagon liked her simple response to the goofy ancient fraud. "The hot sun of the day was relentless; the line moved very slowly. To pass some time, I made up a parable and shared it with some men standing next to me.

"A priest came upon three men who gazed into a well. The priest told these men this was 'The Well of Soul's Desire.' The priest then asked the first man what he desired.

"'To be the wealthiest man on earth.'"

"The priest bent over and gazed into the well. 'Your desire is granted, however, to be the wealthiest man on earth you must give your money away.'

"The first man stared at the priest in stunned disbelief and left mumbling to himself. 'How can I be the wealthiest man on earth by giving it all away? I desire the well to dry up.'

"Then the priest asked the second man what he desired.

"'To have fame and glory.'

"Again, the priest bent over and gazed into the well. 'Your desire is granted; however, you will soon die.'

"The second man walked away in disgust at what the priest told him and said, 'I will die soon? How is this fame and glory? I also desire the well to dry up.'

"The man walked away carrying a spear and shield, off to battle in search of fame and glory.

"Now the third man looked nervous when the priest asked him what he desired. The man pondered all that happened to his friends then spoke. 'I desire to have the water of life pour forth through me, so I can live forever.'

"The priest smiled. 'Your desire is granted.'

"The third man did not hear the priest speak, however, at which time the man leaned over and gazed into the well. Whereby, the priest pushed him into the well and a loud thud could be heard as his body hit the bottom of the dried up well. New water consumed the man, pouring forth from him, bringing water to all. Now the priest marveled at this and yelled down.

"'The well sees the hearts of men and granted your friends' deepest desires, thus the well dried up, but you have it all. Wealth, for the giving of water; fame and glory, for people will come near and far to drink from the wonders of these waters; and your desire to have the water of life pour forth through you and live forever. Though you meant your desire not for good, good it will be, and forever you will live.'"

Dagon paused, and Mary started to speak. He held up his right hand, silencing any of her questions, ideas, suggestions, or comments, at least for now.

"I must give you the meaning of my parable. The first man wanted to be the wealthiest man on earth, but he knew not what true wealth was, so the priest's words were but a curse to him. His deepest desire was known, the drying up of the well, thus denying others happiness.

"The second man wanted fame and glory, but he knew not the cost of fame and glory, for to gain it all, you must risk it all while knowing full well your death cometh soon. This man wanted to live long and reap the rewards of fame and glory without paying the price for the immortality of it. His deepest desire was also known by the drying of the well.

"The third man was yet wise, for he thought before he spoke; but like the previous two, his heart was his judge, and he was found guilty. Yet the judge pardoned him and let his life bear a witness to all, by the giving of water to all who thirst. His life will then live forever, a constant reminder to himself for the price of selfishness and the solution for it.

"Go ahead, step right up and have your fortunes told. You never know, you could become the wealthiest person on earth, have fame and fortune and glory, or we could be drinking from your waters, toasting a cup to you. Goodness knows I could use some water about now. It's hot out here."

Mary laughed. "Dagon, that is amazing. How long did it take you to come up with that?"

"It was all impromptu."

"Really ... amazing."

"Is there anything that jumps out to you about the parable?"

"Love and selfishness."

"And ... what love and what selfishness did I reveal in the present?" *Did she get it right?*

"I'm not good at twenty-one questions."

"I only asked two."

"Oh ya ... well ..."

"The love is ..."

"Me. I'm the beloved you wanted to ask the Pythia about?"

"Yes, and the selfishness was my desire for power and the curse I desire to end."

"I see." She slowly nodded as her gaze drifted across the room.

"Do you?" He doubted she fully understood. How could she.

"Sort of. Did you ever meet the Pythia?"

"Yes, I did."

"Well, what did she say?"

"The line kept slowly meandering through a small narrow path, which led into the temple where the Pythia resided. Priests, whose souls desire wealth, fame and fortune, and not water but wine. All at the expense of the poor souls who waited eagerly. Beautifully carved statues lined the path. These statues were tributes given by the wealthy in honor of Apollo. These brazen priests lined their own pockets and filled the temple's coffers."

"Dagon, what did she say already?"

"Oh that. Mish mosh hibble jibble, that's what she said."

"You couldn't understand anything?"

"Sort of."

"Sort of what?"

Being alone for so long, he dragged the suspense out, but he didn't want to make her mad, just curious.

"If time is moving, then why are you here? For your answer lies beyond, not far, but near."

"Is that what she said?"

"Yep."

"How could anyone understand anything with that?"

"They can't, and that's the point. The double cryptic meaning is a sure-fire scheme to keep the money flowing by having the customers come back again and again."

"Then she didn't help at all."

"She kind of did. She was no more clairvoyant than I expected. True, she did not know when or where I would meet you, but still, I took it to heart. Deducing you were in fact real and out there somewhere."

Mary leaned into his arms.

"What happened to the person who killed your parents?"

"He's in prison."

"What prison is he in?" inquired Dagon.

"He's in Statesville in Joliet."

Dagon kept listening with a poker face though he was grief-stricken and angry. Mary told him that she had seen the man at his trial, and she described what he looked like.

Dagon shifted his attention inside the prison, listening intently for anything regarding the criminal, but it was in vain.

"Mary, it's getting late. I'll come back tomorrow in the morning hours if that is acceptable to you."

"I would love that."

Dagon hugged her goodbye, and Mary opened the door. He glanced over his shoulder at her several times before he melted into the darkness.

MARY FOUGHT the loneliness of night. Her mind reeled from everything she learned. Desperately she clung to the immortality of love and how Dagon placed the image of her into his heart, shielding her from Savila. This outweighed everything else, strange, scary, or otherwise. He was her knight, her superhero knight. Everything in her life had been preparing her heart for him. Night after night when she was little, he would be in her dreams running as if on a treadmill, rarely covering much ground for how fast he appeared to be going. A few nightmares involved kids bullying her or a cruel teacher singling her out in class. In front of a dry erase board she would stand and sweat, the marker in her hand quivering. The teacher would belittle her, telling her she would be less stupid if she studied. Most of the students felt sorry for her, but at the time, it felt like the whole class laughed at her. Perhaps Dagon's presence, his body wrapped in light caused the mean kids to unanimously shut up, their postures stiffening in their seats. These dreams made Dagon appear like Mary could almost touch him. Only a few short years later and her dreams will become hideous in comparison. Like always, Dagon was there, letting her know in some way she was not alone.

Dagon wasn't alone either. He didn't have to be or do anything for Mary to love him, she just did. Deeply, her heart ached for him, not only because of the things he showed her, but also concerning what she couldn't see. Dagon was larger than life, though small too, his knowledge of human life being miniscule. The image of Dagon picking up that massive sword like a twig, contrasted with his fragility. Not only because of the outward wounds, but in his reaction after telling her that he couldn't leave his original home.

One thing which kept crowding her mind besides his feeling trapped was his loneliness. How could he be lonely for over a million years? If that's the case, that's sad. *Ok ... does it really matter that I'm in love with a man who's older than the dinosaurs? He doesn't look that old.* She now saw the impulsive taking of a first aid class as a part of her being able to help Dagon. Somehow this made her think how youthful her parents had looked when Dagon's sword plunged into them in her dream. She wasn't sure exactly why. In youth, all things seem possible, a clean slate of life. Maybe there was a connection between her parents and her present situation.

Now in her bed, she desired to place herself in front of Dagon like a shield of armor. He had placed himself in front of her, protecting her from the dark, cold, stifling place, and she would do the same. *Maybe I can help him with his curse, whatever it is.* With the unburdened mind of youth, she dreamed of Dagon more vibrant than ever before with the immortality of love.

15

The Ninja

Magethna and Dorian made their way up the stairs and into Mark's room. Mystil and Raglen greeted them.

"The boy sleeps," said Mystil.

Sure enough, Mark slept sprawled out, snoring lightly.

"What a lovely time we had," said Magethna, as she reached inside her pocket and took out a pink quill.

Dorian looked at the quill in wonder and asked, "What sort of bird has pink feathers?"

"I decided that I should write with flair and what better way to write, than with a pink quill? I think everything should be pink."

"Wouldn't that be a strange world to have everything pink."

"Not to me." Quick scratches of her quill moved along thin ivory pages.

"Or me," said Mystil with a big grin on her face.

"Guarding Mark. Guarding Mark. Guarding Mark. Guarding Mark." Magethna spoke aloud as she filled in each day. Her quill paused as she wrote silently and solemnly, "Awaiting word about how Mark will end up in the presence of old." Only the scratch of the quill on the paper and the quiet tick of Dorian's watch made any sound now. "Guarding the Bennett house."

PONDERING AND PLANNING occupied Dagon's mind as he walked toward his bench. Dagon's boots barely made a sound on the side-walk as he strolled along. The bandages comforted and yet restricted him at the same time. Had he not chosen a pact with Savila, none of this malevolence would be happening. But then, he never would have known Mary. The rain stopped, but his boots still splashed in dark-ened puddles.

As he approached his bench, Dagon walked past the Seraphs and saluted. Dorian stood still with no visible reaction to Dagon's pres-ence. As usual, none of the Seraphs returned his salute, but Magethna gave him a smile.

Dagon plopped down on the bench, his heart-break hotel. He tried hard to not tell Mary about the Abyss. He couldn't keep stalling on this—she would eventually find out. His mind spun, and his boots dripped, which irked him, for they hadn't been cheap, and he thought Mary liked them. His boots reminded him that he needed to take Mary dancing. They would get their groove on and dance the night away someday.

The Seraphs began to sing, and Dagon listened. He enjoyed it, for even though he had other emotions competing for his attention, for the moment, happiness won. He reckoned that maybe Mary wasn't sick of him. But maybe she had only cleaned his wounds because she felt sorry for him. Still, he would take what he could get. He sat back on his bench and enjoyed living in the light.

With every good image, a bad one followed close behind, including a conversation he had had with Savila when they had walked out of the First Land.

"I think we committed treason," said Dagon

"No, you aided an enemy of the Golden Land. I re-ordered the law."

"How is that not treason?"

"Because I am the law," said Savila.

Dagon fell into silent despair after that. Reeling from the memory, Dagon became angry. In a quick decision, he put on the second veil and took out a lemon drop, rolling it around in his palm. Living in the light by not blocking his mind seemed more for the protection of Mary than seeking vengeance on the man who killed her parents. He thought about transforming into his dragon but changed his mind. The Seraphs could see him, and he wanted to keep this quiet for as long as he could.

While the Seraphs still sang, Dagon puffed out of view and went dark. He snapped his fingers once and summoned Mr. Cool.

Dagon did not know if Savila knew how close he was to his cohorts. He had successfully blocked his mind from her for eons, but he didn't want to take any chances. He ate the revolting tainted candy. *After all this time, I'm still not used to this stuff ... yuck!*

Dagon gave Mr. Cool a black ops mission into the bowels of a Joliet prison.

"That stinks! Why does he get that mission?" said Sledge. "I say let's crash and smash things! Over."

"Love your enthusiasm and passion but not now. You three are guarding my Mary, my most special treasure. Over."

"We know, we know. But ..."

"It will be your butts if you don't shut it! Now gripe less and guard more."

"What happened to living in the light by blocking your mind?"

"Unpredictable, unplanned circumstances is what happened."

"Hypocrite!" shouted all of them.

"Can it, you three. I am taking care of business. Besides, I have something else for you to do."

"TCB to you, too. Get the scuzz bucket." said Friar.

"That's more like it, boys."

Mr. Cool nodded in agreement.

With that settled, Dagon gave Mr. Cool the coordinates.

"That's a far walk, boss. And the mission sounds dangerous. So, cash is king as they say."

"Hitch a ride or whatever you need to do. Yes, cash is king, and you'll get paid. Just keep me posted: where you're at and when you're in."

"Copy that, boss. I can't wait to see the looks on the others faces when I get back. If I get back, that is."

"Think positive. Now go. Over and out."

Under both the veils, Dagon took off his coat and made it into a pillow. Like Alexander the Great, he didn't look back, risking it all to gain it all. For even if Mary only pitied him, he would still give her love. His mind sang the song that Mary had sung in her sleep. The only alteration was the addition of his name. After all, this was his lullaby.

I love him, his name is Dagon.

It wasn't long before Mr. Cool reported in.

"Officer Grossman? Come in, Officer Grossman. Over."

"I am not Officer Grossman. Over."

"Yeah, you are, boss. Anyway ... I've hitched a ride in the back of a pickup truck. Over."

"You what?" Dagon lay down, shifted his body on the bench, then sat up, and rearranged his pillow.

"I hitched. Hey, what's going on?"

"What is going on?" Laying down, Dagon twisted, tugged, and pulled on his sorry excuse for a pillow.

"The road just became bu ... bumpy."

"Where are you?" Dagon sighed, then turned over and punched his coat, causing a prickly scale to be less prickly.

"On the ba ... back of a ye ... yellow ... pickup."

"Just contact me when you're inside," said Dagon.

The bumps stopped. "Will do, Officer Grossman. Don't try to fight it. You know that I am freaking hilarious. Over and out."

Dagon was irritated with this infernal name, but he had to admit that Mr. Cool was funny and resourceful. No time seemed to pass before Mr. Cool radioed back.

"Officer Grossman? Come in, Officer Grossman. Over."

"Just call me 'boss.' Over."

"Whatever you say, Officer Grossman."

"Where are you? You'd better be inside."

"I am, and man is it creepy in here."

"Good. Now, find him."

"I'm looking. Are you sure you have the description, right?"

"Yes, and he's the creepy one."

"They're all creepy."

"Just find him and take care of it and then report back."

"Roger that. Over and out."

MR. COOL stealthily crept along the dimly lit prison hallways, located the target, and radioed his boss.

"Creepy guy found. Over."

"Are you in?"

"More or less."

"Get in now and let me know when it's done."

"Roger that. Over and out."

Mr. Cool crept along like a ninja. The creepy target sat in a cell on the second floor. In one fluid motion, Mr. Cool whipped out his sword, placing the tip of the blade into a crack. Taking out a rope from his coat, he tied sturdy knots in several key places. The sword now served as a ladder, lifting him to the second story. Mr. Cool dissolved through the solid metal bars. He sneaked along inside the cell, finding the prisoner fast asleep. Sitting on a stool, he waited until the prisoner woke up. He would forcefully wake the creep if the prisoner wasted his precious time.

The inmate snored away, and with a loud snort, startled himself awake. Mr. Cool remained silent, watching the man stretch and yawn. Bored, he whistled, frightening the man.

"Who are you?"

"You ask the wrong question. You should have asked why I'm here."

"Why are you here?"

"To kill you," said Mr. Cool calmly.

The man screamed and called for help.

"Screaming will do you no good. Anyone who sees you will see you sitting on your bed; they won't see anything else. No one can help you, but I can by putting you out of your misery."

Shaking and shouting, the inmate looked around to see if anyone reacted to his commotion. No one did.

"You killed the parents of someone very special."

"What are you talking about? Whose parents?"

Mr. Cool stood, making his way over to the prisoner's grimy bunk. The prisoner scooted closer to the wall for whatever protection it would give him.

"Did a woman come to you before you killed her parents? Did you see a woman before you became drunk or after?"

The frightened man screamed, his mind shouting chaos from the barrage of questions. He did not even attempt to answer. He squirmed closer to the wall. Paint chips flaked onto his bunk.

Mr. Cool pulled images from the man's sweaty forehead. Fear and pain radiated from him, and he shook as if he were sick.

"We will watch what happened that awful day."

He whipped his other hand toward the opposite wall. Like a movie, the images played on the wall.

The prisoner sat petrified, watching his memories displayed. Mr. Cool couldn't stifle a smile. He enjoyed seeing the pain this movie evoked. His finger firmly pushed onto the man's forehead, causing excruciating pain. Mr. Cool watched intently to see if Savila had placed an image of Dagon at the scene of the crime. It was not beyond her by any means to frame Dagon for her own crimes. He dug deeply into the man's memories, causing the man to shriek even louder. Re-watching some scenes, he studied for any sign of Savila or Dagon. He didn't see either. In a blink, the images were gone.

"I've already been paying for this for years now. I'm so sorry." The man did his best to convey remorse.

"My name is Mr. Cool, and my boss tells me you have not paid for anything yet, but you will."

Mr. Cool once again placed his finger on the creep's forehead and swiped it, erasing all traces of the memory of their encounter and momentarily dazing him. From his pocket, Mr. Cool pulled out a razor blade. It provided a perfect coverup for this covert operation. With a swipe of the man's forehead, a new memory was placed in his mind. He waited until the man regained some consciousness. With razor precision, the man was sliced dead. Now his death would be considered a suicide.

The soul began fading out of the body, and with his boot, Mr. Cool kicked the soul down into the Abyss.

Another one bites the dust.

Living waters poured over the blade, dissolving all of the blood.

The assassin gripped the rope and slid down it, exiting the cell. He reported his status as he left. "Officer Grossman? Come in, Officer Grossman. Over."

"What is it?"

"Creepy guy is dead and gone."

"What about his memory?"

"It's been erased and replaced."

"What did you replace it with?"

"Suicide."

"Suicide?"

"Yep ... a razor blade."

"That's perfect."

"I thought so, too. Oh, I found no sign of the wicked witch in his memory."

"Get back soon."

"Roger that. Over and out."

Dagon relaxed. The killer was dead, and Savila would not suspect he had done it. If Savila had it her way, she would have had Dagon sexed up, drugged up, liquored up, and smoked up. Basically, screwed up. She wanted him controllable, moldable, and exploitable. She needed Dagon to be just sane enough to fight, but half here, so he would think handing his title over to her would be the best thing for him. Although Dagon did smoke, he couldn't find his beloved while drunk or stoned. No matter how his addictive personality would love to succumb to numb. He refused to risk Mary in that way.

～

ONE OF THE shadow soldiers brought this new soul before Savila and even in death he was quaking. Savila read his mind. *Death not by natural causes.* Savila commanded the soldiers to prod him with pain into the execution room and burn him. He would be made a soldier, but it would not be in glory. His clothes were burned off but would not be placed in ceremonial honor in the Throne Room. The scent of evil scorched like fire over her nose as the man's flesh burned. Within this man and his burning, Savila saw a ruse. Dagon had been blocking his mind with angelic ash. Like Andrana and her bonded mate, Dagon's mind should have been opened to her, but it had not been. She saw this flaw as a remnant of his immortality, but in fact this revelation was flawless, sinisterly beautiful in its origin. With delight, she breathed the power of her dominance. The man's skin burned to dust. Each flake bowing to her supreme authority. Everything worked out just like she planned as protection moved with love in a collision of light and darkness.

～

"OFFICER GROSSMAN? Come in, Officer Grossman. Over."

"I order you to stop calling me that."

"Nah. Hey, I hitched a ride again, and you won't believe what I'm riding in. Now, don't look, let me tell you."

"Okay. I hear wind rushing by."

"You would, for I am riding in a cherry red Ferrari Testarossa ... and flying fast."

"Are you joking?"

"Nope, I'm riding with a balding man. I think this guy thinks he's twenty instead of sixty. He has a big silver chain around his neck, and his shirt is wide open."

"At least he has good taste in cars. Just hurry back."

"Roger that. Over and far out, man."

Soon Mr. Cool was right in front of him, and his greedy hand shot out fast. Dagon sat on his bench, took out two wads of cash, and handed it over. Mr. Cool's money-hungry fingers pocketed the cash before he melted away.

In a few hours, it would be dawn, and he would soon be with Mary. Dagon lay down and fell asleep nice and content, for he had accomplished his mission impossible.

16

Whispering Shadows

The day started out mild and overcast. Under his two protective veils, Dagon took his shirt off and pulled out a set of clean clothes from his coat. With his duffel bag down in the Abyss, he looked around for something to put dirty clothes in. A garbage bag fluttered in the wind, partially caught by brambles in the field.

Half-naked, he walked over to the garbage bag. He carefully removed the bag, trying not to rip it. Once freed, he shook it open, smelled, and examined it. Satisfied, he returned to the "Bench Hotel."

Protecting his bandages, he finished changing. He hoped his fashion choice would earn high marks. With very little to eat at Mary's house, he stopped at a local grocery store.

Wasting no time, he filled a grocery cart with food and cleaning supplies. At the last minute, he picked up a superb Japanese knife set with water-patterned steel. How strange to find this quality of cutlery at a grocery store. Gratified, he made his way over to the checkout counter. Opening his wallet, he placed some money into the cash register while the cashier filled several paper bags with someone else's sundries.

Holding two paper bags, he hung the handle of a bucket over one of his wrists. He whistled as he headed for Mary's house.

"For your callous oversight, this one's for you," The Cherbs guarding Mary's house saluted him crassly with their middle fingers.

"What?"

"The black ops."

"Why I oughta ..."

"You want three middle toes as well? You want us to stick them where the sun doesn't shine?" said Razz.

Dagon threw them a foul look while his elbow rang the doorbell. Disclaimer insults fired from Razz, Sledge, and Friar. Each insult followed by where, when, and how they would shove things if his neglect continued. The words from them dwindled as Mary's quick, hurried steps matched his heartbeat. One of her beautiful blue eyes looked out the peep hole. This time, the door opened quickly.

Standing in the doorway, she started to speak, then stopped. She looked at the bags he carried.

"Good morning, luv. Did you sleep well?"

"Um ... yeah. Was your hotel okay?"

"I'm glad you slept well. My hotel was fine, but the bed is small and too hard for my taste."

"Hopefully you won't be there too long."

"Wouldn't that be nice. You know ... this stuff is a little awkward. Can I bring it inside?"

"Oh, Dagon, I'm sorry." She stepped aside.

"Quite alright, luv."

"You know, you didn't have to buy all that, but it's nice. Thank you," she said as they went inside.

"Why don't we put these things in the kitchen," said Dagon.

"Oh ... ok."

The kitchen was still clean, except for a dirty bowl and spoon in the sink. Dagon put the bags on the counter and hung his coat up in the coat closet. Like a true bonded couple, they put everything away together.

"What are you looking for?" asked Mary.

"Where are your pots and pans?" said Dagon. Maybe he should have bought some at the store.

"Oh, they're over here."

Dagon watched to see where "here" was.

"Why would you keep pans in here?" he asked in astonishment.

"I don't know, the linen closet just seemed to fit."

"Well, let's put them in the kitchen," said Dagon, discretely rolling his eyes.

Together, they picked up pots and pans and brought them into the kitchen. Dagon directed where everything should go and together, they organized the pans.

When they finished, Mary grabbed his hand, and he beamed. But his delight turned to worry, causing his heart to beat faster when she wanted to change his bandages.

On the way upstairs, he found more cobwebs. Instinctively, he reached up but quickly withdrew his hand. Before he could protest, he sat in the bathroom, the first aid kit open and ready to use. Mary tenderly removed the bandages and commented on how good the wound looked, which shocked Dagon. True to her word, she re-cleaned his wounds, repeating the same process right down to the stinging liquid. After bandaging him back up, Mary told him that she would do this again several more times. His wounds and scars didn't seem to bother her, but the recoil of shame would smack him hard when he least expected it.

Back in the kitchen, Mary brought out two mugs, cream (not expired), sugar, and spoons and placed them on the table. Dagon pulled out a chair and tilted his head, squinting at each of the items in front of him.

Sitting across from Dagon, Mary poured each of them a steaming cup, leaving a little room at the top.

"How do you take your coffee?"

"What is coffee, luv?"

"This is called coffee, and some people enjoy the flavor of cream or sugar or both added to it. It's pretty common, lots of people drink it in the morning, but some drink it more often."

She fixed his coffee the same way she liked hers. She watched him take a first sip.

"Do my taste buds detect a familiar flavor in this coffee?" said Dagon.

"You can't tell anyone. This is my secret ingredient."

"What happens if I tell?"

Mary gave Dagon a flirtatious look.

Dagon moved his chair back, went over to Mary, and drew her into his arms.

"I think the benefits outweigh the risk." Mary kissed him and shared her grandmother's secret formula for fabulous coffee. This created a natural opening to learn more about Mary's past. Her grandmother was already old when Mary and her sister came to live in the house with her after their parents died. Mary's great-grandparents were Swedish immigrants. Her grandmother loved to cook, but this talent was not passed down to her and only very little of it to her sister Catherine. The sisters were the only grandchildren, so when she passed, their grandmother left everything to them.

Dagon moved his chair closer to Mary and had a second cup of her special coffee warming his hands. Dagon found Mary staring down at her toes, which kept curling in, and she seemed nervous.

"Um ... Is it okay if I ask you some questions?"

"Yes, luv." He wanted to answer what he could for Mary.

"You said that you are half-human but that you are a man. What does that even mean? I mean, how could you be half-human?"

"Rampart, we have an update on that other job you requested," Friar buzzed in. "The Glynns, friends of the Bennetts, live just down the street. Sending you coordinates. Over."

Dagon fine tuned the image of the Glynn house in his head and listened for any feedback. If he could just adjust the frequency of thought ...

"Dagon? Did you hear what I said? Why are you smiling like that?"

"Yes, I heard you. Why not wear a smile, or would you rather me frown like this?" Dagon gave her his best exaggerated comical frown.

"No, I don't mean that I want you to frown and especially not like that. It didn't look like you heard me."

"Trust me, I did. Now, to answer your question; in many ways, I'm fully human ..."

"Except when it comes to listening."

"To put it plainly, I am all man, and then some. This you will understand when the time is right." Dagon winked several times for emphasis. *This should let her know that physically, I'm all here.* He could tell by her bashful yet alluring expression that she understood, and he continued.

"I can sleep though I do not need to. I don't get tired or need to rest. At one point, I thought that humans died every night only to rise again every morning."

"Really?"

"Yes, I really did."

"Oh, Dagon. That's ... like reversed vampires."

"I guess it is ... I never thought of that." Dagon became somber at the similarity of Savila to vampires. He quickly pushed on, eager to avoid any reminders. "Okay, so I don't have to sleep, I don't have to use the bathroom, I ..."

"You don't have to use the bathroom?" She raised one eyebrow.

"Nope."

"I wish I didn't have to. The lines for the women's bathrooms are always so long. Guys have it easier. Do you know how people use the bathroom?"

Dagon laughed while nodding in affirmation.

"I'm sorry."

"Don't apologize. How else are we going to get to know each other?" He paused between question and response to listen for a moment to the Glynns, who remained silent.

"Yes, I guess you're right."

"I can see through anything, but I purposefully blocked your house the first time I saw you, for your privacy." Dagon touched his ear. "My hearing is virtually limitless, and I can read minds."

Mary seemed unsettled, and he calmed her.

"When I placed you in my heart, I made a vow that I would not read your mind. I placed you in my heart because Savila is evil, and I wanted to protect you and myself. Unfortunately, I made a pact with her that I wish I hadn't. But decisions made for good or for evil all have consequences. I knew that I would be made human to use my title. Savila is trying to seal it to humanity's suffering," Dagon closed his eyes and sighed.

As he continued his reflections, he eventually mentioned she was his bonded mate. He fell in love with her then and would find her. Shockingly, she learned of humanity's doom. A first death, and then an eternal second death of their souls.

The kitchen chair Mary sat in, screeched back as she shot up. What in the ... what are you ..." Wildly, her eyes looked everywhere, but at Dagon. Then, her eyes narrowed at Dagon, her hands balled into fists and with more force than her petite figure would indicate, she smacked the table, causing the coffee mugs to shake, and left the room.

Dagon found her on the couch. She didn't acknowledge him sitting next to her, but she didn't reject him either. "I am not without power, for my title is influential, and Savila wants it for herself. I don't know how to say this without ... well ... just saying it." Dagon hung his head, sighed, and raised his head. "I wish I could make this something it's not, but the cold fact is: The sealing of my title will be set with blood."

"Dagon ... what are you talking about?"

"I know, baby. I never planned on telling you so much so soon, but I think that I need to. Let me continue, luv.

"When Andrana and her mate's minds opened, and they chose evil, they became traitors to the Golden Land. This cursed all of humanity and thus bound all humanity by blood. The bridge that you saw was not exactly metaphor, for truly, no traitors can cross back into the Golden Land ...”

"Then ... we are all doomed to the second death? Me ... my sister?”

"Mary, like I said, my title is powerful. When Savila invested me, I had bequeathed to me one rather large ruby. At some point in time the ruby was cleaved into two pieces. One is the Stone of Kings and the other is the Stone of Power. In 1415, the seal of my title over humanity's suffering began.” Dagon did not dwell on this. “The Stone of Power is in Mark's possession, bequeathed through his family, the Bennetts. The only way to break our bond to Savila is for Mark to deliver the Stone of Power before his death, and after this the Stone of Kings will come ... and then ...”

"The Bennetts? They live one street over from me. I can't even think ... I feel sick.”

"You know them?”

"I'm not literally sick. It's just ... this stuff is hard to grasp. My mind is spinning, that's all.”

"Mary, you are my bonded mate, and you will co-rule with me. Right now, I am bound and so are you, along with all of humanity. We can do more for humanity on a throne than off it, but I must keep our title intact to do this.”

"So, after Mark brings Savila the Stone of Power, the Stone of Kings comes to Savila, then we co-rule?” Between her fingers, Mary twisted a loose thread on the couch.

"After the Stone of Power and the Stone of Kings come into Savila's possession, then yes.”

"Then how can we help humanity?”

"Baby, you are the woman on the bridge, the hope for all humanity. There are things I can't tell you yet. This is to keep you safe.”

"What about you? I don't want to be safe if it's without you.”

Dagon held her, and she leaned against his chest.

"You don't think I'm crazy?” said Dagon.

"No, I don't. You could read my mind if you wanted to?”

Dagon would never tire of looking at her, but he was glad to be on a relatively easy question once again.

"Yes, but I choose not to out of love for you. I saw that Andrana and her mate could not read each other's minds, and I wanted us to have a normal relationship. Being able to read minds is not normal."

"Reading minds is normal for you."

"It is, but it is not normal for a human relationship, and whatever I can do to have a normal relationship with you is what I want to do. Remember how I told you all decisions have consequences?"

"Yes."

"Well, they do, and this is why I did not find you sooner. The choice not to read your mind is a constant one, but the minds of those people connected with you are blocked to me without my choice."

"How could you have known which voice would be mine?"

"Now that's a good question. I knew that my heart would know your voice."

"I believe that our hearts have been prepared for each other."

Dagon swept a stray strand of her hair, curling it between his fingers, pausing just above her ear. "You told me how you had been dreaming of me since you were seven."

"Yes. Every night you were in my dreams, always there waiting for me and protecting me."

Dagon leaned in close, his fingers smoothing the strand of hair behind her ear. "Every night?"

Mary nodded.

"Our hearts have been prepared for each other. Incredible." Dagon placed both of his hands on the sides of her face, drew her closer, and kissed her.

She wrapped her arms around his neck, and he took in the scent of gardenia on her skin, letting it consume him for a moment longer than necessary.

With her arms around his neck, she leaned back. Her sapphire eyes brightly sparkled from the beam of sunshine her upturned crescent shaped lips created. "You really have been protecting me. The supernatural is becoming less super and more natural."

"Do you think me acquiring human ways will be less super and more natural?"

"Yes, I think that for both of us." Mary raised an eyebrow. "Now, where were we? I know, right here." With her hands behind his neck, she guided his mouth to hers.

Dagon whispered in her ear. "I have been looking for you for a very long time, and we found each other. I will always be with you."

"I know," Mary whispered back. Letting go of his neck, she scooted down, and lay her head against his chest. "How did you make that creep at the dance club leave?"

"In the same way that I showed you the images of my history, by placing a finger on your temple. I can also do this without physical contact. I can make someone feel pain if I choose to. After he left, I was happy you had asked about me."

Dagon told Mary that when she lit a cigarette at the same time he did, he felt a connection. Dagon found out Mary began smoking at a young age to try to fit in. This he understood all too well.

"I noticed you check the doors and windows many times. Why?"

Mary abruptly got off the couch, her back to Dagon. "Oh ... well, I do live alone, so that's normal." She squirmed a little while turning to face Dagon. "So, tell me more about your veils."

"How about I show you instead?" Off the couch, Dagon pulled on a veil and poofed out.

"Dagon, where are you?"

"I haven't gone anywhere, I'm right here."

"Where?"

"Here." He took off his veil and grabbed Mary's waist from behind playfully, causing her to jump. "You know, being invisible isn't what it's cracked up to be. I would much rather be visible, especially with you."

He smelled her hair and rested his face into the crook of her neck. "I love you." His words were muffled. Mary turned and kissed him.

Dagon, who had never had affection shown to him, kissed her

tenderly. Her body felt accepting. Long minutes passed as they softly kissed. Dagon pulled away, forcing himself into self-control.

"So ... you said that you never had a girlfriend before?" said Mary, as she gave him several quick pecks on the cheek.

"No, I never have."

"Then, where did you learn to kiss like that? Is there an angelic kissing school?"

He laughed. "No, there is no such school. If there were, would I have received high marks?"

"Definitely. You kiss amazing."

His spirits perked up a little then crashed. "I have never had a relationship of any kind, not even a friend. My relationship skills are not good, I'm afraid."

Tears welled up along Mary's lower eyelids. "That's okay, honey; we can learn together." Mary wiped a tear on her sleeve. "Do you cry?"

"Seraphs do not have tears, so I do not have that ability." *She must know more about relationships than I do.* Though anything together was good for him.

"Does the coat spontaneously transform into a dragon or do you control it?"

"The coat? The coat does not change by itself. I have to change it. I do this by thinking it, as I do with my veils. Mary, I would never let you see that, for I would not want that image of me in your mind. I'm not a dragon, more like ... a pilot."

"I am not afraid of your coat. I find it comforting."

"You do? Why?"

"I think it's because it's something only you can have ... it's protective."

Dagon didn't know how to react to this incredible revelation, so he switched the topic.

"You have the most beautiful eyes. I knew that I would recognize them; they are of unmatched beauty. They give me courage."

"You see, your coat gives me protection, and my eyes give you courage. It's the same thing."

Dagon may have changed the subject, but Mary filled in unspoken gaps. Their minds were connected somehow. Dagon knew how he wanted to react now. He just hoped she would say yes. Wringing his hands and taking a few deep breaths, he said. "Will you be my girlfriend?"

"Yes, I will be your girlfriend!" Mary's face lit up and she wrapped her arms around his waist, laying her head against his chest.

Time froze and flew by all at once. The morning drifted by as did lunch. Strange to her, though not strange to him, he filled his new-bought bucket and started to scrub.

He did not even think to ask her permission, he just took over. He started in Mary's master bathroom, which looked like it had not been scrubbed in years. Dagon saw a cd player on the vanity and numerous cassettes. There weren't too many music groups he liked in her collection. Dagon planned on expanding her music repertoire one day. The prospect unnerved him. Mary seemed to like him just as he was, but how could he explain there's more to him?

He didn't dwell on this. He chose a cd and selected a song. He cranked it up and jumped right into cleaning. Mary walked into a scene like no other, for Dagon acted like he was playing the guitar with the toilet brush. Mary busted up laughing. Dagon winked as he reached over and stopped the player.

"I like rock music, baby."

"I do, too. I have some on my playlist." Mary's excited voice dialed down to a whisper. "Are you cleaning?"

"Is that all right? It's just ... well ... I guess you might as well know. I am what you would call a neat freak."

"Well, I guess I'm not."

Dagon kissed Mary while she stared at his white t-shirt, which said "Rock On, Live On" in black letters.

"It's hard to explain, but since our hearts are connected, this seems right," said Mary.

"Being connected doesn't mean we're the same. Differences are spicy.'"

With this said, the song began. While a cool guitar lick played, Dagon cleaned the toilet.

"Just wait for the part when the singing kicks in. You have to feel it." Then in one rock and roll moment, he spun the brush around three times, cleaning the bowl. "Queens need gloves." He rested the toilet brush inside the bowl then picked up the rubber gloves and placed them onto her hands as if they were made of silk and not rubber.

Dagon watched as Mary bent over to clean the tub, and he found himself cleaning the same section of the toilet over and over again. He shook his head to the timing of the lyrics and forced his gaze away from her twitching behind.

Several songs later, the cleaning duo finished with the master bathroom. Mary bee-bopped to the next song.

He asked Mary if she had one of those sucking machines, motioning to the carpet.

"The vacuum? It's in the hall closet."

With the music blaring, Dagon vacuumed while Mary dusted. Whatever wasn't bolted down got cleaned. Dagon caught Mary looking at his backside.

"Take that, you, diabolical sticky webs." Dagon sucked all the cobwebs up for good.

"If anyone told me that I was going to have a boyfriend, I would have thought they were crazy. If they told me I would have a boyfriend like you, I would have had them locked up by men in white coats."

"Am I that strange?"

"Not strange, just uniquely Dagon."

Eventually, the whole house shone. With a sense of accomplishment, Dagon noticed the lovely ivory curtains and the deep brown couch.

Satisfied, he told Mary that he would make dinner and teach her how to make hamburgers. He wanted to try out his new knife set. Leaning over the counter, Mary watched as Dagon mixed all the ingredients and formed patties. Dagon unsheathed one of the knives used for chopping, like a sword. Showing off, he spun the knife several times with his right hand. Next, he spun the knife in the air behind his back, and he caught it with his other hand. He sliced and then chopped an onion with precision.

"Where did you learn all of that?" asked Mary in amazement.

"In Japan." said Dagon, as he flipped the burgers. "I was there in 1805 in Osaka, known as the national kitchen. I stayed for several weeks, intensely studying. No one saw me. The heart of a Samurai beats in these knives, baby."

After Dagon placed a few more condiments on the table, he looked up and saw Mary analyzing his coat.

"It's okay, Mary, you can examine it."

"I can't even pick it up ... is it made of lead?"

Dagon laughed, but not at her. "I'm sorry, luv, it's just that I never thought my coat was heavy." He picked it up with one hand to show her that it was light to him. "Maybe it's the silver scales."

"Those are scales? They're beautiful."

Dagon was baffled by this. What do you say to someone who keeps surprising you? "Why? Are you serious? Really?"

"Yes, it is beautiful."

Dagon enjoyed having dinner with Mary.

After cleaning the dishes, Dagon suggested going back on the couch and Mary agreed.

"I never found your song list," Dagon asked.

"I got one on my phone. I'll show you."

Mary came back with her cell phone. "See, I touch my music app, and I can listen to my music." Mary swiped her finger through the list and played snippets.

"That's unbelievable. How can songs fit on something so small?"

"I'm not sure how it does." Mary stared down at her phone. "Dagon, why didn't I see you in Oak Park sooner? Did you see me?"

"I didn't see you either. I guess the only explanation is that it just wasn't time yet."

"Why were you gone for two weeks or two seconds?"

Dagon could tell that this was important to her, very important. "Mary, you know how I told you that I am bound to Savila?"

"Yes."

"After we went dancing at your friend's house, Savila summoned my mind, and I had to ... do some things, and I did not have the freedom to be with you."

"What things? And why didn't you have the freedom to see me?"

Dagon didn't say anything.

She let it go at that. "Honey, are you all right?"

"Mary, I'm not used to affection. I witnessed horrible sickness and death during the black plague, and a lot of people died."

"After all you've told me, that I understand."

She lay her head on his chest. His heart beat fast.

"Your heart is soothing, like a lullaby."

"I don't know about that, it's racing."

"Well, either way, it's soothing."

He tenderly stroked her hair. The only thing that mattered was her.

"You can read minds. You can be invisible from people. Your hearing and vision are extraordinary. Those are superhero gifts ... are you a superhero?"

Dagon couldn't help but chuckle at the notion. The Cherbs would like her assessment, for sure. Sweetly, he told Mary that he would be her superhero. He would avenge all wrongs committed against her, so the title fit. Dagon took the time to clarify what he needed Mary to understand about his so-called superhero status.

"Mary, I have powers, not gifts. There is a difference. Although I can read your mind, it is a choice not to be made lightly. For even choices made with good intentions carry consequences. Regrettably, it's getting late. I'll be back tomorrow morning. I can make you breakfast."

"I would love that."

Dagon wanted to stay with Mary instead of being on the hard bench, but he wasn't naive. Staying overnight without it being legal would look bad and would provide free ammunition to be used against him. The worst outcome was their death if Dagon broke the order of events which Savila counted on him doing. Perverting intimacy was one of Savila's favorite manipulation tools.

"What's wrong?" said Dagon tenderly, wiping her tears with his thumb.

"Nothing's wrong, Dagon. Everything is just right."

If everything was all right, then it was right. With this, they lay in each other's arms. Astounded, his thumb was dry, probably due to quick evaporation.

Content, he kissed her goodnight.

Out the front door, the dark night consumed him. The guardian cat peeked through the curtains of the house across the street. With a satisfied smile, he saluted his furry comrade. The Cherbs made kissing sounds, which he ignored.

"Keep good watch, boys," said Dagon.

"Will do, Casanova. See? We told you that we are like superheroes."

Dagon smirked at their wisecracks though he was unsure about the bombs he had dropped on Mary. *Would she have kissed me like that if she didn't love me? Maybe humans need more time in a relationship to say, "I love you." At least she likes me as a superhero.* Whether his bonded mate would ever tell him that she loved him or if he remained only a superhero to her, he could live every day just like that day. One way or another, Mark would surrender the ruby over to Savila.

Dagon saluted the Seraphs as he passed by, but they did not salute back. On his bench, he placed his two veils for privacy. He took off his coat and made his usual pillow of it. His long legs hung awkwardly over his hard bed, but he was happy.

Murderer! You murdered my very soul. The whispering shadows in his mind moved like ghosts through the trees.

The shadows tried to drag him back to the past that he would rather forget, a past that he was glad Mary did not ask him about. *You murdered my very soul!* echoed the dark shadows. The shame and guilt of these words threatened to bring his dagger down to cut the past away. The light and the dark battled in his soul and with sorrow, he let the ghosts lead him back to memories of France where the suffering of humanity flowed with blood. Thorns of torment mocked him, ushering in a new age of darkness.

Dagon did not want Mary to know about his past. It would accomplish nothing except to lose her forever. He only hoped that no more questions would come up about this, so he could let the memories of France and Spain die along with the soldiers on the battlefield. Dagon fought the urge to cut himself, for he respected Mary's generosity in cleaning his new wounds. More than ever, Mary's ignorance about France protected him, for she would not see his skill in archery, only the kill.

17

Captive

Three pairs of smoky hands took Mary from her bed. She screamed and thrashed against the smoky forms that carried her toward the wall. She cried out louder, preparing for a collision.

The next moment, she was inside her parents' car, the very car in which they died. "Dad! Turn around! Turn!" The car moved faster toward a head on collision with her bedroom wall. Unaware, her dad drove on, while her mom reached over to change the radio station.

The wall transformed into a car, barreling toward them. Nothing could change the inertia of the past. Crunching emotional debris was scattered in the present when the cars hit with finite force and jettisoned her parents' bodies into the glass windshield. The windshield shattered into a million pieces, and jagged shards flew out in all directions.

"No!" Mary screamed. Her body zoomed fast, charging into a field. Blades of grass turned into lethal sharp daggers. The ground moved faster toward her, though she descended easily into the surface. Her parents were dead, and she was a captive in a cold, dark, stifling place.

Chained to a wall, her legs dangled above the ground. The skin of her wrists and ankles ached. Black water seeped down the wall behind and around her. Scream after scream echoed off the thick rock walls from torture victims long since gone.

Three captors stood side by side along the wall opposite from her, sinister smiles spread across their lips while tendrils of smoky shadows curl and flicked around them.

A man came through the wall and through the center captor, merging with him, tightening her chains in recognition. Mary thrashed on the wall, as the man continued toward her.

"My husband will be here soon. He will rescue me. He will come, and he won't show you mercy."

The man directly in front of her caused her to cringe. Turning to the side, the man brought up the back of his hand, stroking her cheek.

"Your husband?" the man mocked. "Who is your husband? What is his name? I want to meet him." He stroked her cheek more abrasively, and she flinched. "You will tell me who your husband is." Leaning in closer revealed jaundice-colored teeth. "By the time I'm done with you, I will know more than his name."

Mary clenched her lips, refusing to say a word, partially to keep her chin from trembling, partially in defiance. The man jerked her head to face him.

"Silence is not golden, my lady, and with every word you hold back, your bonds will tighten. If not already, then soon you will desire death." The man kissed Mary on the cheek. "You are awfully pretty."

He kissed her again, inching closer to her mouth. Mary thrashed and tried to scream, but her voice was stifled by the man's foul mouth over hers. Somewhere in the room, a woman in shadow moved closer. In contrast to evil, she was beautiful, serene. Her golden hair moved in supple waves around her face, lighting the room. The shadows became men with blood red eyes that moved toward her. They all laughed, and the woman flew into a rage. Electrically charged sparks flew over coarse shafts of hair. Opening her hand, she produced an apple. Her demeanor switched, offering the apple to Mary.

Mary turned her face away, but she still saw the woman throwing an apple to the ground in disgust and a vaporous sword morphing into her hand. As the blade pierced the apple, it changed into a man than to a woman and then to thousands of humans. Sword held high, the woman screamed as she plunged it into each person.

The man who had been kissing Mary arched his head back and howled with laughter. With his head tilted back, the full weight of his body crowded Mary tighter against the wall and the other two men approached to taste what he had enjoyed.

"My husband will come for me!"

The black rocky wall exploded and jettisoned rocks into the air, leaving a wide hole.

A tall man stepped through the hole. Beams of light rippled over every strand of his hair, casting a glow around his face. Mary could see him clearly. Dagon.

Twirling a sword, he cut Mary's chains and picked her up. She held him tightly, hiding her face in the fold of his shoulder.

"You are safe, luv." He kissed the top of her head, saying, "Rest now."

The evil woman was consumed with fire and ash, flying away in the form of a dragon.

His sword twirled faster. The three men turned around, running.

"Your chains come," Dagon warned.

The men searched for a way out though none appeared. Beating metal struck the ground to the cadence of marching. Rows of blackened chains came out of the walls and marched in flat rows, link after link beating the ground. The chains stopped marching and slithered toward the three men like black vipers, rattling a metallic hiss. Chains undulated back and forth, doubling in strength by an optical illusion from the mirror-like quality of the floor.

Jet black chains marched in military sync toward the men. Dagon's head tilted slowly from side to side. The chains slithering motion mimicked his movements.

"Bind them!" Dagon pointed.

Mary was peaceful in Dagon's arms when the scene changed.

Walking out of a wooded thicket, Mary wore a long silver-flecked white gown with a silver link belt above her waist. The long sleeves billowed past her wrists. A long train trailed behind her, and she wore a silver tiara of looping vines. Black onyx stones were held by pronged vines. The wild underbrush did not hurt her bare feet.

She came to a wide clearing and stopped. White flowers bent over the edge of her train. A knight approached. His armor and horse were jet silver. The horse trotted, and the knight carried his helmet. The horse stopped, and the knight dismounted, walking toward her.

"Welcome home, Love," Mary greeted the knight.

"Home from the battlefield, my queen."

"You are my king."

"Nay, I am your knight, doing battle for your love."

Mary reached up and kissed her knight.

Panting, she woke up. Typically, she would stay asleep during the most horrible dreams and wake up too quickly from the good ones.

Taking a quick shower, the warmth cleared her mind. She appreciated the dream, her superhero knight rescuing her. She couldn't wait to tell Dagon about the dream of how he saved her. Then the steam froze her body, water flowed along her curves. The water suffocated and relieved her thoughts at the same time. How could she tell Dagon about this dream? This cold, dark, stifling place had to be connected to the images of his past. Her Angel Dream, her rescuer, her boyfriend, and perhaps, her future husband, lived in the ground. That was his hotel, his prison. No, this dream Mary would keep to herself for a while at least, or perhaps forever. The dream did have a happy ending at least.

OUTSIDE, Dagon asked the rowdy bunch who were spit-shining their belt buckles and swords how Mary's night had gone and if there had been any more dream crashers.

"Nope, all's fine over here. How about you?"

"I'm great."

The guys paid no more attention to Dagon.

"So, the prison was that dangerous?" Razz said.

"Very dangerous. Villains lurked around every corner and possibly hidden booby traps," said Mr. Cool.

"I would have smashed all those villains," said Sledgehammer as he raised a fist in the air then brought it down hard in front of him.

"I found something you can communicate with, Sledge. Something that you can't break or squirt," said Mr. Cool. "I got the idea from the old guy driving the Ferrari." Mr. Cool gave Sledge a chain link necklace with a bone shaped pendant attached.

"Look it has a name on it, Slugger," said Friar.

"That's me for sure," said Sledgehammer.

Dagon walked toward Mary's house laughing at the thought of Sledge wearing a dog collar. "It's a cool throwback to the London Punk scene, Sledge."

All the guys agreed as they examined the links on the necklace.

MARY PUT her hair in a ponytail when the doorbell rang. She was out of breath, only partly from huffing it down the stairs. When she saw her drop-dead-gorgeous knight in stone-washed jeans standing tall in the doorway, he took her breath away. His flashy blazer was deep blue with silver buttons and a silver satin collar. His shirt, gray with silver flecks and a v-neckline, was accented nicely by a few chest hairs. Mary nipped at her lip with her teeth.

Two infernos collided in a long good-morning kiss. Soon it was over, and she led him back into the bathroom, for some tender loving care. Dagon kept asking if he should make breakfast first.

"After we change your bandages first."

Mary never minded taking care of Dagon, but it still tugged at her heart. She changed his bandages and announced he was practically healed.

Another wonderful meal was done and the dishes again cleaned.

"I want to take some photos of us together." Mary smiled, holding her cell phone.

"Do you have a camera?"

"You can take photos with your phone. See." Mary handed him the phone.

Dagon peered at the phone, turning it over and over. "How do you develop film?"

"You don't need to. The photos instantly appear on the phone. You can even edit your photos." Mary took a few random photos of the room to show him.

Dagon raised an eyebrow. "All with your phone?"

"Yes. If I change the direction of the camera, I can take a selfie."

"Modern technology is amazing." Dagon ran his fingers through his hair.

Mary took selfies of them together and numerous ones of Dagon alone. Mary showed him how to take photos and he took some of her.

"I'm glad I can see you in the photos." Mary swiped the screen.

"Mary, I am not a vampire."

"That's not what I meant." Mary put the phone in her lap and one hand on her hip. "But now that we're on the subject, what about Savila? She seems very much like a vampire to me."

"I wish she were just a vampire. A vampire would be an easy kill. I would enjoy that. I can understand why you would think that she is a vampire. But ... she's worse than that."

Mary flinched.

"It is because of her hold on the blood of humanity that legends like vampires were created. I won't ever let her hurt you, luv."

Dagon would protect her, though she was sure that her face would continually show shock.

The day went by too quickly and being with Dagon blotted out most of her terrifying dream for a while. In fact, many days went by too quickly.

Over two weeks went past and on the days that Mary didn't have to work, Dagon came over to make breakfast, clean, make lunch, clean, make dinner, clean, and then relax. They did, however, find time between cooking and cleaning to talk more about Mary's endless questions.

"Talking isn't like interrogation, is it, baby?" he asked.

"Why would it be?"

"Well you know ... being a woman and all, you know how it is."

"No, tell me."

"Mary ... I'm just saying ... I mean ... while I was still looking for you, I would overhear men talking to women, and they looked like they were being interrogated, but this is not the case with us, is it not?"

"You tell me, Dagon."

"Mary, I am just saying that is what it looked like, that's all."

"Well, maybe you should get your facts straight. Interrogation, really." Mary pulled back, giving him "a look."

Physically, Dagon sat next to her. Communicatively, he might as well had been a million miles from her.

"Maybe it looked like interrogation because the guy wasn't listening. Like you're doing right now!"

"Okay, okay. baby, I'm sorry."

At times, it seemed that their relationship was like any other. She kept forgetting how new Dagon was to human life and to relationships. *My relationship skills are not good ... I'm afraid,* Dagon said this to her roughly two weeks before. In this respect, they had a lot in common. She didn't know much more about relationships than he did.

"Dagon, I'm sorry, too."

With this apology, the million-mile separation shortened. His face and posture relaxed.

As they continued with their coffee and questions, Mary found out more about her house.

"In 1951, being invisible, of course, I would come to this house to watch *I Love Lucy*. Along with the family living here at the time, I sat and watched this new show—"

"You sat with the family here?" She laughed.

"Yep, for a while I had siblings and all that."

More laughter.

"I stretched out and even ate the best roast beef sandwiches on Earth. The family wondered where all their food went, and when they moved, another moved in. In fact, there were four families that occupied this house before you did."

"I never knew that. The real estate agent didn't have much information on this house."

"The other families couldn't cook worth a darn. Rotten tasting excuse for food."

Doubled over with laughter, her stomach cramped.

"I tried making popcorn several times. The first time ... um ... didn't turn out so well."

"What happened?"

"I didn't know the amount of popcorn to use, so it jumped out like hopping beans and burned the bottom of the pot. The whole house smelled burnt for weeks. I quickly learned about using a lid."

The time flew with them laughing their heads off. Mary was glad for this as it broke all the tension, and she enjoyed learning about Dagon and his life before meeting her. Listening to the stories soothed her heart, for he was right there, waiting for her.

"Mary, I love you, I'll be back tomorrow."

He kissed her goodnight and left.

DAGON DIDN'T SPLIT his attention too well around Mary. He hated disappointing her. On a good note, he found out the plans Mark's family made with the Glynns. *I'm not that callous, and I don't want Mary seeing Mark captured.* He would find a way to hide her senses. *This should be easy, I hope.*

18

The Unseen Truth

"Boss, I think the wicked witch is up to something downtown," said Mr. Cool.

"Yeah, I cracked that code," said Dagon.

"Finally, some excitement." Sledge pumped his fist.

"Maybe the babe of your heart should see what Savila's up to," Razz said, inspecting his fingers.

"I just thought of something ..." Dagon said.

"Well, that's a first." Mr. Cool crossed his arms.

"Very funny. So funny. I forgot to laugh." Dagon shook his head.

"Hey, that's good. Where did you hear—" asked Friar.

"From Mary." Dagon said in a haughty tone.

"She's clever. A definite keeper," said Sledge.

"Yes, to all of that. Now, have all of you been taking the doses of lemon drops I prescribed when you infested my life again?"

"How kind of you to be so considerate for *our* well-being," Razz said, spreading his arms out. "We have all been taking the poison ...

oops, I mean ... crap, I mean the bountiful provision you provided us with."

Dagon stomped his foot.

"A lemon drop a day keeps Savila away." Razz snapped his fingers.

Dagon fought the urge not to laugh as he started walking again. Taking Mary's porch steps two at a time, he approached the front door, adjusted his clothes, ran his fingers through his hair, then rang the doorbell. He listened for Mary's characteristic bare footed sound. He waited and waited and waited. Worried, he debated on peering through the walls, when he heard a toilet flush, followed by turning faucets. Closing his eyes, he relished the sounds of her feet. Opening his eyes, he relished the sight of her blue eye squinting through the peep hole. Opening his arms, he embraced Mary as she bounded out the door.

"I know it hasn't been a long time since we saw each other, but I missed you." Dagon said, lifting Mary slightly off the ground.

"I always miss you."

Dagon gingerly placed her back down.

"How about we go for a walk for a change. It's such a nice day to stay indoors. We've been so little outside together." Dagon held one of her hands.

Mary bounced on her toes. "Definitely a good idea and fresh air is good."

"Yes, it is." Dagon leaned down and kissed her cheek.

"Nope, right here." Mary motioned to her lips.

Dagon chuckled and obliged, forgetting about walking anywhere or anything, except...

"I need to get my purse." Mary paused, breathlessly whispering in his ear, then kissed him behind his ear.

"Uh huh ... yes ... that's good."

Mary stopped and left, leaving Dagon momentarily stunned.

"Got it!" Mary slung her purse over her arm. With keys in her hand, she locked the door, jiggling the door knob several times, then placed the keys in her purse. "Let's go!"

Holding hands, they walked down the porch steps toward the sidewalk, and turned left.

"Do you smell smoke?" Mary looked up at Dagon.

"I do," said Dagon without inflection or reaction.

"I see flames!" Mary looked up at Dagon.

He nodded. She stopped.

"We should call 911!" Mary's eyes widened, saucer sized.

"What for?" Dagon asked without inflection or reaction.

"What do you mean what for?" Mary quickly let go of his hand and ran in the opposite direction.

"Where are you going?"

"We're driving!" came her heavy-breathed response.

"She's athletic," said Razz.

"Driving where?"

"Just come on!" Mary ran to the back of the house, fumbled in her purse, pulled out her keys, and unlocked the driver's side door. After unlocking the door for Dagon, she started the car.

Dagon opened the car and peered inside. "We're driving in this?"

The Cherbs bent over laughing.

Mary pounded on the steering wheel. "Get in!"

"All right, I'm getting in." Dagon smiled stiffly, stooped down, and squeezed his tall body into the car.

"What are you doing with that thing?" Dagon stared at the cell phone Mary pulled out of her purse.

"What do you think I'm doing? I'm calling 911!"

"What can one of your friends do?"

Mary looked at Dagon liked he had five heads. "911 is for emergencies, like fires."

"That fire is not any ordinary fire." Dagon waved his hands.

Mary ignored him, dialed 911, and told the dispatcher roughly where she believed a fire was. Hanging up the phone, she tossed it in a cup holder. Mary gripped the steering wheel, Dagon sat frozen, hands in his lap, and the Cherbs rolled on the ground holding their stomachs from laughter. Soon, they were driving down the road.

Mary parked her car a block away from the fire. Grabbing her phone, she and Dagon got out of the car. Mary locked the car, placing the keys in her purse, and ran toward the fire, Dagon following. Sirens could be heard in the distance. In a small park, dozens of trees were on fire. Mary redialed 911, giving the dispatcher the exact location, hung up, and placed the phone in her purse. Flames scorched nearby benches, engulfing them in flames.

"This whole place is on fire! What's taking them so long!" screamed Mary, while looking at her phone.

"This is not a normal fire," Dagon said without inflection or reaction.

"How can you ... here come the firetrucks!"

The firetrucks stopped. Several firefighters got out. "Where is the fire?" asked one of them.

"What's wrong with you? It's right there!" Mary pointed.

"You called a false alarm in? That's illegal." A firefighter sharply pointed a finger at her.

Dagon put on his coat. "Leave," Dagon whispered to the firefighters.

"The park is on fire. Can't all of you see that!" screamed Mary, holding her head.

From unbelief, confusion, fear, or a combination of all three, the men got back into the fire truck.

"Wait, why are you ... why are they leaving?"

"This is no ordinary fire, Mary." He placed his hands on her shoulders.

She shot out from under his hands. "Don't go in there!" She screamed at several people walking through the blazing fire, untouched and unharmed. A few of the people laughed, not paying Mary any attention.

"This can't be. They're not affected by it. They can't see it?"

"In one reality this is happening. Yes, they can't see it, but this is nonetheless, lethal."

A girl sat on one of the benches on fire. Wearing a white hooded cloak, Savila sat next to her. "How innocent she is." Savila's blood red fingernails, raked through the girl's hair.

The girl showed no acknowledgement of Savila. But Mary did. She freaked. Her whole body shook.

"Savila." Mary covered her mouth.

The little girl looked up at Mary and ran off.

"Nice to meet you, Mary." Savila's words came out in a hiss.

Dagon put himself in front of Mary. "Stop with the games, Savila."

"Of course not," Savila said with a smile.

Red hot flames covered parts of Savila's face. Between flickering flames, she smiled. Mary peered around Dagon, then jumped back behind him when Savila vanished into thin air.

Mary shook clinging to Dagon's waist.

THE SERAPHS STOOD LOOKING out Mark's bedroom window at an all too familiar scene: smoke.

"Dagon must be hurt." Magethna looked at Dorian.

"We are not here to ..." said Dorian.

"We can help where we can!" said Magethna, pointing in the direction of the smoke.

In an instant, all the Seraphs froze.

"This is more than smoke ..." said Raglen.

"A park is on fire!" said Mystil.

"This is not just Dagon. We shouldn't let that park burn! Those poor people. I would write this down in my scheduling book." Magethna put her hands on her hips.

"Look, the people are not physically on fire, but it is hard to watch," said Raglen.

"More to the point, it bothers Magethna. The devious desires of Savila bothers all of us," offered Mystil.

"Let's go put it out then." Dorian stood with crossed arms. "I will go with Magethna."

Raglen and Mystil nodded.

DAGON REMAINED SILENT, watching Magethna and Dorian glide into the park with raised swords. Mary stood beside him, facing the direction of the fire.

Their presence veiled from Mary or any humans, Magethna shouted, "Dagon, stop this nonsense!"

"Now, Magethna!" Dorian flashed his sword.

With force, Magethna and Dorian crossed their blades, holding them steady.

The Shadow Kings came out of the ground. Each of them tore two spikes from their crowns and placed them like an X across their chests.

Rays of light shot out of the Seraphs blades, circling the flames.

The Shadow kings flicked one of the blades, gathering some of the flames, and twirling it around the spikes, like cotton candy. The Shadow Kings propelled the coiled flames at the Seraphs.

The Seraphs braced themselves. "You won't win!" shouted Dorian.

The spiraling flame hit the Seraphs swords with fierce electricity. Magethna and Dorian momentarily lost their balance.

"You are defeated." said Lamel.

"Savila did not create light. The One Voice did!" shouted Magethna.

Even stronger radiant light rushed out of the Seraphs blades, quenching the fire in the park.

"She is the created light and can bend it anyway she pleases," sneered Ligon. "No amount of light can deny blood owed to Lady Savila."

"The debt you seek may cost you more than blood," said Magethna.

"We used a fraction of our power, and yet the both of you almost fell," said Listian. "The boy's hour is almost upon him."

The Seraphs did not respond back, their blades still holding. The Shadow Kings sheathed their spikes back in their crowns, glanced at Dagon, and dissolved back into the ground.

"For the record, I didn't start that fire," said Dagon to the Seraphs, but it was Mary who answered him.

"I believe you. I believe all of this." With her mouth pressed against Dagon's dragon coat, her words came out mumbled.

Dagon's body jerked. "Oh ... um ... that is smashing ... I'm glad, luv."

Mary squeezed his waist. Magethna smiled. Dorian raised his chin, his eyes scrutinizing. Both Seraphs sheathed their blades and left.

Mary inched her way around Dagon.

"All is safe." Dagon turned around and held her.

"Like hell it is!" Mary backed out of his arms. "I saw *her.* I'm not sure how. No, don't try and hold me, not now. Answer me, how ... is the fire gone? Seconds ago, everything ... how did this happen?" Her hands touched her lips. She shook, dropped her hands, and darted back behind Dagon.

"What is it?" asked Dagon.

"I saw Mr. Bennett. I can't look at him now. Not with ..." Mary mumbled her lips pressed against Dagon.

Sure enough, Henry stood outside of his jewelry store, looking in their direction.

"So, you do know him," Dagon said as he veiled them. "Don't worry. He can't see us anymore."

Henry turned and went back inside his store.

"I hope he didn't see me. Not like this," said Mary.

Dagon reached for her hand. She threaded trembling fingers through his.

"Don't think this means I don't want answers." Mary said.

"I know." Dagon led her to one of the benches.

Mary touched the bench in several places.

"It is quite cool I can assure you." Dagon said while sitting on the bench.

Mary gently lowered herself, her hands in her lap. She didn't look at Dagon.

"Tell her you put the fire out!" shouted Mr. Cool.

"I won't tell her that. I don't want her thinking I started it," said Dagon.

"I would have helped, boss, but the fire ... too many bad memories." Friar pointed to where his eyebrows used to be.

Dagon nodded and sat sideways on the bench. "Mary ..."

"How did ..."

"Let me explain. Savila started the fire. She wanted you to see it. I'm assuming to frighten you."

Her mouth set as sharp as her body did when she turned her position. Her left knee resting on the bench. "Well, she succeeded."

"I'm sorry about that. Please believe me when I tell you I had no former knowledge of Savila's plan for the fire and for you to see it."

"Then why did you take me here?" Popped veins on her forehead replaced wrinkles.

"Well, truth be told, *you* took *me* here."

She shifted her weight to one foot, her body inching off the bench.

"Please don't leave, let me explain."

She sat.

"Do you think I would have wanted you to see that?" Dagon spread out his arms.

"Actually, no ... but why then?"

"First, I had no choice. Second, what is the human expression for turning a bad situation into good?"

"Oh ... turning lemons into lemonade."

"What is lemonade and what is the origins of this phrase?"

"It's a cold drink made from lemons and sugar. I'll make you some. I'm not sure of the origins, but lemons are sour, but as a drink, it's sweet."

"This then, is what I did, though I would not classify it as a good choice, but maybe unavoidably beneficial. The fire was only a fraction of what Savila is capable of. Only a fraction of what the world has in store. The impending doom is coming. Unfortunately, your mortal eyes needed to see this."

"I believe you, Dagon. I would have to be as dumb as a stump to not see it." Mary stifled a laugh bordering on hysteria.

"Trust me, you are way smarter than a stump."

They both laughed, for a moment, that is.

"I'm truly sorry for all of this. As to how the fire was extinguished, this was accomplished by light."

Mary's eyes eyelids shot up. "Light?"

"Well, you see ... um ... ok ... there are other Seraphs here—"

"Whoa, what? There are more ... here?" She waved her arms.

"Didn't I tell you?" Dagon stroked his chin.

"You most certainly did not!" Her hands flew to her hips; her lips set in a thin line.

"Oh, in that case. There are four Seraphs guarding Mark's house."

"This is good. If they're like you and guarding Mark—"

"They are not like me." Dagon stuck his chin in the air.

"Well ... ok ... but they are guarding Mark, right?"

"Yes, but only to keep him safe, until ..."

Mary waved her hand. "I get it, really wish I didn't'"

"So, the Seraphs can't prevent Mark from being taken?"

"No, but I want to save you from the consequences of death's eternal sting."

She moved her mouth to his ear and whispered. "I love you and believe you. We can try and co-rule and sack that witch."

"My sentiments exactly, and Mary, I love you."

Her hands flew around his neck. Her lips pressed against his.

Dagon wound his fingers in her hair. Her belief helped him to move further toward the light. They kissed and ...

"I know, it needs to be legal. I can wait, for a while at least." Mary batted her eyes.

Dagon leaned down and kissed her cheek.

19

It's All in the Packing, Luv

The shaded trees in the park cooled the heat of the day. Dagon's arms held Mary, her head on his chest as they sat on the bench.

"How do you know the Bennett family?" asked Dagon.

Mary let out a deep sigh. "Francis Bennett and my grandmother were BFFs."

"What does BFF mean?"

"It means best friends forever."

"I see. Did you ever visit them?"

"Many times, me and my sister, Catherine, would go with my grandmother to see them. Their kindness makes this ..."

"Terrible," finished Dagon.

Mary sat up and looked at Dagon. "Could you have put out the fire?"

From terrible to worse ... what else is new? Dagon got off the bench, his back to Mary, hair gently blowing around his neck.

Mary got up, went around, and faced him. Her dainty frame was dwarfed next to Dagon. Sunlight streaked across her face, causing her to squint as she craned her head.

"I could not have prevented or extinguished the fire."

"And ... you made the firefighters leave?"

"Told them ... made them, something like that." Dagon smiled at her.

"Um ... oh ... never mind. Wait, your title is light, isn't it?"

"Yes, but not in this context, I'm sad to say." Dagon's shoulders sagged.

"But for co-ruling, it is." Mary put her hands on her hips.

"With my title, we have a shot." *A long shot, that is.*

"How was I chosen?" asked Mary.

From terrible to worse, to ghastly ... yep, nothing new. "Your kindness and compassion are unsurpassed. You're gentle, and yet, have a take charge personality ..."

"You mean, bossy?" Her hands fisted in the top of her skirt.

"Well, yes, but in a good way." Waving his hands, he continued. "You take care of me and get things done, and you're very brave." Dagon leaned and kissed her cheek.

Her hands went around his waist.

"Tell her she's hot," offered Razz.

"I can't be the only one like this," she pressed. "Why me?"

"She's got a point," said Sledge.

Dagon let out a deep sigh. "I don't want to say what I'm about to say, but regrettably, I must. Remember when we talked about the woman on the bridge and that was you? That's important to remember."

"Yes, I do remember you telling me."

"Of all those people on the bridge, you didn't fall. I knew then that you were unique. Legions of Seraphs and all of humanity fell. Except for you. The purest of hearts. Unfallen."

Mary looked at the floor, brow creased. "Then why Mark? Mark needs to bring Savila that stone, so *we* can save humanity. But why him?"

"Mark is heir to the Stone. Savila wants Mark taken soon. Your part will be easy. You spot Mark and direct him where to go."

At first, she seemed unable to form the words with which to protest. "My part? How is taking an innocent boy easy?"

"He is not innocent."

"How can you think that? Do you believe this?"

"Yes, I do. All humanity is not innocent."

Mary sat back on the bench. Her face blazed red.

"Mary, please, let me explain."

"I don't see how you can explain this."

"Savila cursed humanity, which I played a part in. This curse flows in the blood of humanity. Fundamentally, this curse binds everything to Savila."

"But how does this explain how Mark is not innocent?"

"Let's look at it like genetics. This is a curse of humanity's genetics."

"This still doesn't explain anything."

"Mary, Andrana and her mate made a *choice* for power and knowledge, like I did. Neither of us had to do this."

"And so a wrong decision made by Andrana and her mate affects everyone?"

"The word 'wrong' is a bit tame, but yes, one finite choice has infinite ramifications."

MARY FELT the blood drain out of her face and an increasing saltiness pooled in her mouth. She hid her face in her clammy hands. In a daze, she saw everything Dagon had ever told her merging into this pinnacle moment. Every dream she ever had whizzed by in microseconds, but the most recent dreams slowed down for her to focus on.

"You said I didn't fall. Do I have this genetic curse?"

"Savila took you from the bridge and hid you from me. Hid you within history itself. Hid you until right now. To fulfill her destiny."

More than the endless questions, more than any of the impossibly difficult things that Mary tried to believe, she had to come to grips with a fundamental truth. Did she trust Dagon or not? Yes. He had been protecting her in her dreams, so she had no reason to doubt him. If Dagon said that she must, then she must. Contemplative, she nipped at her lip. Her eyebrows furrowed deeply in concentration. She hugged herself for comfort.

"Can I hold you, baby?"

She let him hold her.

"I am so sorry. If there were any viable way for me to spare you of this burden, believe me, I would."

Mary eased out of his arms slightly, so she could look at him. His eyes were beautiful. They seemed endless and ageless, in contrast to his youthful complexion. She saw the sorrow in the depths of them, in his soul, perhaps.

"I know I've said this before, but it bears repeating. The only way for us to help humanity is for us to co-rule. The only way to break the bonds with Savila is to fulfill them through this undesirable path."

It reassured Mary that there were other Seraphs among them. *How could a boy be allowed to be taken by an evil creature like Savila?* "Meeting Savila only once is enough to know she's pure evil disguised in beauty. Evil and beauty just don't match up."

"It's all in the packaging, luv." Dagon explained Savila used beauty, among other distortions, to ensnare people.

One problem: Dagon was beautiful, the most beautiful man who ever lived. Could Dagon's GQ image, his packaging, be deceiving her? Could she actually refuse this task? Perhaps she was trapped, though she saw tenderness in Dagon, vulnerability even. "All right. What do I need to do?"

"I need you to sign something. Your signature on the document, which would be turned over to Savila."

A signature on a document sounded human enough to Mary, almost too easy and too human. Mary waited for the catch and then it came.

"You won't be signing the document like you would have in the human world, for in the Seraphic world, signatures are emblazoned in gems."

Strangely, she used a pen that Dagon took out of his coat to write her full name on top of Dagon's black onyx. The letters penetrated in blazing heat into the stone. Then when needed, Dagon would place his gem onto the document, and the signature would transfer to its surface.

According to Dagon, her signature blazed away in his ring, though she couldn't see anything in it. Mary squinted and tried to see the signature, but she only saw the smooth reflective surface of the onyx.

"Only Seraphic sight can see the blazing letters, for the gem had been created and invested in the Golden Land," Dagon explained. He stared at her face, his body fidgeting.

"Did Savila place your name and title into the ring?"

"No, Savila did not, but the person who created everything did."

"Who was that?"

"Not was, is. The One Voice."

Mary's mind spun, and she asked Dagon if the One Voice could do anything to stop Savila.

"The law runs with blood, and Savila gains power through the blood. This power Savila has shown to me. But more importantly, you saved me."

"I saved you?"

"Because I love you, I have been spared from being far worse than Savila."

Mary was not sure if she saved Dagon, maybe merely assisted, but undeniably, she was a part of something. Something big. "I love you, too. You also saved me by keeping me in your heart. My heart has always loved you."

"Who gets this new assignment, boss?" said Razz.

"I don't care who does. I'm busy ... don't bother me."

"What?" said Mary.

"I love you, baby," said Dagon.

"Oh ... I love you." echoed Mary.

"All that mushy stuff is revolting ... who is it going to be?" said Friar.

"Jealous?" said Dagon.

"No ... um ... who ..." Mary trailed off and stepped back.

"All right, Friar, you're up. This should be an easy and *fireproof*."

"Should I hitchhike?"

"You don't need to hitch a ride, it's close. Now go!" Dagon snapped his fingers.

"Why did you snap your fingers? Who are you talking to?"

"Just thinking and reacting out loud."

"I do that too sometimes." Mary pushed a stray hair behind her ear.

"You know, I probably saved you from a disastrous mistake with your beloved by intervening. I should get paid for being a chaperone." Mr. Cool pointed to himself.

"Boss?" Friar chimed in.

"That was quick. Well done," praised Dagon.

"I expect payment. My ... um ... leather jacket got a little singed from a Bunsen burner."

"What did you ... is the lab still standing?"

"Yes, it is," said Sledge. "This assignment was not easy and will include hazard pay. No money, no blood kit and definitely none of the knowledge that I garnished. And most important, no way to get a sample of Mark's blood to possibly save Mary if she needed it as insurance. The bone charm is working great, by the way."

Mary stood staring at him, an eyebrow raised. "Friar?"

"Long story. So, unfortunately, baby, I must tell you something else. You will be in an alley and will tell Mark the way is closed. You will not see anything after that. I won't be gone long."

Mary's gripped Dagon's arm.

"I assure you, you'll be safe. I'll come back and bring you home.

My veils will protect you while you're near me. Don't worry, I have this all worked out."

She nodded and opened her purse. "Here, before I forget."

She took out a photo. Dagon was thrilled to hold the first photo of himself. He had no photos of his past. It struck him that maybe his past was not meant to be chronicled, that maybe photos of his past would be too painful. Dagon marveled at the snapshots in brilliant color.

All too soon, the day ended, and Dagon walked Mary back to her house. After giving her a goodnight kiss, he went out the front door. He heard the door lock, then saw one of her beautiful eyes peer out the peep hole. He blew her a kiss, turned around, and walked away. Momentarily, he stopped and saluted Frosty, who lay on the front windowsill, before continuing on his way.

IN PAJAMAS and stretched out on her bed, Mary perused the photos her heart cherished. Tenderly, she drew her finger over Dagon's beautiful face.

Something created everything! The One Voice. Dagon never answered her about whether this One Voice could stop Savila. Just how Savila gains power through the blood, which was creepy. But the creator of everything created Dagon's name and title. This had to mean something.

When did Mary's world change? Was it at seven years old when she had dreams of an angel? When she was being exploited? When her parents died? When her grandmother died? When she bought her own home? When she met Dagon? When she found out he was the angel from her dreams? When had it changed? It changed when Dagon placed her in his heart.

She wasn't exactly sure why or if anyone was really listening, but she thanked the One Voice for helping Dagon to place her into his heart. Maybe someone watched out for them, and maybe Savila did not know about every purpose.

Knowledge of immortality moved through her heart as she hummed the song she composed the day she had learned Dagon's name.

BACK AT HIS BENCH, Dagon soared with love, for Mary had finally told him she loved him. And better yet, she had said her heart had always loved him. That fueled his starving heart.

With just a few hours left to deliver Mary's signature, Dagon told the Cherbs that going into Mark's cell to take a blood sample, undetected by Savila and the shadows, should be relatively easy, like the clandestine assassination in the Joliet prison. The "relatively" stuff didn't sit well with them, especially Friar. Dagon's money, however, did.

Laying out the plan, he told all of them what Mary would be doing and where she would be afterward. Maybe Mary saying she loved him or her signature blazing away in his ring of investiture made him brave, ready to take a leap, the deep plunge. Whatever the reason, Dagon told them he would not block his mind by eating another one of those foul-tasting candies. According to his boys, the lemon drops once tasted good until he infused them with his goofy concoction. Dagon couldn't argue with that.

On a roll, they tallied up all the crazy ways their boss tried hiding Seraphic ash: he placed it in snuff boxes in the 1700's, in pipes, in rolled-up cigarettes. In the 1950's, when the creation of his cigarettes and tobacco were successful, he worried that Savila would detect the strange odor. He experimented with hiding his ancient potpourri blend in benign pieces of candy. He figured Savila always sees him munching on something, and this would be a good way of keeping her in the dark. Over time, he found lemon drops did the trick. Dagon was tired of going down memory lane or into another distracting rabbit hole and told them as much.

"In the light we will move, first with signing the document and then while I am with Mark. I'm choosing Sledge to be with Mary in the alley."

Uncharacteristically, the guys didn't argue but agreed it should be Sledge.

"All of us were thinking ..." said Mr. Cool.

"That's a first." Dagon laughed.

"Already been used." Razz crossed his arms, looking bored.

"Well, what is it?" said Dagon.

"Since Savila can only read mortals minds and no offense, but all of us except *you* are pure immortal," said Mr. Cool.

"What's your point?" Dagon's lips narrowed into a thin line.

"We don't need to eat those crappy lemon drops, that's what!" spat Friar.

"Eating those crappy things was not a request, but an order. I will take no chances with Mary's life or afterlife. Got it?"

"Yeah, we get it. The thought of those things makes me ..." Sledge shivered.

"If all of you don't get it, you will get it." Dagon made a fist. He felt the veins popping out on his forehead.

"Shouldn't we focus on the plan?" Razz spread his arms.

"Boss, you need to stop interrupting the moment. Take your temper down a notch," said Mr. Cool.

Dagon made another fist.

"Or a couple of notches." Friar held up two fingers.

"Back to business. Will this blood save your beloved?" Mr. Cool said.

Dagon's hands unclenched. "Mark's blood is a part of this. Maybe it could be a bargaining chip for Mary if my title is gone, and I'm gone."

"Is it legal?"

"Probably not. Razz, going to Rome is for you."

"A perfect choice, boss," said Razz.

"Why him?" Mr. Cool asked.

"My decision is final," said Dagon.

"We need a code word so that I will know when to come."

"Good thinking. Okay, when I say 'Rampart,' you make your way over to the alley."

"Are you Rampart again?"

"I never was Rampart; it's just a code word, okay?"

Dagon told all of them the rest of the plan, which involved being invisible in the light, some finesse, a hand off, and a send-off. Razz would take the blood sample to the Bank of the Holy Spirit in Rome.

Razz said in no uncertain terms he was not flying coach to Rome or anywhere.

As soon as he agreed to the first-class ticket, Dagon became still.

"What is it, boss?" said Razz.

"Does it not strike anyone as slightly odd that I am the first one Mark will see?"

"Yeah ... we're obviously being framed to take the heat," said Mr. Cool.

"So, here's an insidious plot, which began with Mark seeing my face first in his dream. Me in the coveted starring role, no thank you."

"Yes, but you are dashing," said Mr. Cool.

"Yeah you are, boss," agreed Sledge.

"Yeah, I'm striking all right."

"So, we'll bring on the heat," roared Friar.

Dagon said nothing but nodded his head in agreement.

"So, you're moving in the light? That's insanely brilliant, boss," said Mr. Cool.

"It is at that."

To go into the Abyss without blocking his mind was insane.

Meanwhile, Razz waited patiently, which didn't shock Dagon. Razz dazzled on the outside but stood edgy and brassy enough on the inside to get the job done right.

"You know, boss ... the distance to the airport is too far to walk. Instead of hitching it ... how about getting a car, and I think you know what car I'm talking about." Razz winked. "You can surprise Mary with it and turn her ugly car in for scrap metal."

Dagon's mind moved sports-car fast. Ferrari fast, that is.

"You're seeing it, boss. Aren't you?"

"Yeah, I'm seeing it."

"Since when is grand theft auto a part of living in the light?" said the Mr. Cool.

"For shame," said Friar.

"It isn't stealing," said Dagon.

"Okay, boss, but it's us you're talking to," said Mr. Cool.

"You only steal what you don't own, boys, and ..."

"He's losing it," said Mr. Cool.

"Just shut it," bellowed Dagon.

"Are we going or not?" said Razz.

"We most definitely are."

"Don't say we didn't warn you. In case it comes back around and all," said Sledge.

Ignoring them, Dagon and Razz took off, their sights set on an expensive and exclusive car dealership. A few of the sales staff sat at their desks in the brightly-lit showroom.

"You know, we could just dissolve through the wall," said Razz.

"Yes, but where would be the fun in that? Let's go."

He stood in front of the dealership door and took out a bobby pin. "Clock me."

Razz timed Dagon as he jimmied a bobby pin back and forth into the hole of the lock.

"A thousand and one. A thousand and two. A thousand and three. A thousand and four. A thousand and five ... come on, boss. A thousand and six." Dagon concentrated, while the time rose higher. "A thousand and eight. A thousand and nine. A thousand and ten ..."

At "a thousand and ten." Dagon was in.

"You're rusty, boss. You worked faster with the washer and dryer."

"These locks are harder than the washing machines and dryers. Now, you find the paperwork and the key to the car. I'll change some minds," said Dagon.

Dagon planted a memory into the minds of the sales staff that the car had been sold earlier in the day. Razz found the paperwork for the car and Dagon filled it out. Lastly, he moved his onyx ring over to the signature line.

"How many of Mary's signatures can you use from your ring?"

A fraction of an inch separated a potential blunder. His black gem sparkled with anticipation. Darkened rays held in suspense.

"I'm not sure."

"You're not sure? Isn't this kind of risky?"

"Yes, it's risky, but life is risky."

Assuming the risk, he placed his onyx on the signature line. Smoky golden sparks seeped out. Cooling lettered embers left a black script that read, "Mary Elizabeth Fauston."

"Do you have the key?"

Razz twirled the silver beauty in front of Dagon. "Where are we going to park this car until you spring it on her?"

"It will be stored at an old abandoned house. The house has an even older garage in the middle of practically nowhere. Now we ride in ... wait, I can't believe I forgot about this. You can't drive. We have never sat in a car or been driven in one."

"Mr. Cool told me all about the Ferrari, and I know how that old youthful man worked this fine machine. I'm good."

"Okay, take the car to the abandoned home and place the car carefully in the garage. Contact me when that is done for further orders. Here are the legally falsified papers. Put them in the, what's it called?"

"That's a mitten basket, boss."

"No, no, no. It's a glove box. Here now, put these papers in the glove box." Dagon scoffed at Razz for not knowing proper human terms.

"Are you sure that's what it's called?"

"Don't know and don't care. Just put it in the box."

Razz started the car and revved the engine. He floored it and shot out of the parking lot, maneuvering the gears and streets with speed and finesse. Back at the hotel bench, Dagon pulled an envelope out of his coat with the pictures of Mary and himself.

"This is one bad ride, boss. The pick-up and turns are wicked fast."

Dagon held Mary's photograph, tracing her face. Placing the

photo back into the envelope, he made his way over to the grocery store and purchased two presents. He plunked down the cash, plus tax, and placed the items into his coat.

"I parked it in the garage, which is nasty, though the wood looks fairly sturdy. This place really feels like you're in the middle of nowhere though it's still in Oak Park. I'm looking forward to driving this car to the airport. Over."

"I'm changing the plan slightly. Over," said Dagon.

"What do you mean ... slightly? Over." Razz asked.

"You won't be driving but hitching it to the airport. Over and Out."

Mr. Cool, Sledge, and Friar laughed their heads off when they heard this.

Razz sulked.

Dagon ignored all of them by taking out *the Iliad* from in his coat. Alexander the Great was his hero, and this was his hero's favorite book. Just like Alexander, Dagon would risk it all to gain it all. Laying everything down on a not so imaginary line.

20

A Document of Stone

Well ... *here's to living in the light.* Without taking any of his usual precautions, he left his bench and made his way into the hole of death. It was time for Dagon to give Savila his plan and Mary's signature of agreement.

With several clacks of his heels on the black glass floor, Dagon found himself inside the Execution Room. Legions of shadow royalty and the three Shadow Kings whose spiked crowns glinted like sharp nails waited in formation. Every shadow soldier down to the lowliest was present, which repulsed Dagon.

Charred beams pointed menacingly upward, which brought his attention to Savila, standing commandingly in front of one of them. Dressed as a warrior, she wore a long-sleeved shirt of chain mail and a skirt made of rows of individual throwing knives. Her blonde hair hung loosely down her back. Two braids started at her temples, encircled the top of her head several times, and were held in place by a headpiece of glass shards. Her sword stuck out of its dragon mouth sheath, which hung ready on her hip. Except for the occasional drops of water striking the links of the silver chains, ominous silence seared the room. The air collided with fire and ice when Savila finally spoke.

"You will present everyone here with your proposal by which the boy will be taken into custody, and you will produce your plan of agreement."

"After Mark's family visits the Glynns," Dagon began, both hesitant and eager, "the Bennett family will leave to go home, but Mark will stay back. He will walk back, alone. At that point my bonded mate, Mary Elizabeth Fauston, will be in the alley where she will redirect Mark into the field. This is where the Abyss will prophetically open, as Lady Savila has stated that it would. My bonded mate will send Mark into the field by telling him the road ahead is blocked. As the sun will also be blocked, Mark will not question her and will obey. In the field, Mark will be taken by shadow soldiers into the Abyss. I will question him and then leave."

Savila looked smug with his presentation. "His family would never allow him to walk back alone. How do you propose to get him to leave the protection of the Glynns?"

Savila waved her hand, producing a bat with needle-like fangs. The bat spread its wings in her palm.

Savila's hissed a command, and the bat flew across the Execution Room and into the hands of King Lamel. The wings of the bat beat harshly and then the bat thrust its wings over its head, transforming itself into a document of thin but dense stone.

Dagon headed toward the document, the echoes of his heels clacking eerily on the glass. Clack after lonely clack, his boots made their way to the document. King Lamel stood tall and defiant, holding the document of stone with immortal firmness. The Execution Room sizzled in silent suspense as Dagon faced the document inches from its hard surface. The shadowy crowd sneered and cackled. For a change, Dagon was glad he wore his dragon scale coat. It thickened his skin for the cheers felt more like jeers directed at him.

"Where is the signature line?"

With two firm yanks, Savila took two of the throwing knives from her skirt. Her mouth set like a vise, she threw the knives with force and precision at the document, but Dagon was in the line of fire.

The air behind Dagon seared as fast whizzing metal flew toward him. Instinctively, he turned sideways, letting the knives sail past him. The knives impaled the hardened stone just inches from Dagon.

"There are your lines. Both of your signatures are required."

Ticked, Dagon removed the knives from the stone. With flair, he spun around and threw one knife over-handed and the other one under-handed back at Savila, his coat swirling around his body.

With ease, Savila caught her knives and placed them back into her skirt. A low rumble of chanting started among the shadows as Dagon placed his ring where one of the knives had created a signature line. Black flaming sparks came out of his ring and blazed onto the stone, cutting deep letters into it. His name and title still steamed when he placed his ring on the next signature line. More sparks came out of his ring, while the letters of Mary's name etched deeply into the stony surface. Unlike the paperwork for the Ferrari, the letters did not cool, but grew hotter.

A loud chant of victory broke out, and Savila walked over to Dagon. Savila scraped each letter, her clawed fingernails digging into the hard surface with ease. With a wave of her hand over the stone, the lines blazed on the surface, as did Dagon's publicly declared agreement.

"King Lamel will read this proclamation of law to the treasonous Seraphs who guard the boy. As agreed upon, when the sun is blotted out, this boy will be taken into custody. The Golden Land will be defeated and torn to shreds." Savila, raised her claws, flicking them in defiance at the Golden Land.

Savila waved her hand over the stone document and it transformed back into a bat, perched in the palm of King Lamel. The wings of the bat beat faster, and claws extended and contracted. King Lamel closed his hand, and the bat disappeared.

"You must wait above for King Lamel. Together, you will present the document to the Seraphs. You will stay where the Abyss will open until after the boy is taken," said Savila.

Without showing it, Dagon was overjoyed yet petrified with worry. These thoughts and emotions would be saved until he entered his private quarters. The ceremony concluded, and everyone dispersed at Savila's command.

Once again, Savila managed to punish him for loving Mary and now his unfulfillable promise pierced his heart. Savila wanted him kept far enough from Mary so she would have to suffer through every detail of that horrible night, alone.

He wasn't thrilled about being the one to draw Mark out. Even being pragmatic, he would not bodily abduct Mark. Right now, this was the least of his problems. Dagon scrambled to find another plan to prevent Mary from seeing or hearing the inevitable. Even Alexander the Great would adopt a new strategy on the fly and flawlessly. Dagon wished he could discuss strategy with Alexander, for he feared his plan might somehow flop. He wished he would have met his hero in person and not merely from a distance. Out of respect, Dagon rarely looked in on the strategy sessions, and Dagon never gazed into Alexander's private quarters. He had chosen not to listen to Alexander's thoughts, for Dagon would want that same respect given to him.

He envisioned holding her and her wanting him, a pleasant thought, though torturous. He had never touched or been touched before Mary, except by Savila's blade when she enjoyed seeing his body in pain, just to see how his humanity would respond. Savila cut him many times with human weapons when he wasn't expecting it. She would always heal what she inflicted upon him, but the pain remained. It would sink in deeply, though no outward wounds showed. No chances would be taken with Mary's safety though he saw his life to be expendable.

Would the Seraphs think I wanted to have Mary's name on the stone document? Would Mary leave me if she thought I was making this all up. If she leaves, we're dead. We're all dead. If she stays, but doesn't want me, and live separate lives, we have a chance. Not a great one, but a chance, and perhaps only one chance. I would rather live apart and know she will be safe.

Conveniently, only Dagon's name and title appeared on the stone, for Savila's title had been confiscated. Savila cut the letters deeper. *Big whoop as my name goes down in a blaze of glory. Even Alexander wouldn't want his name to go down in history like that.*

Dagon had the good sense to tell Sledge to keep Mary in the alley. Dagon wouldn't tell Mary about his veils having the ability to shield her because the distance made it a moot point. In her mind he was a superhero, so she may not understand that he did have limitations.

Internally, Dagon struggled between love, repulsion, joy, shame, guilt, and remorse. He never expected to receive love for himself, only to give it to his beloved. He wasn't sure why Mary loved him. It didn't seem possible she could love him. The jeering in the execution room seemed fitting. He deserved it, a kind of penance.

What was the light good for? Mary took such careful measures to heal his wounds. His control slipped away as the stone document would for all eternity bear Mary's name and his name together. He and Mary would reign together over humanity for all eternity with Savila remaining in ultimate authority. None of this seemed to matter back when he desired power, but now he knew he was being used and abused. Besides his and Mary's names, other words were etched in the document under Savila's claw marks. It may have been nothing, or Savila wanted him to think that.

He reached down and unsheathed the dagger from his boot. He looked at the blade closely, and he saw the razor-sharp edges hungry for his skin. How could Mary not see his coat as the physical manifestation of his shame? At that moment, repulsion, shame, guilt, and remorse won the battle for his tormented mind, and he slashed his dagger against the coat sleeve and let the blood surge down his arm.

"Ahhh," came his muffled scream. Hot, excruciating throbbing ripped through his skin. Shame, control, and being alive emptied from the red-hot lesion. He deserved this. If he purged his past and paid atonement, maybe Mary would see someone worth loving.

In control again, he took off his coat and wrapped his shirt around his arm. In his familiar ritual, he burned his shirt and its memory in a cloud of smoke.

From the closet, he put several expensive suits and other clothing items into his coat. Once done, he could finally relax. Thanks to Emperor Claudius and his Roman bath, Dagon *really* could relax.

After his bath he went to work creating Mary's gift from his purchases. Studying the gifts, he was pleased with them. Right on cue, Savila ordered him to go above. Wasting no time, Dagon scanned his room and left.

It was so much brighter up here but with heavier air. Dagon found out from the Rat Pack that Mary slept. Dagon told them to keep watch and report back.

Back in Mark's room, Magethna wrote in her daily planner when she and the other Seraphs heard a faint voice riding on the surges of smoke. It faded in and out, then broke up, "shame ... I deserve ... Mary's love ... not worthy."

Magethna's quill flew on the fine ivory pages of her daily planner. Jotting down these words, which sounded less like a cry for help and more like a cry of regret.

Dagon sent the signals. The smoke disappeared just as Dagon appeared from the ground. Walking over to his usual bench, he sat, lost in his own thoughts.

Dorian mentally contacted Henry with the latest development while Magethna's quill moved efficiently on the pages, documenting what she saw.

"We continue to watch," said Dorian.

"And write," said Magethna.

All the Seraphs watched in readiness, and they saw King Lamel approach Lord Dagon. Fast quill scratches wrote down the time and date the proclamation would be read. Magethna put her daily planner and quill back into her pocket, which must have sensed the urgency because it stitched up rapidly.

The moon dangled in full view over the Bennett house when Dagon's heels mournfully and yet joyfully struck the sidewalk of

Forest Avenue. After the last clack of his heels, six blades unsheathed at their presence in front of the gate.

Lord Dagon unsheathed his sword, characteristically twirling it, while King Lamel opened his hand and the bat appeared. A hiss rose and rumbled from the Abyss as the two immortals gripped the hilts of their swords with eternal strength in response to the sound from the pit of death. That defiled sound, which once rode upon a whisper in the Golden Land, thundered and called forth this winged creature of the night. With angry, deliberate flaps, the bat flew toward Dorian. He allowed the creature to land in his palm. The wings of the bat beat several times before it thrust its wings up over its head, transforming into the stone document.

Formally, King Lamel read the document aloud from where he stood behind the gate.

"On Memorial Day, Lord Dagon's ..."

King Lamel's voice faded. Dagon added the rest of the script.

Bonded mate, Mary Elizabeth Fauston will send Mark Bennett into the field ... Mary will be in an alley ... The sun will also be blocked.

Magethna watched Lord Dagon, whose mind echoed a part of the script. The sparks of the signatures filled the eyes of the two immortals, pulling Dagon back to the present. *Are there names in the document? If so, what names?*

All around the signatures lay the deep scratches Savila had made.

Nuvila's bare feet moved silently over the grass, though no blade moved. Fabric of pure light barely skimmed its surface. The shadows parted in her presence. She stood behind William, whispering like the sound of the breeze. "On the eve, Dagon will deceive."

"Who is involved?" William didn't turn around.

"Mary Fauston, the new neighbor."

As soon as William left, Nuvila walked over to where the Seraphs stood. The signatures of Dagon, the once-guardian of the First Land and his mate, were sealed in stone, hammered into law by her sister's hand. With delight, she saw the names blaze together with the title that Dagon still bore.

Nuvila removed one of her veils, while a hiss came from the Abyss beneath her feet. Everyone was astonished to see Nuvila, her timing being perfect for this moment.

The wings of the bat began to beat rapidly, flying back into the hand of King Lamel. The Shadow King shot a scornful look at the sister of his master.

Nuvila simply smiled in return. "My sister was always ambitious and ..."

"That's putting it mildly," said Dagon.

"You were also ambitious, were you not?"

"That's also putting it mildly," said Dagon. King Lamel laughed, an unpleasant sound to hear, for it was like metal grating over metal.

Magethna kept her expression contemplative yet relaxed. She glanced over to Dorian, whose expression mirrored hers.

"And now the signatures blaze unto a seal for all humanity who inhabit the Second Land. This document of stone sets words of law into motion, which calls the boy to his appointed time." No sooner had Nuvila's last word escaped her mouth when everything ended.

Nuvila, Lord Dagon, and King Lamel disappeared, covered in Seraphic invisibility as six blades sheathed.

BACK AT MARY'S HOUSE, the Cherbs griped about getting paid. They slaved away while Dagon dawdled, and they planned to tell him so.

Sitting on Mary's porch swing, Dagon propped his boots up onto the porch railing. They ranted and raved about being denied the basics of life. Between shouts of "Slave driver!" and "Tyrant!" the Cherbs said that they would take ten carats or gold-plated smokes as payment, but Dagon just ignored them. They kept throwing out more bombs. "Dictator!"

21

Spectacles

"It's going to be a scorcher under partly cloudy skies. A stray shower may be possible, especially during the afternoon hours," the local weatherman reported on the television in the Bennett house. Magethna thought it was rather loud.

At 10 o'clock, Mark finished his breakfast and got dressed. He was in a good mood, for his family was going to spend the day at the house of Bryan Glynn, Mark's best friend, to celebrate Memorial Day.

Within the quiet bedroom, Mark's patchwork quilt hung lopsided off the corner of the lumpy bed, despite the effort Mark made to straighten it. The Seraphs saw the lonely book with its evidence of recent use lying on the nightstand. The cover pictured a sword with a ruby on top of the hilt. The wise old writing desk guarded the ruby while waiting for an absolution. With an animated gleam, the sword seemed razor sharp in its illustration, drawing attention to the title, *The Princely Stone*.

Mark's family drove off eagerly to begin their festivities, and the

Seraphs were alone to guard the house. With immortal vision, they watched the family arrive at the Glynns' and carry in bags of food and other items the Seraphs didn't recognize.

Throughout the day, Magethna opened her pink planner and moved her quill to the rhythm of the musical instruments being played by people in colorful suits. Flags waved in the crowd which lined the avenue as cars decorated with flowers inched their way along the parade route. Buntings in red, white, and blue hung from windows and porches.

Drums beat, people cheered, and feet marched past as men in uniforms waved to the crowd. Soldiers young and old marched past with somber faces in stark contrast to the people cheering along the streets.

These soldiers, who had escaped the crossfires of war, spoke loudly through their silence that they marched for those who had gave their lives. The Seraphs watched as some of the soldiers rode by in chairs with wheels.

Smoke billowed over trees around the area. With relief, it was welcome as a call to eat. They inhaled the aroma which rode on the strands of smoke. Families eating and reminiscing of old times.

Magethna's daily planner became more like a daily journal. The nib of her quill solemnly stopped in a moment of silence for this day of memorials. Mark and his family laughed together at their friends' house.

The Seraphs sang in perfect harmony, like wind-chimed bells, as unmatched freedom marched into a war, triumphant and victorious, in a memorial of infinite days.

Temporarily, Magethna put her daily planner and quill back into her pocket, for in keeping with the mood of the day, the Seraphs unsheathed their swords in honor of those soldiers and the soldiers yet to come. In a blinding flash, their swords shot up. The gleam of the sun raced down their blades and then shot back up again, radiantly reflecting the glory around them.

"To glory! To glory!"

Sheathing their swords, Dorian spoke. "Nuvila comes in light, pointing to the hour bearing witness to a greater hope."

Magethna clapped her hands in agreement.

DAGON WATCHED Mark arrive with his family at the Glynns' house.

I don't want Mary to pay the price with her memories. Dagon only planned for Mary not being able to see. He didn't want her hearing the horrible event either. How to get around this? He wasn't sure, so he fretted over it.

"Hey, you still owe us cash," said Mr. Cool.

Dagon winced at the not-quite harmony and then got off the porch swing to take out his wallet. He opened it and threw many bills into the wind. The greedy guys chased them.

"Remember ... pay as you go, and you'll never owe."

Dagon walked back to the porch swing and sat. He did his best to ignore them as they flicked the money several times in joy.

A wonderful sound then replaced his money-hungry henchmen. His attention diverted to drawers opening and closing followed by the trickling of water. Mary was in the shower. His mind trailed off, which he berated himself over.

Yes, my bonded mate is ... his imagination tumbled over again, so he stood up, attempting to distract himself. He took off his coat and lay it on the porch swing, but the swing rocked violently under the weight of the coat. He was about to put the porch swing under the veil, when a ruckus coming from inside startled him. Cautiously, Mary moved the curtains out of her way and searched the front of the house. Quickly, Dagon stopped the porch swing and then reversed his veils. The curtains closed as she went back to whatever she was doing. Seeing her made Dagon's temperature rise.

The veiled porch swing swung back and forth gently. Dagon removed his long-sleeved shirt and placed it on the swing next to his coat. Shirtless, he leaned over his coat and rummaged through the pockets looking for a short-sleeved shirt. Mary again parted the curtain and looked.

The hairs of his chest and arms prickled from embarrassment. Mary couldn't see him, but it made him blush. Unsure why she stood at the window, he looked around. He didn't hear any noises except his guys telling him to show some decency and get a shirt on. With delight, he enjoyed Mary's smile. Then out of impulse, Dagon went to the window and traced her face with his finger. Her breath gently fogged up the glass in front of her as his fingers traced the contours of her face. Losing whatever sense of decency that still clung to him, he outlined some of her body parts, but the curtains closed, and she was gone.

"For shame," Mr. Cool scolded.

Dagon happily ignored him. He found a plain shirt, with a deep V neckline.

Dagon somberly watched the Memorial Day celebrations around him as his mind searched for a way to have Mary's hearing somehow blocked.

"Hey, get a move on. The hot ... 'you know who' is inside, not outside." The four jesters teased. Funny thing, they were right.

Dagon only smiled. Just then, a man jogged by, singing away. The pitch and lyrics sounded jerky with the jolt of the jogger's feet hitting the pavement. The jogger was out of human view, but Dagon could see and hear both him and the music device attached to his clothes. This gave Dagon a brilliant idea. Walking in place and out of breath, the jogger took out a phone like Mary's and with a touch of his finger, he selected a song before singing and jogging again.

PLACING her folded clothes in a laundry basket, Mary picked up a wadded up white top sheet from the floor and shook it. The sheet would probably never be as clean as the garments her Angel Dream wore. In an odd way, she was cleaning him, or at least his wounds.

She went into the kitchen to start a pot of coffee. With a sly grin,

Abyss of the Fallen

she added her secret ingredient. While waiting for it to brew, she took the laundry basket to put her folded clothes away. She paused a moment before heading upstairs to peek out the porch window to investigate a strange sound. Seeing only the creaking porch swing, she continued to her bedroom. Drawer after practically empty drawer opened and closed, for she hadn't done laundry in many days. With the laundry basket empty, she sat on her bed. Everything around her confirmed that Dagon was real.

Mary went back to the porch window. The bright sunlight hurt her eyes. Dagon's brilliant blond hair sometimes caused her eyes to squint. A combination of beauty and sadness. She could almost smell his musky scent.

For a second, she thought she saw Dagon standing with his coat over his arm and running his fingers through his hair. The doorbell rang. Startled, Mary flew to the peep hole, and with joy, saw Dagon's face smiling at her.

She yanked the door open and threw herself into his arms. Dagon's coat scrunched in as Mary's body clung to him and he clung back.

"I missed you," said Mary in a muffled voice, her face buried in his neck as she breathed the deep heady musk on his skin.

"I missed you too, baby."

Holding Dagon by the hand, Mary backed up, and Dagon followed her. Dagon kicked the door shut behind him with his foot, and he pulled Mary back to himself and kissed her. Mary's fingers slid into his hair. Dagon reluctantly pulled back.

"Luv, things need to be done properly, with proper timing." His body shook.

"The timing is just right." Mary snapped her fingers and swayed her hips.

Dagon accepted her kiss with a controlled and reserved effort.

Dagon's lips skimmed her neck. "It will be, soon."

Mary exposed more of her neck. "It better."

"Uh huh," Dagon slurred.

Mary pulled away slightly. "You look hot."

"Oh ... um ... yeah, I ..."

"It's so hot outside," said Mary.

Dagon drooped. "Oh, you mean the temperature."

"Well? Aren't you hot?" Mary repeated. Her eyes raked over the deep V neckline of his shirt. Unlike the last time, there was more to see and appreciate.

Dagon looked down at his chest and back up at Mary.

"Isn't that coat too hot for this weather?"

"No, but my face and other exposed extremities are affected by temperature changes." Dagon sighed awkwardly. "Must I always use the word 'exposed'?"

Mary just laughed as she led him over to the coat closet. She tried to take the coat from him to hang it up, but it wouldn't budge. The weight of the seemingly leather coat astounded her. His short-sleeved shirt revealed his wrists, so he shoved the other arm under his coat.

"You look good, luv, nice and cool."

"You look good, too, but do you ..."

"But do I ... what?" said Dagon, his body shook slightly.

"Do you have shorts?"

"What are shorts? Or are 'shorts' a ... um ... a condition?"

Mary put her hand to her mouth and stifled a laugh.

"Did I say something funny?"

"I'm sorry ... I'm sometimes surprised by what you know and what you don't know, that's all."

"Oh."

"I'm wearing shorts, see? And you wear them when it's hot outside, like today."

"Do they only come in pink?"

Mary giggled again and explained they come in all kinds of colors and even styles for men.

"We can buy some soon for you if you'd like," said Mary.

"I'd like that, thank you."

Anything which involved being with Dagon was all right with her.

"You are so beautiful, Mary, so beautiful. My eyes are weak. I think I may need spectacles."

Dagon's voice had a smooth romantic veneer to it, which made Mary swoon as she tilted her head up.

"Spectacles?" repeated Mary. She became quiet and stared at him, speechless, with his use of the outdated word.

"You know, corrective eye wear?" he said.

"You mean glasses."

"If glasses are corrective eye wear, then yes, I mean glasses."

"You have superhero eyes, remember, honey? You don't need glasses or spectacles."

"I think I do, but I think even with corrective eye wear, I still wouldn't see your full beauty, for it is deeper still than every inch of your radiant skin."

"Dagon, do all Seraphs talk like this?"

"What are you referring to?"

"Dagon, coffee!" Mary walked quickly toward the kitchen, talking as she went. "I put it on a while ago ... do you want some?"

"Yes, I would love some; I could smell it from outside."

"You did?"

"Yes, my sense of smell is very good."

"Dagon, do you have a car?"

"Baby, let's just have some of that coffee, for I have several surprises for you."

He hugged her, and she didn't let go. Wanting some coffee, her hand slid down his chest, and his muscles flexed. Mary took his hand and led him into the kitchen.

Sitting at the table with glasses of iced coffee, Mary wanted to ask about her surprises but decided to wait and let him bring it up.

"This is just as good as hot coffee," Dagon said after a few sips. "Imagine that. Coffee for every season."

"Do all Seraphs talk like you?"

"You've asked before about Seraphic speech. Seraphs don't learn how to talk in any specific way, we just utter our thoughts."

"See, like that."

"Like what?"

"Like how you said 'utter.' It's romantic."

"Well, I don't know much about romance, but I know my love for you is deeper than any ocean."

"See? Romantic. Sometimes, but not all the time, you use outdated words, like when you told me your name. You used the word 'tis,' and just now the word 'spectacles.' But mostly, it's the way you say things as a whole. It's antique, but not exactly outdated. Do you understand what I'm trying to say?"

"You remembered that?"

"Yes."

"As long as I've been on Earth, or the Second Land, I have not spent a lot of time with people, and so my speech reflects this, I'm afraid."

"I love it."

"I'm glad, but maybe your friends would find it ... I don't know ... strange?" Dagon cringed.

"I don't care what my friends think, but I also don't want you to feel badly. I think our two hearts are better than one, don't you?"

"Yes, luv, I agree."

SHE DOESN'T MIND *my oddities ... she doesn't want me feeling badly ... two hearts are better than one ... wow.* "Baby, what's wrong?"

"I know what has to be done, but it's difficult. I know we can't get out of it, but Mark's family, well, it's just so hard."

"Yes, I know, and I wish that I could change it for you, luv. I wish that I could go back through time and undo what I agreed to. I know that in doing so, I would never have known you, but the alternative under these circumstances is agonizing."

"But, Dagon, I'm glad we found each other."

"I'm glad too, very glad."

"I was wondering, do you work?"

"Kind of."

"What do you mean, 'kind of?'"

"Well ... I ... follow the stock market ... and acquire money in that way."

"So, you trade and sell stocks?"

"Yes."

"Are you a broker?" Mary raised an eyebrow.

"No."

"Is it legal?"

"Now, why would you think that it was illegal?" Dagon winked.

"Well, since you can read minds ..."

"Reading minds isn't illegal."

"No ... I know that, Dagon. But it's just ... your life is not like mine. You don't seem to have many limits. You are exciting."

He heard her heart race. "I'm exciting?"

"Yes, very."

"Well, there is more excitement coming. I can hear tips going down about stocks, so I capitalize on it. I've been exchanging money and buying and selling stocks for centuries."

"Centuries?"

"Yes, when empires would fall or rulers would change, I capitalized on it. A bit of arbitrage here and there, you know, normal stuff." Dagon smiled.

Mary's mouth hung open.

"Baby, I'm rich," said Dagon in a slow, accentuated tone, showing Mary a stack from his pocket.

"I never saw a stack of money like that. What is that one on top? I never saw one like that before?"

"It's a thousand-dollar bill. I'm what you would call, 'old money.'"

Mary smiled. "Most of my money is in the bank. I work part-time at the Pines Restaurant. With the insurance money, I never had to work more than that. I live frugally—that's how I was raised."

"I see."

"You know how you told me you're a neat freak?"

"Yes."

"Well ... I'm not. I'm more of a generational pack rat."

After the word "pack rat" his eyes darted around the room. "Did it bother you when I cleaned here?"

"It was strange."

"Am I strange?" Chair legs screeched and the table wobbled, sloshing coffee when he pushed back and shot up.

"Don't put words in my mouth. I never said you were strange!" Chair legs screeched and the table wobbled, and more coffee spilled, when Mary got up and left the kitchen.

Dagon found her sitting on the porch swing. Her face fire red.

Dagon stood next to her. "I'm sorry ... I ..."

"You should be!" Mary glared up at him. The situation is strange. I mean, what guy cleans his girlfriend's house anyway!" A tear streaked her cheek. "It made me feel bad about myself."

"You didn't let on like it bothered you." Dagon folded his arms.

Mary hit the bench with her hand. "Well it did! I just didn't show it."

Dagon hung his head. "I have lots to learn. I'm sorry, Mary, about my outburst, and I would never want you to feel bad about yourself, like I do."

"Aren't we the pair." Mary giggled while she pushed the porch swing.

Dagon sat next to her, his hands in his lap. "I guess we are."

Mary touched his leg. "I don't know how to explain this, but I don't think you are strange ... it's just ..."

"I think I understand. Not everything can be explained."

"Let's just start over. Want some coffee?" Mary got up.

"Can we clean the mess on the table first?"

"Yes." Mary helped him up.

Hand in hand they went back into the kitchen.

This human life is hard. He wanted to draw this moment out as much as possible, before Mark became a memory.

22

Private Affection

Mary insisted that Dagon should hang up his coat, which apparently, he didn't want to do. He reluctantly gave in.

"Dagon! What happened to your arm?"

"Oh that ... that's nothing ... it's just red."

"That is not 'nothing' and of course it's red—it looks infected. Honey, how did that happen?"

"It's fine. I cleaned it with soap and water."

Mary didn't probe further but took his hand and led him up to her makeshift hospital, the master bathroom.

"But, Mary, I've already cleaned it."

"Dagon Guardian, I'm going to clean your wounds now, and that's that."

Halfway up the stairs, he stopped cold, his mind reeling with Mary's words.

"What surname did you call me ... I mean, last name?"

"I didn't say any last name. You don't have one."

"Yeah ... you did. I have a last name now."

Mary's eyebrows furrowed.

"When you introduce me to people, I will have a last name," said Dagon, excitement growing. He never factored meeting other people, but with Mary in the human world, this would be unavoidable.

"I guess you do. I think your title must have stuck in my mind. Well, it is like your last name, your title and all, isn't it?"

"I suppose it is."

Once Dagon was cleaned and bandaged, nurse Mary opened a vanity drawer and pulled out a silver tube. She took off the cap and twisted the bottom of the tube, making a red stick appear. Mary wrote "I love you" on his bandage in red letters, the same color as her lips were right now.

The simple act moved Dagon, and he hid her words deeply in his heart. He reached up and kissed her, bringing her onto his lap.

"We're on the toilet, not the most romantic setting," she observed.

"I figure mortal life must be lived anywhere and at any time. I love you, all the time."

"I love you the same."

This act of private affection raked over his soul, bringing the shame of his act of private blood to the surface.

"Dagon, what document is my signature on? The agreement, I mean."

"It's just a piece of stone. Nothing more, nothing less," he said, trying to get out of any more questions regarding the stone. Not wanting to lose momentum, he led her downstairs. He hesitated in front of the couch.

"It's clean, honey," said Mary.

"Trust me, baby, it's not."

"Where is the dirt, then?"

"Everywhere."

"I don't see it," said Mary in a sing song voice.

"I know you don't, but it's there," said Dagon in the same sing song voice. "Now, you sit, while I fetch your gift."

Dagon came back over to the couch with something hidden

under his shirt. He brushed off the couch with his hand and eased himself down.

"I can get my present from under your shirt if you like."

"Just close your eyes." He wasn't sure how much his hormones could take with Mary's persistence.

"Okay, you can open your eyes now."

Her mouth hung open at her surprise.

"Cigarettes and a lighter?"

He wasn't sure if her look projected disappointment or approval.

"And not just any cigarettes; these are no ordinary smokes. You will be smoking Dagon. That sounded better in private. On second thought, that didn't sound good either. I don't think I'll ever get the knack of this human life."

Mary bust up laughing. "Are your home-made cigarettes in my pack?" she asked between breathless gasps.

"Yep, none other," he said, then laughed.

"Do I tap it to light it?"

"Nope, I rigged you a new lighter. Now, this flame will never run out, but it only works on metal.

"Only on ... oh never mind." She placed a cigarette in her mouth, and with her new lighter, she lit the end.

"Looking back, I guess it wasn't the best gift to give."

She took a drag off the cigarette and exhaled. "If it's from you, then it's fine. Does it refill by itself?"

Dagon kissed her cheek. "Yes, it does," he whispered in her ear.

With one hand she grabbed a fistful of his hair and brought her mouth to his. The fingers of her other hand cradled the cigarette. The smoke from it lazily spiraled in the air.

"Why must you always pull away like that?"

"Mary ..."

"Please don't feel bad, but I'm trying to quit smoking."

Seeing her gently stroke a stray hair of his between her fingers, diffused the awkward interruptions and boomerang conversation shifts.

"Why would I feel bad about that?"

"Because you gave me these as a gift."

"Gift or no gift, your health is more important."

"Have you thought about quitting ever? Your health is important to me as well."

"No, not really. I'm too far gone."

"No, you're not. Why would you say something like that?"

"Why wouldn't I?"

"The fact we found each other after centuries would be a clue, that's why."

His kiss said everything he couldn't.

"You know, the gift does smell nice."

"That's all right, luv, you don't have to spare my feelings."

"Dagon, it's ..." Mary held the shrinking cigarette between her fingers.

"It's all right, that's what it is. You and I may be the only ones who think they smell even remotely pleasant."

"Really?"

"Yes. It's hard for me to believe, but I sometimes forget what we have and have not talked about, for our conversations have taken so many unexpected twists and turns. Maybe I'm more human than I think." He paused. "I'm not saying that you have a bad memory. I'm just drawing a correlation with analysis, between human and Seraphic natural qualities."

"What?" Her face trembled, her eyelashes fluttering. Her cigarette bobbed up and down

"Let me put out the cigarette, Ok?" Mary handed it to him, and he flicked it out. "We've covered a lot of ground, that's all."

"How do you figure? You have centuries on me."

"For me, we've covered a lot of ground."

"Yes, I guess we have." Mary winked.

Dagon blushed and forged ahead, covering more ground, or perhaps, the ground should cover him up. "There are two Seraphs, who I've known for ... well ... for a very long time and ..."

"The ones who are guarding Mark?"

"Yes, you remember. Well, they don't think that my smoke is pleasant at all." Dagon smirked.

"Maybe because I have been dreaming of you since I was young, it's easier to believe in Seraphs. But the thought of others around here is harder to grasp."

"Totally understandable."

Her shoulders slumped.

Now what?

"Do they really not have a choice but to let him go?"

"They will fight, but they won't win."

"This One Voice that you mentioned many days ago … I think … He's powerful. I remember you saying that he is the creator of everything. Can't he do anything about this?"

"Mary, for now, Savila has dominion over the Second Land. Humanity is bound to her, and so is Mark. Savila told me that blood beyond Mark's will be claimed. Human blood is guilty and thus stained, so the only thing which could happen is that Savila will rise to power."

"The ruler with the Stone of Kings?"

"Now that's a good possibility and one I never thought of."

"Really, you've never thought of this? Didn't you mention how the Stone of Kings will follow the Stone of Power?"

"I did, but I assumed it would be the prince from the Golden Land." He clapped his hands. "Ah … what if the strike is merely symbolic to cut at the heart of the Golden Land through an earthly ruler? *A coup de grâce.*"

"What does that mean?"

"A final blow." His mouth dried and puckered, emphasizing the incontrovertible truth.

Mary trembled, and Dagon placed his hand on her shoulder.

"There is a prince of the Golden Land?"

"There is."

"Is he an angel like you?"

"There are more than angels in the Golden Land. He is ruler and nothing like me." He said the last words through clenched teeth.

"Maybe the prince can do something."

"He is not human."

"Maybe that's the point. You're not human."

"Thank you for drawing *that* point out."

"You know what I mean." She smacked his shoulder.

"I'm also half-human, the prince is not. I know the Golden Land will try and defeat Savila."

"Is this possible?"

"No, a finite impossibility." Dagon sighed. *Why wouldn't Mary want to know about all of this? I would if it were me.* "The laws are the laws. The blood of humanity is both tainted and bound."

"And the prince?"

"To clean, to reverse the laws. My title is powerful; why else would Savila need it?"

"Isn't there another way out of this without bloodshed? There has to be a way to prevent Savila from rising to power."

"It is prophecy. Unchangeable prophecy."

"Are the Seraphs guarding Mark good or evil?"

Crestfallen, Dagon stood and walked over to the window. Taking a deep breath, he plunged ahead, taking this opportunity to explain an emotional truth.

"This is hard to explain and harder yet to say. In a manner of speaking, I guess they are good. Before they gave me the old heave ho out of the Golden Land, I told everyone I was sorry for what I did. No one helped or came to my defense; they just watched me walk away. Not even the One Voice did anything, nothing. I became a pariah."

Mary walked over to where he stood and put her arms around him. "I'm sorry, honey."

"I know you are, but the consequence is the same."

"Yes, but it brought you to me."

Dagon turned sharply around. "Do you not think if I could, I would turn back time and spare you from all of this?"

"But we would never be together."

"Yes, but what is love if it only seeks for the sake of oneself? Do not misunderstand what I'm saying, but if I could, I would take back everything I did to save you. Even if it meant I would never be with you. I love you very much."

"I could never misunderstand that. I would do the same for you. I love you. Still, we were meant to be together."

"Yes. You are my bonded mate and with us co-ruling, we have a chance, but without it, we don't."

"About this bonded mate stuff, what does that mean, really?"

"Mary, you are my wife."

"I'm your what?"

"My wife. Though it has not yet been made legal in human courts."

"We are married?"

"Yes."

Mary opened her mouth, but Dagon held up his hand.

"Luv, before I found you, as per my agreement with Savila, I knew I would have a bonded mate though at that time, I knew you not. Not until after I clinched the deal, so to speak, did I see you on the bridge. I fell in love with you and hid you in my heart. It was then that I saw my fatal mistake. I knew that I would be made half human, because my title of light is for humanity. Savila told me my title would have to be sealed over humanity and likened unto them and likewise, my bonded mate would be bound to me. At that time, I did not love, only thirsted for dominance. My love for you aside, that does not change what I agreed to." Dagon paused, allowing Mary time to understand.

"What happens if we are not properly bound?"

"We would die, and we would have no chance of helping humanity. Even your sister would suffer a similar fate."

"Catherine." Mary put her hands over her face, then dropped them slowly. "I have not been a good big sister. She's always been stronger than me in many ways. I've been hiding from hurt."

"I would like to meet your sister very much. Do you favor each other?"

"Wait, I'll find a photo of her." Mary smiled and left the room.

She returned holding a photo in her hand. "It's not current." She handed the photo to Dagon.

Dagon looked at the photo. "You do favor each other."

"Yes, I guess we do. We are similar height and build, but her hair is straighter than mine."

"So, she's stronger than you? How? You have a strong personality." Dagon's eyebrows crested.

"I know, bossy."

"Mary ..."

Mary waved her hands. "Ok. Catherine just has a stronger sense of herself. She came out kicking my mom said." Mary looked at the photo with Dagon. "I miss her and don't want anything to happen to her. We must save her."

Dagon placed the photo on the couch and held Mary. "This is the cold truth: Mark is tied to you, we are tied to each other, and we are tied to Savila. Each fate rests on and changes with the other, but whatever we can do to protect Catherine, we will."

"Will I be immortal then?"

"Yes, I believe that you will be, for I am immortal and our reign, like Savila's, will be eternal."

Mary seemed somewhat content, yet her expression still seemed torn. When she finally spoke, Dagon's throat constricted. "Do you need me to rule with you, Dagon?"

"Baby, why would you ask that?"

"I don't know, I just wondered."

"Among many things, this has plagued me. The answer to your question, and I hope that it does not sound manipulative, is 'No.'"

"No?"

"Mary, this is likened unto a marital alliance of old. I need you for the title and rule with me you may, but without trying to sound callous, it is not necessary."

Mary stiffened, her shrunken cigarette bobbing in her hand. "So I get knocked off in the end. I can't believe that I—" Mary fell to her knees, crying.

Dagon stood there, helpless. He may only be half a man, but right now, he needed to be more. He knelt and cradled her. To his relief, she fell into his arms.

"I would never hurt you. If I could cry right now, I would. You have to believe that I would never hurt you," said Dagon, as he rocked Mary gently.

Mary sobbed, and her tears flowed into the forest of his chest, when Dagon groaned loudly in pain.

"Are you all right? What's wrong?"

"I don't know. I feel something ... moving ... inside my chest."

"What ... what is it?"

"Not sure, but it has subsided."

"Is it your heart?"

"No ... maybe I don't have one."

"Of course you have a heart."

Mary snuggled against his chest. She ran her fingers through his chest hair, which Dagon enjoyed. Maybe they had a chance.

What is going on inside of me?

Something again moved around inside his chest. *There are songs which could be written about this stuff. Pieces in the heart ... stuck in my heart.*

"Dagon, my tears are going into your chest." She propped herself on her arm, tracing the area where her tears once were. "And..." She sat up; her eyes open wide. "And ... they're glowing as they disappear. What's happening? How is this possible?"

Dagon examined his shirt and chest. "Quite simple, I'm your knight. My heart is but your shield. Your tears are now inside of me, I believe. I will carry your pain, joy, love, fear, everything. I would die for you ... repeatedly, if need be. I would come back to life to give it again for you, over and again."

"How is that simple? You're my knight?"

"Not in shining armor, but yes, I'm yours.

"I will carry your pain, joy, love, fear, and everything. I'm yours too. Are my tears really inside of you?"

"Yes, I believe so. You can't carry my burdens. They're too heavy, but I'm glad you're mine.

She sat straight as a board. "Look here, Dagon, if we're together, then we're together. That means helping each other and sharing."

Dagon just nodded.

"Are my tears causing you pain?" Her eyebrows furrowed. Her nursing fingers examined his chest.

"The pain, I believe, was my heart warring against itself, warring from the bad decisions that I have made, against the goodness of your love within me."

"Your heart is good. Why should it war?" Mary moved her hand over his heart.

"My old memories are fighting. But I'm strong, baby, strong for you."

"I'm strong, too." She pushed him onto the floor and kissed him.

His heart, hormones, and emotions warred, but he would win this battle. Holding onto her hips, he lifted her up and set her beside him.

"We're married."

"Mary, I want to … I *really* do, but it needs to be fully legal. I don't care what people think, but we are being watched … and …"

"We are being watched?" Mary looked toward the window.

"Not like that, luv. To protect your memories, your joy, your peace, I want everything right. As far as us being watched, I don't want to give ammunition where it is not needed. I don't want to be trapped by a hidden loophole. Our marriage being legal is for you, for us."

That evening, the semi-married couple lay together on the floor. Mary's head lay on his chest. "I'm listening to *your* heartbeat. A heart of gold, of silk, of substance, of love, and of armor."

"Your heart beats with strength, kindness, and compassion." Dagon stroked her hair.

He listened to Mary's hidden memories in his heart. Vivid memories of sadness, pain, and regret for not being a better big sister. Some of joy, which now lay in pieces, free floating within the very depths of his being. Hollow voices from the past remained as agonized whispers. *Please, leave me alone … Help me … I love you, Mom and Dad …*

Catherine. These voices mixed with his memories. *Murderer... I have been paying ...*

He didn't want Mary to know about the teardrop voices or the pain they caused him. He didn't want her to deal with anymore, so he stoically kept quiet. The voices screamed on within his heart, though the most troubling voices pumped fresh blood of fury into his veins. *Please leave me alone ... Help me.* Did someone hurt her? His blood boiled while Mary nestled on his chest, fast asleep.

23

It's Time, Luv

"You guys better have a good reason for leaving Mary vulnerable," Dagon shouted at Mr. Cool, Razz, Sledge, and Friar.

"We did our job, boss. Look at her, how does she look?" Mr. Cool asked.

"Well, I guess she does look peaceful."

Mary groggily called his name, and Dagon reassured her. She told him she dreamt of being a character in *Dracula*, a book she read long ago.

"Mary, it's just a dream."

"Someone owes us an apology in shades of green, isn't that right, boys?" Friar said.

"Yep, someone does," said Mr. Cool.

Verbal ping-pong ceased when the Bennetts left for home. With trepidation, he told Mary that it was almost time. She reacted with a deep sigh as Dagon stroked her hair.

Offering his hand to Mary, she stood and placed the gifts in her purse.

"Can I do a load of laundry? It's easier than hot-wiring the laundromat machines and carrying all those coins ... what a pain, plus coins are petty." Dagon dropped his laundry bag next to the washing machine.

"What in the world! You want to do this now? With everything about to happen. Wait, you hot-wire machines? Let me get this straight. My boyfriend-husband is a rich, older-than-the-dinosaurs angel with superpowers who steals?"

"You think I'm older than the dinosaurs?"

"Well, you are. That's beside the point. What about stealing and petty stuff?"

"But at least I look young."

"Dagon, just answer the question!"

"Oh, all right. Picking locks are fun, breaks up boredom. And coins are petty; that's just the way of it."

"So, not only do you hotwire machines, you pick locks?"

Dagon held up his hand. Mary froze.

"Mary, it's time to—"

"To what? I'm afraid to ask. I'm not ready."

"There is no being ready for something like this. I can be with you in the alley at first, but then I have to go into the field."

"Are you going to be the one to take him?" Mary was visibly shaken, and he held her.

"Well ... no, but I do have to be there."

Mary got up, shaking her hands. "If you go into the field, I'll be alone in the alley?"

"All you have to do is whisper, and I will hear you."

"At least you have good hearing. Is it good enough to hear me from that far?"

"Yes, I can, but there may be other noises. Use the music on your phone and wear those ear things."

"They're called ear buds. Wait ... Oh, Dagon, is this to drown out Mark's screams?" She ran upstairs.

Dagon listened as her feet moved frantically about. Drawers opened and closed loudly. First, Mary was in her closet, then her dresser opened, then back to her closet, then to her nightstand, and again back to her dresser.

"Can you hear me, honey?" Mary asked in a soft whisper.

Dagon laughed to himself. "Loud and clear, baby."

"Found it! They were under the bed." Mary returned, the cords of her earbuds dangling from her hand.

The washer came to a sharp stop. Together, they placed the clothes in the dryer.

"I know, but here we are." With flare, he intentionally sang off key to try to lighten the moment and contact Sledge. "Ramparts we watch."

Mary looked at him, an eyebrow raised at his impromptu performance.

"Ramparts we watch," Dagon repeated. He kept smiling on the outside but fumed on the inside.

"You changed the code word," said Sledge.

"That's part of the National Anthem," said Mary. "It goes like this—".

Dagon waved his hands, cutting her off. "Lovely voice, but we don't have time for a concert."

"You started it."

"You know, boss, you could have just spoken to my mind," said Sledge.

"I'm patriotic, now get going."

Savila sat on her throne as Dagon and Mary walked toward the alley, hand in hand. Mark was at the Glynns' home. Savila licked her lips and rested her hand on her sword.

Magethna's pink quill scratched as she wrote out the last details of the day, then stopped, the quill pausing over the thin, onion skin paper.

The Seraphs saw Mary and Dagon in the alley.

"It begins," said Dorian. "The fire was but a foretaste of what is coming."

All the Seraphs looked at Dorian.

"What is Dagon planning to do?" said Mystil.

"He's leaving Mary in the alley," said Raglen, looking at Dorian.

Magethna held the nib inches from the parchment, still because the words which could not be erased, changed, or edited. She glanced toward the door as William walked into Mark's bedroom.

Sledge walked toward the alley. Dagon told Mary he would communicate to her when and what to say. The stage was set. Dagon was antsy.

"It's going to be all right. It will," Mary said.

For as fragile as his bonded mate was in her mortality, she was stronger than him.

"Now, it will be like I'm with you even while I'm over in the field. I will bring you home after, so wait for me," said Dagon.

"Okay."

"I will take care of her, boss," said Sledge, uncharacteristically serious.

Dagon relaxed as much as he could under the circumstances. Sledge made an emphatic point when he unsheathed his sword and twirled it. Cascades of gleaming silver light meant business in safe-guarding Mary. For extra crashing, smashing, and wrecking power, Sledge took out his namesake, a sledgehammer from his pocket. "Either way, whoever tries anything will get it."

Dagon kissed Mary, who looked so innocent and sweet with her ear buds in. Mary wrapped her arms around his waist and kissed him back.

"I love you, honey."

"And I love you." Dagon stood there, frozen.

"Honey, I'll be fine."

"Yes, you will," was all that he could say. He kissed her again and left.

"THE KEY IS GLOWING!" William shook the key at the Seraphs. He made his way to the writing desk, key hovering near the lock.

"That is not for you to open," said Dorian.

"Didn't the proclamation read by King Lamel state that Dagon would be stationed in the field?" said Raglen.

"Yes, it did," said Mystil. "But he's heading to ..."

"The Glynns," said Dorian. He leaned his hands against the windowsill and slumped his shoulders.

"The proclamation has been altered," said Magethna. Her quill moved furiously across the paper.

"What's that supposed to mean?" said William. He stood next to the window. "Dorian, what is that supposed to mean?"

Dorian stared down at his hands. "It means Dagon altered the proclamation. Mark will be taken tonight."

"No, that's not going to happen," said William. He backed away from the window.

"William, it's already too late," said Dorian.

"No! We can't just sit here and do nothing!" He turned on his heel and raced out the door.

Magethna and the other Seraphs exchanged glances and followed him.

William thundered downstairs, passing his parents, who were sitting on the sofa, heads lowered and holding hands. Without a word, William bolted toward his car.

DAGON LEANED against a large oak tree in the Glynns' front yard, watching Mark mill around inside the house with his friend. Glancing back in Mary's direction, he took out a cigarette. The nicotine failed to calm him this time. Leaving Mary stung. Through a screen of smoke, he planted a thought in Mark's mind. "Mark, come out, I have something to show you."

Sure enough, Mark appeared in the window, squinting in Dagon's direction. Dagon felt a pang at how young Mark looked, especially in light of what was about to happen. Out of the mist of smoke, Dagon beckoned to Mark. A moment later, like all curious children, Mark walked out but kept some distance away from Dagon.

"Your friend isn't here." Dagon flicked out the cigarette and stepped toward Mark.

"Why are *you* here?" Mark backed up and almost fell over.

"You know, you're the only one who ever asks the right questions. Bring me the Stone."

"I know you. You're the homeless man who sleeps in the park."

Dagon glance down at himself. "You've seen me in the park? You're a gifted lad indeed."

Mark started to shake. "But I've seen you somewhere else ... you are ..."

"Dagon, Guardian of Light. The star of your dream." Dagon bowed with a flourish.

"This can't be. That was just a dream."

"Well, it's happening. Tell me, would you like to see your dad again?"

"My dad is ..."

"Dead. But with the Stone, you can possibly see him again. Go fetch it. You're the only one who can."

"I can't. The key doesn't work. Besides, my Uncle Henry has the key."

"We don't have time for all your problems. Now go get it. Your family ..."

"What about my family?"

"Your family has been lying to you. The key works for the bearer of the Stone, and that's you. The Stone and the key work together."

In a blink of black vapor, King Lamel appeared between them. He pointed the smoky tip of his sword at the Glynns' house. Dagon could hear Mark's heart pounding as Mark's eyes darted between Lamel and Dagon.

"If you want your friends to live, you'll get that Stone," said Lamel.

With a cry, Mark ran down Forest Avenue in the direction of his house.

"Remember your father," Dagon called after him.

THE THREE SHADOW KINGS and their entourage appeared like smoke from the concrete of Forest Avenue.

With grating hisses, the Shadow Kings ordered the shadow soldiers to kneel, which they did in obedient unison. King Lamel told the shadows to lie down and sink partially into the ground, creating what looked like holes. The three kings took the form of road barriers and staggered themselves along the street.

Even for shadows, the pageantry impressed Dagon as they transformed themselves into obstacles.

Dagon then relayed to Mary what to say, for Mark approached.

"Hey, the road is completely closed ahead. You'll have to go across the street and walk through the field to get to where you're going," said Mary, strangely calm.

Mark panted and searched both directions then ran across Forest Avenue and into the field.

Dagon watched him trudge along, for in some places the grass was high, and beneath the grass lay hidden snares of brambles and thorny weeds.

The wind violently churned around Mark.

A scream rang out. "Who can help you now?" The sound of shattering glass echoed in the winds.

Even the music blaring in Mary's ears couldn't possibly keep out this nightmarish sound. Mary hunched down, her curls whipping her in the face.

Mark walked faster when a soft purring sound pierced the night air. Dagon sneered when he saw Henry's only son, William. clutching the steering wheel. *He sure has an irritating knack of showing up at the wrong time.*

The wind picked up, causing William to grip the wheel tighter. William's eyes diverted to Mark.

You'll see how it feels to not be able to help those you love. Dagon glowered at William, then dodged an empty cigarette pack blowing into his face. "Not the best time for a smoke."

"Boss, something's going on over here."

"I can hear everything!" Mary screamed.

Dagon scrambled to come up with a way to intercede. He had an idea, maybe not a good one, and maybe kind of corny, but an idea none-the-less.

"Just keep repeating over and over again how much I love you ... I can't control ..."

"Dagon loves me, Dagon loves me ..." Mary kept repeating and then she changed the wording. "I love Dagon, I love Dagon."

"That works, too," said Dagon.

Mary nodded her head and continued switching her words every so often between, "Dagon loves me," and, "I love Dagon."

"No chanting will protect your sight. Now you will see my power commence," Savila said.

"I can see everything! My eyes are closed, but ... Dagon, help me!"

"Luv, I can't ... all be over ... baby, I ..." his words blew away on the wind.

Sledge searched for anyone to stab, jab, or smash.

William parked the car and bolted out. He barely took a few steps when the wind blew him backward.

Mary clenched her eyelids shut and put her hands over her ears.

All Dagon's planning was trumped by Savila. Dagon swore.

Hideous screaming shrilled through the field.

I can't believe I used that word. What else can go wrong?

Mary frantically changed songs. Quick blurbs of singers whooshed by.

Dagon hoped she would find a comforting song. He listened to a song about devils running.

You've got to be joking ... a song like that?

"Mark, don't look back! Run, just run!" said William.

"William, help me!" Mark screamed, thorns and thistles snagging Mark's clothes and skin as he ran through the tall prairie grass.

"Mark!" William braced his body against the wind.

"You are not alone." Magethna touched William's shoulder, which caused him to jump.

The Seraphs held their swords up, ready for a battle already lost.

Dagon bristled. "Trying to change prophecy now, are we?" he shouted at them through the fury. "Now all of you will know how *this* feels. Not being able to control events for those you care about!"

And then Savila stood before Dagon, sword at his sternum. Her triumphant eyes bearing into his heart. "You know that feeling better than anyone."

The wind flew in violent gusts all around him. But for Dagon, the moment silenced everything around him as Savila eased the tip of her sword into the skin over his heart. He heard Mary scream his name. Then Mr. Cool and Friar knocked him to the ground. The air came rushing into his lungs.

"We got you, boss," Mr. Cool knelt over him, a hand over the red stain darkening the white of his shirt. Dorian and Magethna now stood between Dagon and Savila, the other two Seraphs flanking them.

"This is a violation of the contract, Savila," Dorian's voice boomed through the velocity of the wind. His sword and Magethna's raised at the ready.

"Not at all, dear Dorian," Savila's eyes narrowed as she examined the blood on the tip of her sword. "Lunion is dead. Have you ever wondered how one kills the immortal?"

Dorian and Magethna stared at Savila, then they both turned to look at Dagon. Dagon scrambled to his feet, Mr. Cool and Friar bracing him on either side. His eyes searched and found Mark, still clawing his way through the field, William desperately trying to reach him but failing.

Although Mark was losing his fight to escape, all Seraphic eyes had locked onto Dagon.

"Let me show you," said Savila. In one slow arc, she sliced her blade at the nearest Seraph.

"Mystil!" cried Magethna.

Mystil brought her sword up just in time to block Savila's blow. Savila flashed her sword horizontally as Mystil parried and pivoted away, the tip of Savila's blade grazing Mystil's upper arm. Mystil stumbled, confusion on her face as she touched the thin red line on her sleeve. She fell to her knees.

Dorian and Magethna rushed to her side as the fourth Seraph, Raglen, caught her and eased her to the ground.

In that moment, Dagon's vision darkened, and he realized he couldn't breathe. The battlefield at Agincourt covered his vision.

"King Lunion desires your title," whispered Savila into Dagon's ear. She caressed his neck with the tip of an arrow.

Dagon didn't even flinch as she drew blood. *Drew blood.*

"No," Dagon breathed, the horror of the present crashing back into his brain.

"She's gone," said Raglen, disbelief aging his ageless face. "She's dead."

Mystil disintegrated into ashes and disappeared.

"All this time," whispered Dagon. "I thought you had enchanted the arrow that killed Lunion. My blood. That's why you keep me alive. My blood kills Seraphs."

"Ahh," said Savila. "A little slow, but we're catching up. Don't be so hard on yourself, Dagon. Filtered just right, your blood heals."

As she spoke, the blood, his blood, traveled in rivulets down her sword, through the hilt, and up through her hand, smoothing her wrinkled skin until it glowed.

Dagon turned to Magethna. His vision blurred. "I didn't know. I swear to you, I did not know."

Magethna reached out as if to touch his face. "Tears. You're crying, Dagon."

"Don't," said Dorian, pulling Magethna back. "A Seraph with tears? Another Seraph dead? This is all impossible, and yet ... we don't know what you are, Dagon."

Mary paled, leaned over, and dry heaved.

Smoke chased Mark, smoke with fluorescent eyes. The smoke thickened and then moved in waves like shadowy dominoes.

William moved into the field then stopped. An unseen barrier prevented him from moving further.

"Do something!" William screamed at the Seraphs.

Magethna sheathed her sword, the other Seraphs following suit, their defeat way more painful than Dagon had ever imagined.

"Mark, run!" said William. He collapsed, clawing at the unseen barrier.

The Seraphs abandoned Dagon and ran to William. Magethna wrapped her arms around him. "I'm sorry," she whispered. "I'm so sorry."

Mark fell, and hands of smoke dragged him away.

In a violent wrench, Mary finally threw up.

"Please let me go! Please! Ahh! Help me!"

"Mark? Mark! Where are you? Oh, my God, help us!" said William.

Mary yelled out, "Leave him alone! Let him go! Dagon, help him! Someone, please help him!"

Savila laughed. The wind drowned out Mary's cries.

Mary grabbed her hair at the temples and hands shook rapidly. "Not again, please not again."

Dagon was torn. Mark's capture would help free them, but to hear Mary scream and watch her be sick was dreadful. Her hidden past pierced his chest and caused him pain. His own pain engulfed him at the realization of his cursed blood. Mary had signed the agreement and told him she understood, but nothing could have prepared her for this.

Dagon heard Mark's last words in the Second Land as claws came out of the smoke.

"William, hel—"

The smoky claws grabbed Mark as the field split open, and they dragged him down, Savila and her army vanishing with him.

Mary shook, kneeling in the alley. Sledge stood next to her. He glanced between her and Dagon.

To Dagon, Mark's cries for help had sounded more like "hell." Dagon was helpless.

The gusty wind subsided into a lonely breeze. Dagon wanted to run toward Mary, who sat trembling, but he stood in place, not even taking a step.

"Dagon cannot leave the field," said Magethna. "The barrier goes both ways."

William faced Dagon. "You knew all along, didn't you? That's why you went to the Glynns'. Guardian of the Light! You can't guard anything. You can't protect anybody."

Dagon said nothing.

"Your silence is your witness and your judge, and you are found guilty," said William.

The Seraphs witnessed every incriminating thing. William had spoken the truth, for even with all his powers, Dagon could not save Mary. He could not save anyone.

"That woman saw and heard everything," said William pointing at Mary. "Now she's sitting in darkness, and you have destroyed her life."

Still, Dagon remained silent. He let the tears fall, not bothering to wipe them away.

"You, who willingly agreed to Savila's plot, started what has now been fulfilled. His family, my parents, will grieve in hopeless darkness. This should shred your heart if you even have one. It would have been better if the One Voice had never created you at all to spare them from what just happened. Can't you talk? You got nothing to say?"

With all the destructive words William shot at him, Dagon held to the notion that with silence, there is dignity, for at least this hole won't dig itself deeper.

William simmered, Mary sobbed, and Dagon stood in the field, just as he had been ordered to do.

Mary shook her head, rubbed her neck, and trudged home on wobbly legs. She didn't even flinch when William's car zoomed past. Mary left the alley without looking at Dagon.

Dagon stood silent and lifeless when Mary left. Without saying a word, Sledge followed Mary home. Once again, the Seraphs faced Dagon. Again, their ancient noses puckered as he lit a cigarette. Smoke trailed behind him as he walked into the Abyss.

24

Shattered Pieces

Shattered pieces, shattered past, shattered memories that seem to last, glistening bright in an array of dreams, which scatter over lives tossed on stormy seas.

D agon approached Mark's cell and stopped. Two shadow soldiers stood guard. No prisoner could leave the Abyss. Two watchdogs glared at Dagon. Three more babysitters waited for him inside Mark's cell.

Outside and inside the cell, the vile shadows bowed to Dagon, their superior. His authority put an end to the shadow soldiers cruel prodding and joking at Mark's expense. Mark's clothes hung in tatters from being dragged. Fresh cuts oozed blood on his face and limbs. Seeing his wounds pricked Dagon's conscience, or was it watching Mary's reaction, or both?

Mark moved closer toward the wall for its meager protection. Drawing his knees tightly to his chest, he hid his face.

Dagon reached down and jerked the boy's head up, tilting it back. The scales of his dragon coat tightened, ready to strike. Even Dagon couldn't deny what the coat craved: punitive vengeance.

"Do you know why you are here?" said Dagon.

Mark shook his head.

"Let me tell you where you are," whispered Dagon, while the shadow soldiers' sharp silver teeth gleamed in triumph. "You are in the Abyss, a place of death in the domain controlled by the law of death and in death you will stay."

Mark's body went rigid. Only his breath and the rattling of his chains echoed off the musty, scarred walls. The silence broke with blood-curdling screams after Dagon yanked Mark's head back even further. With blinding speed, Dagon unsheathed his sword and put it against the boy's throat. *Yes, he's only a boy. Can't think about that … think about Mary … freedom.*

"It is to this death that you, your family, and all of humanity are bound, for in treason, your inheritance will spill with your blood." Dagon's voice mirrored the sharpness of his blade.

Tears moved down Mark's cheeks. He seemed detached from the moment, listening to something perhaps. His face looked calm, too calm in this place of death, like he was being comforted somehow. This possibility, if it was a possibility at all, baffled Dagon. He reversed both of his veils.

"Mark, they don't see or hear what is going on now. They continue to see my blade at your throat, and they only hear what I want them to think that I am saying."

Dagon, help him! Screamed the memory of Mary's words.

"Hold out your hands," Dagon told Mark. "You and your family are thieves, and as thieves you shall die!" Dagon shouted for the benefit of the shadow soldiers.

Mark brought his hands up in submission.

"I cannot remove your bonds any more than I can remove mine, but I can loosen them some."

"Thank you," Mark said as tears streaked dirt and blood down his cheeks. "Why did I see you in my dream?"

"That is complicated, and I do not have time to socialize, though suffice it to say, you and I are linked."

"Why are you here now?" said Mark.

"To live."

"Why, then," gulped Mark, "am I here?"

"To die," Dagon replied, which made Mark flinch.

Dagon rummaged through his coat, making a loud ruckus. The boy froze at the sight of a large needle.

"Don't ... why are you doing this?"

"I must for freedom. Though this is my first try at phlebotomy, it shouldn't hurt ... well ... not too much at least."

Mark barely winced. Either the boy had good pain tolerance and was used to being in hospitals for *something*—hopefully nothing catchy—or Dagon was, in fact, quite skilled.

With the blood in a clear capped tube, he placed a piece of gauze in the crook of Mark's elbow. Dagon spun the tube, causing varying shades of red to swirl, and placed it back in his coat. Dagon removed the blood-stained gauze from Mark's arm and placed it and the used needle back inside the blood kit and back into his coat. Lastly, Dagon put a drop of living waters on Mark's arm, and it healed instantly.

"Now you will see and hear what the shadows have seen and heard."

"What ... what are those things?"

"They are shadow soldiers, and they are dead. You are still alive." Mark looked relieved.

"Will I ... will I see you again?"

"Assuredly. How old are you?" said Dagon.

"Thirteen. How old are *you*?"

"Old. Though I have been told that I look to be around twenty, what do you think?"

"Yeah ... I would ... say that sounds right."

"Are you saying that just to be kind? Because I was also told I'm older than dinosaurs." Dagon appreciated Mark's unbiased confirmation of his youthful looks.

The shadows would hear Mark screaming, insisting he didn't have anything of Dagon's.

Dagon posed in his original position, the sword at Mark's neck for the benefit of the shadows, then sheathed his sword and left his cell.

Once out of the Abyss, Dagon burned the gauze.

SLOWLY, Mary sat up on the couch, the couch that reminded her of the man she wanted to forget. Her head spun. Sitting weak as a newborn kitten, she took a deep breath. Placing her face into her clammy hands, she took more deep breaths. She wanted to forget what she had done, but her mind wouldn't release her. *What were those things?* They went far beyond creepy. *Did Dagon know about those things? Where had they taken Mark?*

Beads of perspiration trickled down her forehead as she steadied herself. She understood now, more than ever, that Dagon moved in immortal circles, that she would have to try to forget about him. She had to move on. She wanted to hold on to the embers which warmed her heart into a new existence. Just how does one move on with their life when their life has been affected by someone like Dagon?

Mary steeled herself to be alone forever. Maybe she was never meant to be married. Maybe the dreams of him, the nesting and meeting him, were designed to help her live with herself. She wondered how long she would live because Dagon told her they were as good as dead without each other. But Mary already had lived most of her life as a walking corpse, going through life invisible and isolated, though at a casual glance, it would appear otherwise.

Carefully, she walked into the laundry room, opened Dagon's laundry bag, and pulled out his black rock n roll t-shirt. She didn't care if it was dirty. It would serve as a reminder to never let love in again. Love is too painful.

As soon as she could emotionally do it, she planned to dispose of everything that reminded her of him, except the t-shirt and the photos. She wondered how she could dispose of her heart so deeply moved by love.

DAGON PASSED the Seraphs who could not see him. They were singing, which was inappropriate because of what happened, their melodic song a lament.

In Mary's front yard, Sledge sheathed his sword and put his sledgehammer back in his pocket. His body sagging, his face was covered in frown-shaped wrinkles.

"What's wrong? Is she safe?" said Dagon anxiously.

"She's safe ... but she's angry. Really angry, and I can't say I blame her, though I know that you couldn't help her."

"At least she's safe."

"I would highly suggest, that is, it would be wise for you to not stand in front of her in a darkened alley. Like where she was tonight," said Razz.

"She couldn't be that mad."

"Yeah ... but she is."

Dagon blew him off and gave Razz the vial and the blood kit and told him to dispose of the kit before heading to Rome.

"Everything is disposed of, and I'm sitting in a taxi. Over." said Razz.

"Already?"

"Yes already, and would it please you to know that I'm sitting on vinyl?"

"No, but it pleases us," said Mr. Cool.

"Heard that."

"We hoped that you would," said Sledge.

"For that, I will be bringing back no Italian chocolates."

Mr. Cool, Sledge, and Friar quickly recanted, trying to apologize.

"I may be sitting on vinyl, but I'm going to Rome. Uh ... boss ... what if there are no airplanes going to Rome?" Razz asked.

"How would you exist without me?" said Dagon.

"Can we try?" said Friar.

Dagon glared at the Cherbs and told Razz to get on the first plane flying to Europe and then take a train to Rome if need be.

Dagon rang Mary's doorbell. After multiple pushes of the doorbell, Mary stomped across the floor with more force than usual. Then an eye peered into the peephole.

"It's me, baby."

"Go away, Dagon Guardian. And don't come back."

"Baby, just open the door. What do you mean, don't come back?"

"You heard what I said ... go away, now!"

"Mary?" said Dagon, more confused than hurt.

"Don't you 'Mary' me. Please leave."

"Okay, just let me explain, please?"

Mary banged her fist on the door. "What do you not understand? Leave me alone!"

"You can't be serious!"

"I heard and saw everything, Dagon! Do you understand me? Everything!"

"Yes, I know, but—"

"Dagon!"

"I didn't know, baby, let me explain, please!"

"Did you hear me yelling for help? Did you?" Mary pounded on the door.

"Yes, I did, but—"

"You heard ... yet you did nothing, just like ... Dagon, get out of my life, now. Just leave!"

"You can't mean that ... you can't!"

"I do mean it. Leave me alone. Forever."

"We will die, Mary ... die!"

"I've been dead most of my life, what's the difference? Please don't make this harder than it already is. Just go." She spoke with a voice like the undead, with more death than life moving through her.

"I love you, Mary. Always have and always will." Dagon walked away. In darkness, Dagon turned around and looked back at the house of his beloved.

"I guess our guarding days are done," said Friar.

"No, all of you will keep protecting her."

"For how long?"

"Without end. You boys just may get to see what living without me is like, for the door to my death will soon close," said Dagon in dreary certainty.

"Look on the bright side. At least you know it's coming."

"And how is that a bright side, exactly?"

"The more you know, the more you grow," Mr. Cool said.

"You know, you may have something there, that's really good."

"Good? Man, it's inspired."

"I think I may coin that line," said Dagon.

"Well, that would be plagiarism, and it will cost you."

"You know, the three of you might be a teensy-weensy bit understanding, since I'm dying and all."

The guys gathered around and conferred amongst themselves, whispering and gesturing.

"We decided to be understanding and give you a deathly discount, redeemable between now and the time of your untimely demise. After you have expired, well, the discount would also be expired."

"Thanks, I guess."

"No problem. In fact, we have loads of clever inspirational, relational, and perspirational sayings, just waiting to be plucked from the vast troves of our brains," said Mr. Cool.

"Oh, brother. What's this perspirational stuff?" said Dagon, uncertain that he wanted to know.

"Oh, those are brilliant words designed as quick-witted comebacks, to make the sorry person wish that they had never opened their traps in the first place." Sledge slammed his fist into his other hand.

"You know, you guys could go into the greeting card business."

"What a wonderful idea! I'm glad we thought of it."

"Hey, I thought of it. Isn't that plagiarism?"

"Nah. That's business."

Dagon just sighed, "I am dead, yet hopefully, she will live. Maybe, I was never meant to be with her, but to help save her. With this, I can die. Razz is on his way to Rome. Her life insurance by blood will be in the lock box. Locked away for when she needs it. My love for her will keep all of you around to guard her the best you can."

"We'll do more than our best. Better give us all your cash since the dead can't use it."

This was as sentimental as it gets as far as these guys were concerned.

"Well, all of you are probably right."

"We're always right."

Dagon sighed. *Why did Mary say she was already dead? Did she want to be already dead to me? Well, I can't blame her for that.*

Dagon, a walking dead man, didn't even try to conceal himself from the Seraphs. He didn't care anymore. Somehow, he found his bench home and with a lonely thud, sat staring ahead into nothingness. Mark sat in a cell below, and together they waited for their death sentences.

HOLLOW AND GUTTED, Mary sat, her eyes fixed on nothing. Her mind and heart were fixed on everything. She lost so many people in her short life. Mark, taken below ... gone ... Dagon her love ... gone. Her past emotional relationships were easy to dispose of. But Dagon was different, very different. With the few guys she dated, she would have never invited them to her house. Other guys' quirks disgusted her, yet she could discuss these things with Dagon. His spontaneity excited her. Most importantly, she felt alive in his presence. How had she been since he had been in her life? Better perhaps? Yes. He made her feel safe, wanted, and respected. Fresh tears coursed down her cheeks. Truth be told, Mary missed him. Dagon tried to explain what happened, but in a heated emotional state, she kicked him to the curb. A man who had been looking for her for centuries. A man who had loved her before she was even born.

Chills ran down her spine with the image of those smoky creatures dragging Mark under the dark, cold earth. Things started becoming clear. Is this the dark, cold, stifling place she saw when Dagon showed her images of his past? Or when she had the dream where she was the captive? The smoky creatures, the images of Dagon and her dreams, validated that Dagon indeed lived in the ground. If so, Dagon being "in between houses" actually meant that he waited to be with her when her house would become their house. Their marital home. How could she let him go just like that? Even with everything that happened, Dagon wouldn't leave her. Terrible things happen in life, but love is forever. What did Dagon say to her earlier when she could hear everything? Words of love, that's what. *Just keep repeating over and over again how much I love you. Dagon said something else ... what was it ... oh yes ... I can't control ... Can't control what?*

Once again, she returned to the dark, cold, stifling place. A bottomless pit, an abyss of loneliness for Dagon to fall into while cast out. A pariah. Didn't she cast him out? The feeling that he was trapped never left Mary. They stood better together, stronger, and he said he would never leave her. Two hearts will always be better than one. That place below, if it existed, Mary named, "The Abyss of the Fallen."

Her mind ricocheted back and forth. Focusing on large and minute details as best she could. Adrenaline was replaced with calm. Her heart beat steady. With Dagon in her heart, she got up from the floor. She stood steady. She was in love. She had lovingly cleaned and bandaged his flesh wounds, the wounds she could see. What about the wounds she couldn't see? Only love and time could heal those. Whatever it took, no matter how long it took, she would love him without end.

Maybe, just maybe, she was meant to come to life, to bring him to life. Whatever Dagon couldn't control, she was going to let him explain. Together they would save his title, her sister, Mark, Dagon, and herself if possible. Hope coursed through her once hopeless body. She was in control of herself, her emotions, and opening the door. Into the inky black world of night, she whispered.

"Dagon."

GET HELP - HELP OTHERS

If you or someone you know is at risk:

NAMI: National Alliance on Mental Health. Helpline: 1-800-950-6264

National Suicide Prevention. Lifeline: 1-800-273-TALK (8255)

Crisis Text Line: Text NAMI to 741-741

Website: www.nami.org

ALSO BY DIANA ESTELL

Please Enjoy a Preview of What's to Come in Book II-

ASHES OF THE FALLEN

Book II

CHAPTER 1 - ASHES OF THE FALLEN

Blood Immortal

Forgiveness and reflection mixed with perfect fusion in tendrils of twilight smoke and ash. Memorial Day was almost over. The only remainder of this festive day smoldered in charred remains from neighborhood fire pits. Thin trails of smoke curled over the treetops as people lounged with friends and family on this summer kick-off.

Mangled parade bunting drifted down streets and tangled in fences. Even with immortal powers, the Seraphs could not protect Mark from the law of the earth, Savila. Defeat did not bring them back into Mark Bennett's bedroom. Hope did. Mark's dream had brought the Seraphs to his house for his protection a few months ago. Now Mark resided captive in the realm of death, the Abyss.

The immortals began singing a lament of Mark's capture and the death of their beloved friend, Mystil. A lament for Mark's Uncle Henry, Aunt Francis, and Cousin William, who had tried desperately to save Mark and now mourned in the parlor below. The duality of hope and grief, victory and surrender, loyalty and rebellion, freedom and prisoner of war, filled the spontaneous singing with anguish.

As Magethna's gaze drifted out the window toward Dagon, her singing trailed off then stopped. The others stopped as well. She placed a hand on the window. "He's a casualty of Savila's war. We all heard Mary's blistering words."

"I hate to admit it, but seeing Dagon slouched on his bench in such a state feels ... uncomfortable." Dorian rubbed his forehead. "I'm not sure what to do with this."

Magethna turned and looked at Dorian. "Well, we have to start somewhere. Wait, remember that large parchment we saw in a window a few paths over? It offered services to understand and master human emotions." Magethna took out her daily planner and thumbed through several pages. "Here it is. 'Willow Galgrins. Professional counselor, life coach, and yoga instructor. No emotion is too hard to soften.'"

"I think I'll pass. Besides, how successful can such services be, when so many feel unhappy here in the Second Land?"

Magethna shared a sketch from her planner. "This woman, Willow, on the parchment is all smiles, and I love the green color of her shawl, very peaceful. She looks so sincerely sparkly, maybe she could help others feel that good too."

"I don't know about her." Dorian shook his head. "She looks too happy, maybe even happier than you,"

"See, then there is hope for everyone." Magethna beamed and put her daily planner back in her pocket, which stitched itself up.

"Still, her references should be checked," Dorian said.

Sssh ... click ... sssh ...

Magethna turned to Raglen as he repeatedly unsheathed his sword about a hand width, then dropped it back in ... *click.*

"I have been holding back my words for far too long. Mystil is dead, and I knew her the longest. You two," Raglen said, pointing at Magethna and Dorian, "pine over Dagon as if Dagon and Mystil were equals!"

"Raglen ..."

Raglen held an open palm out toward Dorian's face. "Just stop! Let me remind you what we all know. Dagon is *not* a casualty of war. He was there from the beginning. He *participated* in humanity's doom. He was an invested knight who turned evil."

"We do not know Dagon's path, but we do know justice was served," Dorian said. "The scale of guilt tips more to Savila."

"He was guilty then, and he's guilty now." Raglen said. "Savila's law, written in stone, bound Dagon, but he went above and beyond that law when he took matters into his own hands by luring Mark out of the Glynns' house. He even used and abandoned his beloved Mary in her time of need."

"What if Dagon didn't alter the document of stone, and it was Savila who commanded him to the Glynns?" Magethna said. "I'm sure he tried to block Mary's senses and Savila stopped him,"

"We have no proof either way," said Dorian. "Incrimination is not based on mere action. Strangely, we didn't detect anything near Mary when Mark was captured,"

"What if—"

"Magethna, we have no—"

Magethna spun to the side, facing Dorian, shooing him with her hand.

"Let me finish. We have Mystil ..." Her words abruptly ceased as she bowed her head.

Dorian and Raglen placed their hands on her shoulders.

"I wish I could cry like Dagon did," Magethna said. "Perhaps he can shed tears because he's half human."

"About that. We don't know *what* Dagon is. His blood is immortally lethal." Dorian removed his hand from her shoulder and folded his arms over his chest. "That means Savila could use it to kill any of us. *Dagon* could kill any of us."

Raglen's hand slid off Magethna's shoulder when she turned and walked over to Mark's bed. With her back to the other Seraphs, she placed a hand on one of the patches on the quilt, lifted her hand, and turned. "Dagon was just as shocked as we were when Mystil ... died. He's remorseful."

"Or a skilled actor," said Raglen.

"Love is hope—"

"Magethna, you have to concede that Dagon may be evil and is forever lost." Dorian came over to Magethna and, once again, placed his hand on her shoulder.

"And hope is love," is all she said as she looked into Dorian's eyes.

She drifted back to the window and stood next to Raglen. Dorian followed to stand on the other side of her.

"I will always miss Mystil," Magethna said.

"We all will," Dorian said. "What we can do now is help Mary."

Raglen nodded.

Just then, Mary came outside her house and whispered Dagon's name. A musical sound to Magethna.

At the same time, Henry and Francis wept.

"There will be a way to bring Dagon to justice!" William vowed between sobs.

ICE COLD STEAM followed Savila when she left the throne room, making her way to Mark's cell. Her glass stilettos rang as they struck the black glass floor. With her mind, she changed her wardrobe to an outfit the boy would never forget. Her chain mail shirt, throwing-knife skirt, and glass boots transformed into a silvery gray floor-length dress and open-toed matching high heels. Rows of softly-draped, scalloped edges cascaded like flowing water; her sword concealed within. The dragon-head hilt rocked gently to the fluctuations of her swaying hips as she walked toward the cell. Braids underneath her glass headpiece loosened and became smooth within the rest of her shiny blonde hair, trailing down her back and partially over her shoulders. The headpiece transformed into a thin band, set in a half moon shape on top of her head like a gleaming tiara.

The shadow soldiers bowed when Savila entered the cell. She paid no attention to the soldiers. Mark sat on the floor, hugging his knees. Blood and sweat matted his hair. Savila walked over and stood in front of Mark. The boy looked up with red-rimmed eyes. She folded her hands and stretched her lips into a wide grin. Reaching down, she patted his head.

The boy flinched, cowering beneath her hand. Leaning back, his forehead furrowed as he stared at her face. "I saw you ... in my ... dream. Who are you?"

"Although you already know, I will answer your curiosity. My name is Lady Savila, and this is my dominion. This is where you will remain."

"Please. Let me go. Someone, help me!" Mark's eyes darted erratically around the room. His fetters snapped and grated, his body lifting, as if somehow, emotionally, he needed to be as strong or stronger than his captive chains.

"Who would help you now?" The shadow soldiers said in unison then howled in laughter.

"Death," Savila said.

Tears mixed with sweat streaked his cheeks. Her fingers raked his hair. Mark, recoiled from her touch as her nails began digging and scraping his scalp. Her fingernails grew longer and sharper ... and black. Her toenails resembled claws.

In one quick movement, she flung his head back and stared at his face, causing Mark to cry out.

"You look so much like your father," she said, softening her tone.

"You knew my father? How?" Mark trembled in her grasp.

"Not your pathetic human father, your father!" Mirrored in his eyes, her pupils elongated, the color changing to blood red.

Mark repeated as if to himself, *"Fear not ... Fear not."*

In her reflection, her skin pulled taught, revealing her bones.

"Dagon!" Mark screamed. "Let me see Dagon."

Savila released his head so quickly it whiplashed forward. She unsheathed a sword and lifted it into the air above her head.

Mark shuddered. His chains shook. Three shadows materialized through the blackened walls. These shadows were bigger than the other soldiers, and they had crowns with large nail-like spikes.

Savila leaned down. Her dress changing into scales. Her words blistered like flames. "The Shadow Kings come to bear witness. What did Lord Dagon do while he was in here with you?" She placed the blade of her sword against Mark's throat. Seething heat radiated from the blade.

"He didn't do anything to me. He just asked me questions."

"Let's see about that." She sheathed her sword and pressed her blackened nails against his forehead, pulling images from his mind. "Did you see Lord Dagon take anything from here?"

"No, Lady Savila," reported one of the shadows when Mark didn't answer. "We saw Lord Dagon take nothing. He only asked questions with his blade at the boy's throat."

With a hiss, she released her fingers, and Mark wrenched forward, gasping.

"Hold out your arms."

He held his arms out, his eyes welling as he continued to gasp.

"Your bonds are loosened. Did Lord Dagon try to remove your chains?"

"No! I begged for help, but no one would help me!"

She tightened his shackles. Mark winced as she pulled his arms out for further inspection, her reptilian hand came under his elbows and locked them up straight. Her black, shiny claw traced methodically along the path that her eyes had just scoured. Black clawed fingers scraped the skin along his veins, drawing no blood yet she thirsted. Her mouth watered, and her parched lips began to crack.

"I'm anxious for the completion of what is mine." She turned away from Mark and whispered to one of the crowned shadows. "I find no evidence on the boy's skin. His skin smells like iron. Could the boy be covering for Dagon? No, that is an impossibility. Dagon is more likely stealing blood for his own power."

Smiling, she spoke in a tone which, while neither pleasant nor unpleasant, hardened like truth set in concrete. She placed her sword near his left cheek to emphasis her point.

"You will satisfy many things, but if I could satisfy my thirst, I would. Alas, this is not yet to be."

Mark only shook his head, his breath hitching in short gasps.

"What you bear will carry you into death, as your blood will satisfy laws and my bonds of thirst. After yours, more blood will come as my eternal dominion over humanity will never be broken."

With a reptilian hiss, she flicked her body up. Part of her scales rose slightly, then lowered back into place.

Without another word or glance, Savila, the Shadow Kings and the three shadow soldiers left Mark's cell, and with a sharp clang, his cell door closed.

She ordered the shadow soldiers to leave them but her kin, the Shadow Kings, stayed with her in front of Mark's cell door.

"One of the four Cherbs loyal to Lord Dagon heads to Rome with a vial of Mark's blood."

"How is his mind not revealing itself? Ligon asked.

"With angelic ash, but I have foreseen all of this," said Savila.

"We have enough evidence to cast Dagon into isolation, Lady Savila," said Lamel. "He has committed treason."

"May we arrest the Cherb before he gets to Rome?" said Listian.

"No, for Lord Dagon's own ploy for power will be his undoing, as the price tag of love will tighten ever more around his neck and the neck of his beloved. No, we will let things play out, for his death will be better served on a platter, chilled by the loneliness of his passing."

"He is no longer with her, so he will die," gloated Lamel and his brothers, Ligon and Listian, laughed.

"Vengeance is almost at hand, my kin. So, Lord Dagon wants to live in the light? Then by all means, he shall, for the revelation of pain he will know. His beloved has no real proof of his innocence, only his word."

The three kings walked back to their private quarters while Savila went back into the Throne Room. She sat on her throne and stroked the winged armrest of her chair with her black claws changing back to shiny red fingernails.

With her mind, Savila scanned the skies looking for the Cherb, though she saw it not. Stolen blood moved toward Rome. With joy, Dagon was on the road he would take to his own death. For the blood stolen would not come back void. She waited in triumph as blood waves crashed beneath the glass floor. He and his precious human bonded mate would soon be writhing in pain as their lives, the life of Mark and all of humanity are bound to Savila, through the law of blood.

ABOUT THE AUTHOR

Thank you for reading the preview of Book II. Please follow Diana's journey at her website: DianaEstell.com for release dates, launch team news and more. If you enjoyed the title please consider taking a moment to leave an honest review on Amazon and Goodreads! These are especially helpful for authors! Thank You!

Since a very young age, Diana traveled the world exploring new cultures, history, and art. These experiences fuel her writing. Since the age of seven, dictionaries became her playgrounds for learning new words and crafting her own unique ones. By age eleven she wanted to be a ninja, so she studied hard and earned a black belt in three different styles of martial arts. Later in life, she earned a degree in Cultural Anthropology. Diana's inspirations include gothic art, architecture, and world history.

She enjoys reading fantasy novels, science fiction, and biographies. Bram Stoker's *Dracula* remains her favorite novel to this day. Since her parents would not get her a dragon as a child, she writes about them. Currently, she lives in the Chicago suburbs with her family. Diana's first novel, *Abyss of the Fallen,* is the first book in a trilogy.

facebook.com/DianaEstellAuthor
twitter.com/DSEstell
instagram.com/dianaestellauthor